THE M[illegible]
OF THE
LUCKY CAT

Cozy English crime fiction at its best

Book #2 in the Quentin Cadbury Investigations

Christine McHaines

Published by The Book Folks

London, 2023

This book is a work of fiction. Names, characters, businesses, organizations, places and events are either the product of the author's imagination or are used fictitiously. Any resemblance to actual persons, living or dead, events or locales is entirely coincidental. The spelling is British English.

ISBN 978-1-80462-106-6

www.thebookfolks.com

THE MYSTERY OF THE LUCKY CAT is the second standalone cozy mystery novel in this series by Christine McHaines. Details about the other books can be found at the back.

Chapter One

September 2006

Quentin Cadbury had never seen a dead cat before. When he came downstairs one Saturday morning and found the poor creature stretched out and stiff on the kitchen floor his heart thumped erratically.

'Oh my God, Magpie!' he gasped, clutching at the worktop for support.

'Meow!'

Quentin turned to see his own cat, Magpie, padding in from the lounge. Relief swamped him, along with a sense of foolishness. Of course it wasn't Magpie lying there – Magpie was black and white, like the birds he was named after. The dead animal was nearly all black, with a few white patches. It was his neighbour's cat, Lucky, that he was looking after while she was on holiday. Kneeling, he prodded the cat to satisfy himself that it was really dead. The furry body felt cold. Quentin recoiled, then got to his feet.

'Bloody hell,' he groaned, staring at his neighbour's pet. 'Now what do I do?'

Magpie sat nearby, gazed at the body and mewed.

'Sorry, boy,' Quentin said, fondling his ears. 'Looks like our visitor's had it. Poor old thing.'

Magpie drew away, looked at him disdainfully, then swished his tail and stalked off.

'Hey,' Quentin called after him. 'Don't go blaming me. It's not my fault he's upped and died on us.' Stepping over the dead cat, he found the telephone handset and punched the keypad.

'Wanda,' he said when a sleepy voice answered. 'I thought you might still be asleep, that's why I didn't come in.'

Wanda, his partner in their newly formed detective agency, also friend and sometimes more than friend, lived next door. Most of the time anyway. When she was being more than a friend, she stayed over with Quentin in the terraced house in Greenwich where he'd lived for two years.

'You woke me anyway, so you might as well have come in,' Wanda complained. 'What do you want?'

'It's Lucky.'

'What is?'

'Not what; who. Lucky, Mrs Freeman's cat.'

'What about it?'

'It's dead.'

There was a long pause before Wanda said, 'What a shame. He was a nice old thing.'

'Yes,' agreed Quentin. 'The thing is, what shall I do?'

'What do you mean?' Wanda still sounded sleepy. Quentin glanced at the clock. Nearly nine. Well, it was the weekend, and he knew Wanda got up at six on a work day.

'I mean I can't just get rid of him without telling her, can I?'

'Of course you can't. She worships that cat. Give me time to wake up and I'll come over.'

Quentin heard a swishing sound and guessed she was getting out of bed. For once the visual image he held of Wanda in bed failed to excite him. He ended the call and went to switch the kettle on.

'Sorry to be disrespectful, old thing,' he murmured as he stepped over the dead animal again, 'but I need sustenance.'

He was on his second cup of tea before he heard the front door open. Wanda had keys to his house, and he had a set to hers. It was an arrangement they'd come to the previous year, when they'd inadvertently been involved in a crime that led them to investigate an international criminal organisation.

'Morning.' He greeted Wanda as she appeared, looking cool and fresh in cream linen trousers and an apple-green top. Her blonde hair, still damp from the shower, fell to her slender neck in a perfectly cut bob.

'Morning. Oh, poor Lucky,' Wanda said when she spotted the cat stretched out in the kitchen.

Quentin gave her a wry smile. 'Not so lucky after all. Looks like his luck ran out.'

'Not funny. The poor thing. You'll have to move him, you can't leave him there.'

Taking the blanket from Magpie's basket Quentin wrapped it round the dead cat. He did it gently, as though it might still feel pain or discomfort. Then he placed it in the corner.

'What happened?' Wanda said, watching him.

'Nothing happened. He just died. He was getting on a bit.'

Wanda pulled a face. 'So am I, but I'm not planning to drop dead any time soon.'

'I should hope not! Anyway, I'd hardly call thirty-nine getting on.'

'Nearly forty, and it is compared to a twenty-five-year-old.'

Quentin sighed. Yet another reminder of their age difference. Ignoring her comment, he washed his hands then poured tea into a china cup and placed it on a matching saucer. It was a ritual he knew she appreciated – mugs for him, his late aunt's Spode teacups for her.

'What am I going to do about poor Lucky?' he asked.

Wanda frowned. 'Didn't Mrs Freeman leave a contact number?'

'No. She's on a coach tour of Italy. She left the vet's number, in case of any medical problems, but that's no good now, is it?'

Taking the tea that Quentin proffered, Wanda said, 'It might be. Some of these places have storage facilities. Give them a ring and find out.'

'And say what? Can you look after my neighbour's dead cat? They'll think I'm taking the mickey.'

'I'll do it.' Wanda sounded impatient. 'Give me the phone.'

After passing her the handset Quentin went in search of Magpie. He found him upstairs, curled up on the bed in a patch of sunlight. 'Hey,' he said. 'You know you're not allowed up here.'

Making no attempt to move him, Quentin perched on the bed and patted him. 'That gave me quite a turn, boy. For a minute I thought I'd lost you.'

Magpie rubbed his head against Quentin's hand and purred. Stupid of me, Quentin thought. Who'd have imagined I'd become so attached to a cat. If anyone had told me a year ago that I'd even take a cat in, let alone get fond of it, I'd have laughed.

But Magpie wasn't just a pet, he realized. He was a symbol of his new life, the life he had made for himself since his parents had emigrated to Australia. Magpie had been instrumental in solving the mystery which had led to him and Wanda setting up their detective agency.

'We'll do that. Thank you so much.' Wanda's voice reached him from downstairs, and Quentin thought how low and sensual it sounded; as his mother had called it, a Lauren Bacall voice. Leaving Magpie on the bed, he went to join her.

'What did they say?'

'They were very sympathetic. They knew Lucky well – he's been there a few times recently. Mrs Freeman's one of their best clients.'

'Never mind that – what did they think we should do?'

'They said to take him over there and they'll put him in cold storage until Mrs Freeman gets back.'

Quentin sucked his cheeks in. 'Take him there? What in?'

'Your car, of course, unless you want to hire a hearse.'

'I mean what shall we put him in?'

Wanda shot him an incredulous look. 'Find a small suitcase or a holdall. Some detective you are, Quentin, if you can't even work out what to do with a dead cat.'

She was right, of course. He had recently foiled the plans of a criminal, survived being beaten up, saved a police officer's life and rescued Wanda from danger, but dealing with the death of an animal in his care was in a different category.

As though sensing his distaste Wanda continued, 'You're not used to pets dying, are you?'

Quentin shook his head. 'I never had a pet. My father wouldn't allow it.'

Wanda nodded. 'I don't know what I would have done without Mozart when Gerry died. We always had dogs, but Mozart's the best of all of them. Anyway, you've got Magpie now, and your dad's ten thousand miles away.'

Quentin stiffened. 'He's not my dad – I mean I've never called him Dad. He always insisted on Father.'

Wanda sent him a shrewd look. 'Yes, well, he is a bit Victorian, or he was when I met him. Go and find something to put poor Lucky in. The sooner he's gone the better we'll feel.'

After locating a small black holdall, Quentin lifted the dead animal into it, the blanket still in place.

'Will you come to the vet's with me?' he asked.

'Yes. Did you have breakfast?'

'Only a cup of tea. Funny how a dead cat puts you off your food.'

'The vet's in Eltham apparently,' Wanda said when she'd scrambled some eggs. 'Not exactly local, is it?'

'That's where Mrs Freeman used to live. It's not far.'

Wanda looked at her watch. 'It's twenty to eleven. They close at one o'clock on Saturdays and the traffic might be bad. We can't use my car, it's still in having the brake pads changed.'

'Mine's in the lock-up,' Quentin said, thinking of his BMW a few streets away in a rented garage.

Inherited from his mother on her move, the BMW series 3 model was one of his prized possessions – that, and the running machine taking up a corner of his lounge.

'I'll walk round and get it,' he said, standing up.

'I'll get my coat and feed Mozart while you're gone.' Wanda started towards the door.

'Hold on. Take Lucky with you. I'll pick you up in fifteen minutes.'

Wanda screwed up her face as she picked up the holdall. 'Not the best thing I've had to carry,' she murmured as she left.

Quentin knew she was imagining what it would be like if it was Mozart lying dead in a holdall. Wanda's West Highland terrier, named after her favourite composer, had been her constant companion since the death of her husband.

Checking his appearance in the bathroom mirror, Quentin frowned. He hadn't shaved, and he didn't think so-called designer stubble suited him. He ran his hand over his chin and the heart shaped mole by his ear, then donned his jacket and started on the ten-minute walk to the lock-up. It was a sparkling September day, but the east wind struck cold as he broke into a run. When he reached the lock-up he slid into the car and cursed when the engine didn't respond. He tried again. Nothing.

'Bloody hell!' He jabbed a finger at the dashboard. 'Flat battery!'

Muttering to himself, he connected the battery to the wall-mounted charger. It would be fine in a few hours, but was absolutely useless at the moment.

'No go,' he told Wanda when he'd run back. 'Flat battery.'

'Oh for goodness' sake,' Wanda said, rolling her eyes. 'If we don't get him there by one, you'll have to keep him till Monday. There's no underground to Eltham so it's the bus or a taxi.'

Quentin flinched. 'Take a dead cat on the bus? No way! We'll get a taxi.'

When the taxi arrived, they went to meet it. The driver jumped out and reached for the holdall. 'I'll chuck that in the boot for you, mate.'

'No!' cried Wanda.

'We'll keep it with us,' Quentin said, horrified at the thought of Lucky being chucked anywhere. They got in, the holdall on the seat between them.

Three quarters of an hour later they sat staring at the traffic queue ahead. The road was jam-packed with vehicles edging forward a few inches at a time. The meter ticked ominously and Quentin glanced at it, frustrated.

Wanda followed his gaze. 'The vet said they weren't far from the railway station.' She pointed to the main-line station ahead. 'It might be quicker to walk.'

Quentin nodded. 'Pull in here,' he called.

When it had crawled another few yards, the taxi swung into Eltham station and came to a halt in the taxi rank.

'Fifteen quid!' Quentin muttered when he'd paid the driver and carefully lifted out the holdall. 'We should have opened a taxi firm instead of a detective agency.'

'This is awful,' Wanda said, looking around her as they stepped away from the taxi rank. Hordes of people crowded the station, many with coloured scarves and shirts. Football, Quentin realized. Mainly Millwall supporters, judging by the number of blue shirts on view. The place was a seething mass of blue, contrasting with the red of the buses parked in the centre of the enclosed square that made up the concourse.

'Come on,' Wanda urged as people pushed past her to get to the ticket hall. 'Let's get out of this crowd.'

Taking hold of Wanda's arm, Quentin tried to guide her to where the crowd was thinner.

After a few paces he noticed a middle-aged man in a grey coat and a green woollen scarf gazing around as if looking for someone. He's got no chance in this lot, Quentin thought as they walked by him, then turned as he heard a moan and a thud. Wanda turned too, then wrenched her arm free of his hand, stepped forward and bent over the man, who was now lying on the ground. He lay on his front, having fallen on top of a bag he'd been carrying. What they could see of his face was grey against the green of the scarf, and his eyes were closed.

Setting his holdall on the ground, Quentin leaned over him, alarmed at the possibility of seeing a second dead body that morning. The rise and fall of the man's shoulders told him otherwise, and he stood back and pulled out his mobile phone.

'Better not move him,' he said. 'I'll ring for an ambulance.'

A little knot of people gathered round, some looking genuinely concerned, others just curious. One woman stayed after the others had dispersed and knelt down on the other side of the man, feeling for his pulse.

'I've had some first aid training,' she explained. 'We should get him into the recovery position.'

At that moment another large group of people joined the ever-growing crowd trying to get to the platform. They surged past Quentin, practically lifting him off his feet and carrying him forward. After he'd broken free, he whirled round, worried that Wanda may have been pushed over in the crush. He was relieved to see her with the newly arrived woman kneeling by the stricken man, their holdall still in place next to her. He took a few steps towards her, then gasped as a figure came from nowhere, scooped up the holdall and made off into the sea of people ahead.

Wanda looked up at him, incredulity showing on her face. For a breathless moment they gazed at each other, at a loss for words. Then Wanda raised her eyebrows. 'Am I dreaming, or did someone just steal our cat?'

Chapter Two

Quentin stood there, trying to process what had happened. All that had registered was a tall streak of blue topped with a dark head snatching a black bag – his bag. Then the adrenaline kicked in.

'Hey!' he shouted.

Running into the mass of people shuffling towards the ticket hall he elbowed his way through, trying to locate the thief. Most of the people in the crowd wore football shirts, and three quarters of them were blue. He spotted a dark-haired man, slightly taller than most, trying to fast-track his way through the entrance to the ticket hall.

That's him, Quentin thought as he watched him go through the glass doors and on to the turnstile at the barrier.

With people still pressing around him, Quentin took several minutes to force his way to the turnstile, pushing other travellers aside, muttering apologies and fumbling for his Oyster card. Then he was on the platform, looking left and right, scanning the crowd. But it was no good. The person he'd thought was the thief was nowhere in sight.

Frustrated, Quentin weaved in and out of the hordes of people, glancing down and hoping to see someone with a black holdall. There were rucksacks and cases on wheels, but no black holdalls carried by anyone wearing blue. A robotic voice announced the approach of the next train, and the people on the platform shunted forward. Quentin stood against the wall hoping to catch sight of the thief. As he saw a wave of blue move aside to let passengers alight from the train, he felt suddenly ridiculous. Why on earth was he chasing someone with a dead cat, especially when a man was lying outside, sick, possibly dying? Stupid, he thought, and hopeless in this lot.

Just then someone darted from the toilets and joined the mass trying to board the train. From his position by the wall Quentin only saw one side of the dark-haired male figure dressed in blue, but recognized what the man was carrying.

Anger stirred in him, and he rushed forward. It didn't matter what was in the holdall, it was his, and this bloke wasn't going to get away if Quentin could help it. He leapt forward, pushing sideways towards the man, catching him just before he stepped up into the train. Grabbing the bag by the handles he yanked hard, kneeing the unsuspecting thief in the leg at the same time. The thief's legs buckled and his grip loosened. Quentin staggered backwards as the bag was suddenly freed. People who hadn't seen what was going on were still pressing forward and Quentin, tottering with the bag clutched to him, was pushed to the ground.

'You all right, mate?' said a cockney voice beside him.

'I think so,' he said, dazed.

He stood up just in time to see the head and shoulders of the man he'd tackled turning away from the open train doors as if trying to get to him, his progress impeded by other travellers. Jumping back, Quentin caught the arm of a passing guard, pointed to the thief and shouted, 'That man tried to rob me!'

Immediately the thief turned back to the train and squeezed into the already full carriage. His body was obscured by surrounding football fans, but as he stepped up to the doorway Quentin could see his face in profile – a sharp nose and a prominent chin. As soon as he was on board the doors slid shut.

'He tried to rob you?' the guard said, looking startled. 'I'll stop the train.'

'Hold on a minute,' interrupted a female voice from behind. They both turned to see a middle-aged woman in a trouser suit and glasses looking purposefully at Quentin. 'I just saw this man steal that bag from someone who was getting on the train.'

The guard frowned. '*This* man stole the bag?'

'I was on the train before all those football louts got on. While I was waiting for a chance to get off, I saw him grab the bag from another man.'

'But he stole it from me in the first place,' Quentin insisted. 'And now he's getting away.'

They watched as the train pulled away. The guard, a pleasant-looking black man with close-cropped hair, looked uncomfortable when he realized he'd failed to stop the train from leaving. He looked from Quentin to the woman, obviously unsure who to believe or what to do.

'I'll call the police,' he said. 'They can sort it out.'

Quentin shrugged. 'Fine by me. I've got a witness to my bag being stolen.'

When he'd explained how the bag had been taken, the woman looked crestfallen, as though her good deed for the day had been undone.

'I'm only telling you what I saw,' she said.

'Right,' said the guard, 'come with me, both of you.'

'Why?' asked Quentin. 'I've told you what happened and I can tell you what's in the bag. How would I know that if it wasn't my bag?'

'Tell me in the office,' said the guard. 'I need to report this.'

All three of them made their way along the busy platform to a small room which served as an office, where the guard spoke to a female member of staff in a British Rail tabard.

'We need to report an incident,' the guard told her.

'Another incident?' the girl said. 'We've already had a man collapse outside.'

'There, I told you,' Quentin said. Looking at the female worker, he continued, 'What's happened to him?'

She shrugged. 'Apparently someone's already called an ambulance.'

'That'll be me,' Quentin said triumphantly.

'We still need to report what's happened,' said the guard, gesturing towards the trouser-suited woman. 'This lady's made an allegation.'

'Please yourself,' Quentin said, 'but why don't you check out the witnesses first? Or the bag? There's only a–'

His attempt to tell them about Lucky was interrupted as the door opened and another guard appeared with Wanda.

'Here you are! I've been looking for you,' Wanda said. Turning to the guard beside her she continued, 'Thanks for your help.'

The man withdrew and Quentin breathed a sigh of relief. 'Wanda! Would you please tell these people what happened to our bag.'

When Wanda had repeated what had happened on the concourse, the trouser-suited woman shook her head. 'But I saw your friend take this bag from someone who was getting on the train,' she insisted.

'Well, of course. He was just trying to get back what was ours.'

'Tell them what's in the bag,' Quentin suggested.

'A cat,' Wanda said.

'My neighbour's cat,' Quentin went on. Seeing the disbelief on their faces, he explained the situation.

The trouser-suited woman gave an exasperated huff. 'All this over a dead cat? That's the last time I'm public-spirited enough to report a crime, I can tell you. I'll be late for my appointment, thanks to you.'

She strode out of the room, muttering to herself.

Trying to suppress a grin, Quentin said, 'Can we take poor Lucky away now? Or you can look inside if you like, just to be sure? I don't suppose Lucky will mind. He's mainly black with white patches, and he's wrapped in a brown blanket.'

After a moment's hesitation, the guard picked up the holdall and pulled the zip halfway open. He paused, as though not relishing the idea of viewing a dead cat. He put his hand in, seemed to feel something, then withdrew his hand and held the bag away, his lips curled in distaste.

'Can we go now?' Wanda asked. 'We might still make the vet's before they close.'

'Just give us a description of this man and we'll pass it on to the railway police,' said the female worker. 'He may be on our system as a regular thief. There could be something on CCTV. They'll check that, too, and keep an eye out for him.'

Quentin described the thief as best he could. Then, with the holdall once more in their possession, they left the office.

'What's happened to the bloke who collapsed?' Quentin asked Wanda. 'Did the ambulance come?'

Wanda nodded. 'Yes, but they had a wasted journey. He came round, said he'd had these attacks before and insisted he'd be all right. He just grabbed his bag, staggered off and got into a taxi. The lady who stopped to help wasn't too impressed, but she said maybe the illness made him grouchy.'

'Right, well we did what we could. OK then, next stop the vet's.'

Walking as fast as they could, they left the station, finally getting to the surgery at one-fifteen.

'Closed!' Wanda cried.

'I expect there's still someone here,' Quentin said. He banged on the door but there was no response. 'There must be somebody here. They knew we were coming, and they wouldn't leave animals over the weekend. Hold on to this a minute.'

Wanda took the bag while Quentin moved to the edge of the pavement and looked up, wondering if the vet lived above the surgery. The curtains at the window were drawn.

'Perhaps they haven't got any overnighters this weekend,' Wanda said. 'Leave it, Quentin. We'll come back on Monday.'

'Go through all this again? Not on your life.' Quentin banged the door harder, but there was still no response. He looked for a separate door or bell for the flat above but found neither. Defeated, he gave up and called a taxi.

All the way back Wanda was silent. The bag sat beside Quentin, a faint odour coming from it. Poor Lucky, he thought, wrinkling his nose. The traffic had cleared a little, so the journey back was quicker, and after he'd paid the fare Wanda followed him into his house.

'What's up?' Quentin asked as he placed the holdall on the lounge floor. 'Don't worry, it doesn't matter if we take Lucky on Monday. I'll make us some tea, then you'll feel better.'

'Quentin… I didn't want to say anything in the taxi, but are you sure this is your bag? It seems… different.'

'Does it?' Quentin eyed the bag, then moved closer. Black, with two side pockets, chrome tags on the zips. Chrome? Didn't his bag have brass tags?

He lifted it carefully, trying to judge the weight. Did it feel different, or was it his imagination? In the chaos at the station and the rush to get to the vet's in time, he hadn't noticed anything unfamiliar. But now…

Placing the holdall on a chair, he grasped the tag and pulled the main zip open. A relieved sigh escaped him when he glimpsed something dark and furry. Then he frowned. He'd wrapped Lucky in a brown blanket, not this soft, fleecy blanket, which was covering something very un-catlike. His hand hovered over the opening for a long moment before he snatched at the blanket and pulled it aside.

His eyes widened and he gasped as he saw what was underneath.

Chapter Three

'Oh my God,' breathed Wanda as she peered over his shoulder. 'That's definitely not Lucky.'

For a few seconds neither of them spoke. Then Quentin said, 'It depends on your point of view. Most people would think it was pretty lucky to find this amount of money.'

Still staring into the bag, Wanda asked, 'How much do think is here?'

'A lot.' Quentin reached in and pulled out a bundle of notes. He counted out a thousand pounds in twenty-pound notes. Other bundles were made up in different denominations, some still wrapped in packaging as though they'd come straight from the bank. Tipping all the bundles out onto the chair, Quentin did a quick calculation.

'From the look of it, there's over a hundred thousand, maybe about a hundred and thirty.' He fingered the mole by his ear. 'What I don't understand is how we ended up with it. I thought I just took back the holdall that was nicked from us.'

'There're only two possibilities,' Wanda reasoned. 'Either it's not the same holdall, which means the guy you took this from wasn't the guy who took Lucky, or our thief dumped poor Lucky somewhere and put the money in.'

'It's not my holdall. It's very similar, but mine had gold-coloured tags. I didn't notice before. But it was the same man, I'm sure of it, and he had a holdall.'

'Two,' said Wanda, gripping his arm. 'It's coming back to me now. He had two holdalls when he ran away.'

'Did he? I didn't notice that. And you didn't think to mention this at the station?'

'I've only just remembered. It all happened so quickly. I was confused, but now I think about it I'm sure he had something in each hand.'

Frowning, Quentin tried to recall the image of the fleeing man. All he could remember was a flash of blue, and a black holdall – the holdall he'd snatched from the ground. Had he been carrying another bag? Quentin had been so focused on poor Lucky being whisked off to heaven knows where, he hadn't really noticed much else. On the platform he'd only seen the man from one side. Could he have had a second holdall in his other hand?

'Well, if he swiped ours, perhaps he swiped someone else's as well. The guard said they had regular railway thieves. Our thief probably didn't know what was in either of them. Now we've got this, and he's got our cat.'

Wanda shook her head. 'But it's not our cat! Poor Lucky – stuffed into a holdall, carted through London, now he's been kidnapped. Not a very dignified end to his life, is it?'

'No, but imagine the look on that guy's face when he opens the bag and finds a dead cat.'

Quentin saw a grin spread over Wanda's face, and the next minute they were both convulsed with laughter.

'Oh my word,' Quentin choked. 'How I'd like to be there when he does. That'll teach him to swipe other people's belongings. What a fiasco – fifteen quid for a cab to get someone else's cat stolen, and more than a hundred thousand in return. You couldn't make it up, could you?'

'What will you tell Mrs Freeman?' Wanda said when she recovered. 'Sorry, Mrs Freeman, I couldn't look after your cat even when it was dead?'

'That's the least of my worries at the moment. The thing is, what are we going to do about this lot?'

Wanda grimaced. 'I don't know, but if I don't have a cup of tea soon I'm going to faint. I'll put the kettle on.'

Twenty minutes later they sat on Quentin's sofa sipping tea and eating sandwiches. When he'd munched his way through cheese and pickle in granary bread Quentin sighed. 'We should probably hand it in.'

'Probably?'

'Well, it's a lot of money. You don't pay for your weekly shop with that much, do you? You don't pay for anything pricey with cash these days, unless it's for something illegal.'

Wanda looked at him expectantly.

'What?' he asked when she said nothing.

'Go on,' she urged. 'Say what you were going to say.'

'What was I going to say?'

'That we could investigate it ourselves. After all, we are a bona fide detective agency now, and you know how stretched the police are.'

Quentin thought of the two rooms above a bakery on the main Greenwich road where they'd set up their business, and the mundane, mostly domestic cases they'd handled since they'd started. He longed for the excitement he'd felt during their first case. Their work had been so dull recently he was beginning to think Wanda was losing interest in the agency.

'I don't think that justifies us holding on to a hundred-odd thousand pounds though, Wanda.'

'Really? I seem to remember someone finding a pot of money and deciding to keep it.'

The sarcasm in her voice wasn't lost on Quentin, and despite his twenty-five years and the success in the case that had brought them together, he flushed.

'That was different – it was family money. I didn't hear you complain when I put most of it in to start up our agency. Anyway, it was nowhere near this amount. We shouldn't really keep this.'

'I didn't say we should,' Wanda said. 'But we could hang on to it for a while and try to find out about it. As you said, it might be for something illegal.'

'Yeah. Suppose he didn't swipe it, the bloke I chased. Suppose he brought it to pay for something, drugs say, or stolen goods of some sort. Perhaps he was meant to exchange the money for something.'

'A straight swap, you mean, at the station? Just change bags?'

'Why not?' Quentin said, slipping into detective mode. 'Busy place on a busy day, dress like hundreds of others and blend into the crowd when you've made the exchange – what could be easier?'

'Except he didn't make an exchange. He just took our bag and ran off. Why would he do that?'

Quentin frowned, going over the events as he remembered them. 'Perhaps our holdall was like the one he was expecting to see, the one he was going to exchange it with.'

'But…' Wanda paused for a moment before continuing. 'He wouldn't just take it if the person who was meant to hand it over wasn't there. He could have been taking any old bag.'

'Yeah, but perhaps the person who was meant to make the exchange was there. Think. Where was our holdall when it was snatched?'

'On the ground next to me.'

'You and who else?'

Wanda stared at him. 'The man on the ground! He had a bag, but he was lying on top of it. You mean–'

'Well, it makes sense. Suppose you turned up with over a hundred thousand in cash to buy something and the bloke you were meant to buy from is out cold on the deck with a holdall next to him. Wouldn't you think the goods you wanted were in there, especially if that's the only bag you could see? You wouldn't leave it there for bystanders or paramedics to rummage through and find whatever it was you were paying for, and you certainly wouldn't leave the money. You'd grab the goodie bag so its contents wouldn't be found then make off with both bags.'

Wanda pushed a strand of hair from her forehead. 'Let me get this straight. You're saying the bloke who collapsed was a crook who had dodgy goods in a bag that he was meant to exchange for a bag full of money.'

'I'm saying it's a possibility. Or it could just be a random bag-snatcher who managed to steal two bags and one just happened to be full of cash.'

Wanda shook her head. 'Maybe, but I don't think he would risk taking two bags at the same station at the same time. He'd double his chances of being caught.'

'Unless he got the first bag somewhere else,' Quentin countered, 'then tried his luck at the station. But if he stole the first one somewhere else, he'd have looked in it, surely? Once he'd found the money, he'd hardly bother to steal anything else.'

'If your first theory's right it would explain why he had two holdalls,' Wanda said slowly. 'He was carrying the one with the money in, then snatched ours and disappeared into the crowd.'

'Yeah, he moved pretty damned quick too.'

'True, but if he brought the money with him to pay for something, why would he let it go without more of a fight? That's if he did bring the money with him. We're only making assumptions.'

'Well,' said Quentin, 'I think it's a start. It's unlikely he was just an opportunist on the lookout for a quick profit. Even if he was, there's still the question of why he had so much money, where it came from and what it was going to be used for. Either way, we have a mystery on our hands, so what are we going to do about it?'

Wanda pursed her lips. 'You know what we're going to do. You've already decided.'

Quentin interlocked his fingers and leaned his chin on them. 'We'll investigate. And we'll hand the money in, but not just yet. We need to have a good look at the bag and the money to see if we can learn anything.'

'Really, Sherlock? Got your fingerprint kit and magnifying glass handy?'

'You know what I mean,' Quentin snapped, impatient at her flippancy. 'There could be something in the pockets or the lining to give us a clue. Come on, Wanda. I know you're just as keen to take this on as I am.'

'Well,' Wanda said, looking directly into his eyes, 'it beats trying to track down garden gnomes. We need something to stimulate our brains.'

A tacit understanding settled between them, and Quentin felt a surge of elation.

'OK,' Wanda went on. 'We'll examine the bag and record any findings. Take some photos too. Did you get a look at the bag-snatcher?'

'Not enough to give a good description. I think I'd know him again if I saw him. What about our man on the floor? All I can remember is he had a grey coat and a green scarf. You saw him more than me.'

Wanda screwed up her face. 'He was pretty ordinary-looking. Middle-aged, mousy hair. Pale, but then he would be if he was ill.'

'You'd know him again though? And what about his holdall? What did that look like?'

'Just an ordinary black holdall.'

The door swung open and Magpie strutted in. He sat at Quentin's feet for a few moments, then rose and went to sniff at the holdall, which sat on the floor next to the chair where Quentin had tipped the money. When he'd finished sniffing, Magpie clawed at it.

'Leave it, boy,' Quentin said, pulling him back. 'Come on, I'll get your dinner.'

Wanda stood up. 'I should go and let Mozart out. Poor dog's been in all morning. I'll get my camera while I'm there.'

'Got anything in for dinner?' Quentin asked hopefully. 'I was going to go shopping this afternoon, but I don't feel like it now.'

Wanda nodded. 'I expect I can rustle something up.'

'Oh, I don't mind cooking,' Quentin told her, recalling his mother having to cook every day for his demanding father. 'I just don't feel like shopping.'

'It's all right, I'm happy to do it. I'm meant to be seeing Colin, but I think I'll ring and put him off. Do you want to come to mine, or shall we eat in here?'

'I don't mind,' Quentin answered, pleased that she seemed to want to stay with him rather than meet up with his rival for her affections. Colin was an old friend of her late husband's and, if Quentin's suspicions were correct, Wanda's ex-lover. She saw much less of him since she'd moved to Greenwich and met Quentin, but he couldn't help the jealousy that rose in him whenever Colin was mentioned.

'Mine then,' Wanda decided. 'I'd rather cook in my own kitchen. I'll just go and walk Mozart round the block and I'll be back.'

She bent down to pick up her handbag, exposing the swell of her breasts. Quentin's pulse quickened and he felt a tingle of desire. In spite of her thirty-nine years, Wanda was everything he admired in a woman – attractive, sophisticated, quick-witted, good fun yet somehow mysterious. Sometimes he felt he didn't know her at all. He certainly didn't know how she really felt about him. She was tender towards him, made love to him, accepted him as a business partner, but when he'd asked her to live with him she'd refused point blank.

After Wanda had left he went into the kitchen, followed by Magpie, who waited patiently while he squeezed chunks of fish out of a pouch into his food bowl.

'Well now, boy,' Quentin said. 'It looks like we've got ourselves a decent case. What do you think about that?'

Magpie ignored his food long enough to give him a haughty stare.

'No need to look like that, boy, just because we lost poor Lucky. I look after *you* well enough, don't I?'

Magpie turned his head, sniffed at his bowl, and looked back at Quentin before he deigned to nibble at his meal.

'Be like that then, you fickle feline,' Quentin huffed. 'Just be grateful I adopted you, or you could still be raiding bins for your food.'

* * *

While he was waiting for Wanda, Quentin examined the holdall. The faint smell he'd noticed in the taxi and assumed was coming from his neighbour's dead cat was still there, but he couldn't put his finger on what it was. There was nothing inside or in the two pockets to give any clue as to where it might have come from or who it had belonged to.

Magpie came in and rubbed against his legs. 'So you love me now then? Ugh, you stink of fish. Fish! That's it!'

Side-stepping the cat, he picked up the holdall and held it to his face. Yes, that faint odour was definitely fishy – not strong enough to be identified immediately, but sometime in its life it had been near a fish. Or lots of fish. Or had fish inside it.

'So what?' said Wanda when she returned. 'I mean, it hardly narrows the field, does it?'

Quentin shrugged. 'It might. It could be that whoever owned the bag comes from a fishing port, or somewhere where they handle fish.'

'Right. Or maybe they carried the shopping in it one day, or put it down next to the fish counter at Sainsbury's. We need a more substantial clue than that. Wasn't there anything inside?'

'No. You can have a look if you like.'

Wanda knelt on the floor and peered into the bag. She put her hand in and felt all around, drawing out the stiffened bottom panel, turning it over and feeling underneath. 'Nothing,' she said, replacing the bottom panel and searching the two side pockets. 'Nothing there either.' Turning the holdall upside down, she examined the base. Four metal studs were positioned so as to keep the canvas from touching the ground.

'Pity,' Quentin said, guessing her thoughts. 'If it weren't for them there might have been some tell-tale signs on the bottom, you know, scraps of material or scratches, something to show where it's been.'

Wanda nodded. 'I daresay the police could come up with something with all their equipment. Still, that doesn't help us, does it?'

She stood up and placed the holdall on the table. Then she reached for her camera and took photos from various angles.

'That's enough,' Quentin said after several snaps of the shutter. 'We're not trying to sell it on e-bay.'

'You never know,' Wanda said, snapping again. 'These photos may be useful. What about the money?'

'What about it? You mean photograph it, just to remind ourselves what that much money looks like?'

Wanda looked exasperated. 'I mean do you think there could be anything in the bundles to give us a clue?'

'Such as?'

'I don't know. A bit of paper, a matchstick or something.'

'Shouldn't think so, but I suppose we could check the bundles that aren't wrapped, the ones that aren't straight from the bank. Actually, that's a good idea. We can count it at the same time.'

Thirty minutes later Quentin placed the money back in the holdall and gave a low whistle. 'A hundred and fifty thousand! Fancy walking around with all that on you.'

‘Risky,’ agreed Wanda, covering the money with the fleecy blanket Quentin had mistaken for fur. ‘Suppose he lost it, or got mugged.’

‘Yeah, or had some guy snatch it at the railway station! I wouldn’t do it, that’s for sure. Not that I’m ever likely to have that much money.’

There was a short silence as they both tried to think what to do next. Wanda spoke first. ‘If it weren’t for that fleece, the guard at the station would have realized it wasn’t a cat he was touching.’

‘Mmm. I guess he didn’t fancy examining a dead cat,’ Quentin said. ‘Can’t say I blame him.’

‘You do know we’ll probably have to explain how our fingerprints got all over the money?’ Wanda asked. ‘I mean, of course they would be on the bag. But the money? It’ll be as clear as day to the police that we’ve handled the money as well.’

‘Well, who wouldn’t? Surely anyone would want to know how much it was once they knew it was there.’

‘I’m not sure everybody would. Sensible people would take it straight to the police.’

Quentin spread his hands. ‘Or keep it. Some of it anyway. Still, when we do hand it in, I don’t think I’ll take it to the local nick.’

Wanda looked at him. ‘You’re taking it to Philmore, aren’t you? Why? This has got nothing to do with the case we worked on last year.’

‘No, but he knows us and I’d feel happier explaining the situation to him.’ Quentin thought of Detective Inspector Steve Philmore, with whom he had collaborated on their first case. ‘And I promised I’d give him any information I had.’

‘Yes, about that Whitelaw who got away, the mastermind or whatever he was,’ Wanda said with a toss of her head, ‘not every dodgy deal we come across.’

‘This is more than some dodgy deal, I’m sure of it. That amount of money wasn’t destined for any Del Boy down at the market. Anyway, I think we should take it to Philmore. He'll know what to do with it, how to get it analysed and everything.'

'Perhaps you're right. You won't get hold of him till Monday though. I don't suppose he'll be working at the weekend, unless he's on a special job.'

Quentin didn't answer. He still had Philmore's mobile number from the previous year. Should he call him now? He could be at a wedding, at the races or simply enjoying a quiet weekend with his family. It wouldn't hurt to leave it until Monday. After all, no one was going to come after the money. The man he'd taken the bag from had never seen him until today, and he may not even know about the money. If he'd snatched the holdall from someone at the station like he'd snatched Quentin's perhaps he hadn't looked inside and had no idea what was in it.

Yes. It would be safe enough to leave it until Monday. Or Tuesday. After all, they might have found a lead by then.

Chapter Four

After Wanda had left to prepare the meal, Quentin spent twenty minutes on his running machine. Usually, if the weather was good, he ran several circuits around Greenwich Park, but today he didn't feel like negotiating the uphill slope and road junctions to get there. He wanted to keep his mind on the day's events. Running helped him to think, helped him deal with any stress he may be feeling as well as improving his fitness. Afterwards he shaved, showered, dressed in fresh clothes and felt better. Refreshed, he went to Wanda's for dinner that evening with the bag in tow.

'I didn't feel comfortable leaving it unguarded,' he told her. 'You never know.'

'No,' she agreed. 'After all, you've been burgled before.'

'Yeah. Well, I've set the alarm, just in case.'

Wanda raised a perfectly arched eyebrow. 'In case you're burgled during dinner or in case you don't go home?'

Quentin grinned. 'I wasn't planning on going home.' Setting the holdall on a chair, he pulled her to him and nibbled at her ear.

'Hmm,' she said, pushing him away. 'We'll have to see about that. *After* we've eaten.'

'Can I help?' he called as she disappeared into the kitchen.

'No, I'm more or less organised.'

Wanda's West Highland terrier, Mozart, trotted into the room. 'Hello, Mozart,' Quentin said, stroking him. 'How are you then?'

The dog yapped and went to sniff at the holdall. Quentin pulled him back. 'Hey! Stop that. There's nothing in there for you.'

When the dog had settled down at his feet, Quentin glanced around the room. The house was a mirror image of his own, two bedrooms upstairs with the bathroom on the ground floor. In the year that Wanda had been here the lounge had been made bigger by a dividing wall being removed, as his had been. The fireplace had been opened up and a log burner installed, giving the place a cosy glow on winter evenings. She had made other tasteful changes, and still had some of the antique furniture from her late husband's shop. Having grown up with mature, traditionally minded parents, Quentin appreciated its beauty and craftsmanship. He was particularly fond of the green velvet chaise longue, where he and Wanda had shared their first kiss.

He spotted a picture of Wanda with her late husband, Gerry, and for the umpteenth time thanked him silently for his timely death.

'Sorry, mate,' he murmured, 'but you really did me an enormous favour.'

'What was that?' Wanda asked, carrying a tray of dishes to the table.

'I was admiring your décor. I really must get round to doing my place.'

'Well, I've offered to help enough times. Sit down, then, I don't want this getting cold.'

As usual the meal was delicious, but Quentin's mind wasn't on the food. It was torn between the delights he hoped to share with Wanda and how a hundred and fifty thousand pounds had come to be sitting in a holdall in the same room as them.

'The only lead we can follow is your guy in the green scarf,' he said, helping himself to more wine. 'The one who collapsed.'

'My guy?'

'Well, you stayed with him. He went off in a taxi, you said. So that's where we'll start.'

'Track down the taxi driver you mean, find out where he took him?'

'Yep. First job tomorrow.'

Wanda gave him a mischievous smile. 'Or we could go now? Taxi drivers don't finish at five.'

The lighting was subtle and the music soft, and there was a note of amusement in Wanda's voice.

'Tomorrow's soon enough,' Quentin said.

Over coffee, Wanda played one of their favourite CDs, one by Leonard Cohen. Quentin's pulse quickened as he recognized the coded message. Ever since their first dinner together, Leonard Cohen had been a cue for their love-making.

He stood up and caught Wanda to him as she turned from the CD player. They swayed to the music and listened to the words for a few minutes before Quentin tilted her face to his and kissed her. The thought of what lay ahead filled him with urgent desire, and as he followed her up the stairs all thoughts of the money fled from his mind.

* * *

'This is stupid,' he said when he took Wanda a cup of tea the next morning.

Wanda rubbed the sleep from her eyes. 'What is?'

'Me sleeping in here, or you sleeping at mine when we could be living in the same house.'

Sighing, Wanda sat up. 'We've been through this. As much as we like each other, it's no good you getting shacked up with me. When you're thirty I'll be forty-five. Think about it.'

'I have thought about it.'

'Well think again. You need to meet someone your own age.'

'I've met lots of girls my own age. I couldn't stay with any of them for more than a few dates. I–'

His words were drowned out by the shrill of the doorbell. Wanda jumped up and reached for her dressing gown.

'Who could that be at nine-thirty on a Sunday morning?' Quentin said, going to the window and peering out. His heart plummeted as his plans for a cosy breakfast with Wanda, possibly followed by a repeat of the previous night's activities, faded like the light on a winter's evening.

'It's Colin,' he grumbled, seeing the lean shape and balding head of the man below. 'What the hell does he want?'

'He probably just wants to see how I am,' Wanda said, pushing past him. 'I told him I wasn't well last night.'

As Quentin pulled on his jeans and donned his shirt, he heard Wanda talking to Colin downstairs, though their voices were indistinct. Annoyed though he was at Colin's interruption, he felt mildly guilty at the way he always thought of him – a boring quantity surveyor whose redundancy had turned him into a persistent nuisance.

For a moment he wondered whether to stay upstairs out of sight. 'What the hell,' he muttered to himself. 'He already knows about me and Wanda. What's the point of hiding it?'

Clattering down the stairs, he saw Colin's face change when he realized he was there.

'Morning, Colin.'

'Quentin!' Colin's grey eyes narrowed and his gaze slid over Quentin as though he expected to see a badge with "Guess where I've been?" written on it. He turned to Wanda, an accusing look on his face. 'You said you weren't well last night. That's why you told me not to come round.'

'That's true, Colin. I didn't feel well.'

'But well enough to…' Colin's voice tailed off as he inclined his head towards the remains of the meal on the table.

'It's sweet of you to worry about me, Colin, but I still needed to eat and Quentin was with me all day yesterday anyway. Not that I should have to explain myself – to either of you,' Wanda said pointedly. 'Now if you gentlemen will excuse me, I'm going to have a shower.'

As she swept past them an uneasy silence descended on the room. Quentin cast a surreptitious glance at Colin. He was dressed in his usual attire of casual trousers, trainers and a short-sleeved shirt which fell to his hips. Removing his glasses, he lifted the bottom of his shirt and rubbed at them vigorously, something Quentin knew he did when he was anxious or angry.

'Look,' Quentin said at last. 'I know you're fond of Wanda, and I know you promised Gerry you'd look after her, but she's quite capable of making her own choices.'

Colin shook his head. 'It won't last, you know, you and her. You're too young for her.'

'Probably,' Quentin agreed, 'but I can't help myself. I'm going to spend as much time as I can with her. Anyway, she's my business partner now.'

Replacing his glasses, Colin snorted. 'Business partner! Setting up a detective agency just because of that case last year. All you've done since then is look for missing dogs and try to catch adulterers in compromising situations. Fat lot of good a law degree's done you.'

Quentin cringed inwardly, relieved that Colin didn't know he'd dropped out of university before getting his degree.

'How about you?' he asked in an attempt to change the subject. 'Had any luck with a job yet?'

'No. Fortunately I've still got some of my redundancy money left. Anyway, I can see I've outstayed my welcome and I'm on my way to my daughter's, so I'll leave you and Wanda to your cosy tête-à-tête.'

He sounded so despondent Quentin felt quite sorry for him. In his heart he could understand Colin's feelings about his relationship with Wanda.

'At least have a cup of tea before you go,' he offered, moving towards the kitchen.

While the kettle hissed its way to boiling, he found some cups and put teabags into Wanda's china teapot. He'd just poured in the hot water when he heard Colin's voice, though he couldn't make out what he was saying.

'What was that, Colin?'

'I said, I see you know where everything is then. Don't bother with the tea, I'm off. Tell Wanda that Emma will let her know about the dress.'

What dress? Quentin wondered. Then the house shook as the front door slammed shut. Please yourself, Quentin thought. Colin really should be a more gracious loser.

'Has he gone?' Wanda asked, emerging from the bathroom wrapped in a towel.

'Yeah. He went off in a huff. Not that I blame him. Still, he should be used to the idea of us by now.'

'He'll be all right,' Wanda said. 'I'll talk him round. We're old friends.'

'He said Emma would let you know about the dress, whatever that means.'

'My wedding dress,' Wanda explained. 'His daughter's getting married and I said she could borrow it if she wanted to. Oh, for goodness' sake.'

'What is it?'

Wanda rolled her eyes. 'He's left it here.'

'Where?'

'There, on the floor by that chair, in that holdall. I gave it to him when he came in.'

'Holdall? You mean that navy-blue holdall?'

'Yes, Quentin, that navy–' Wanda stopped, her eyes sweeping round the room before meeting Quentin's.

Red heat crept up Quentin's neck, and he stared at Wanda with the same horrified look as she was giving him.

Chapter Five

Wanda let out a long moan. 'Oh no. Colin's taken the wrong bag.'

A swathe of emotions swamped Quentin. He saw his chance of another big case disappearing.

'It's all right,' Wanda said, breaking the silence. 'We'll just ring him and explain.'

'Explain he's walked off with a hundred and fifty grand?'

'No, just say he's got the wrong bag and we need it. He probably thinks your overnight things are in it. Unless we take him into our confidence. He *is* an old friend, after all. I'd trust him with my life.'

'Your life, yes, but a hundred and fifty grand? I'm going after him – he can't have got far. What's his daughter's address, do you know?'

'Yes, but–'

'Give it to me, Wanda, quickly.'

He watched while Wanda wrote the address and telephone number on a piece of paper. 'Aren't you forgetting something?' she said as she handed it to him.

Shrugging on his jacket, Quentin asked, 'What?'

'How are you going to go after him? My car's not here and yours has a flat battery.'

'It'll be charged by now. I'll go round and get it.'

'You'll never catch him. He'll be at Emma's before you're even halfway.'

Quentin clicked his tongue. 'That's what I'm afraid of. If I can catch him before he gets there, give him the right bag, he'll have no need to open ours. But his daughter will want to look at the dress.'

'Of course she will. Sit down, Quentin. It's no use rushing around – he's got too much of a head start. I'll ring him, explain about him taking your bag and that we're coming to get it. Wait till I'm dressed, then we'll walk to the lock-up together.'

'Makes sense I suppose, but what if he opens the bag even if you ring him?'

'Why should he? I'm sure he's got better things to do than rummage through your things. He might realize it's not the right bag – the one he should have taken is navy blue. The one he took is black.'

Quentin harrumphed. 'Stupid man. Can't he tell blue from black?'

Giving him an impatient look Wanda said, 'Navy blue looks black in some lights. He probably picked up the nearest one.'

'We're supposed to be investigating it,' Quentin said through tight lips. 'If Colin gets hold of it, we'll have to involve him.'

'He'd like to be involved,' Wanda said, rounding on him. 'You know he would.'

'Well, I don't want him involved. All right, so he helped us before, or at least he tried, but… it's *our* detective agency, yours and mine, not his. Anyway, we've already decided the money's dodgy. It could be dangerous.'

'That's true,' Wanda conceded. 'All right, I'll ring him and hope he answers before he gets to Emma's and opens the holdall.' She reached for the phone and rang Colin's mobile. 'He won't pick up if he's driving, but he might call me back before he goes in. Ah, I'm getting his voice mail.'

After leaving a message she dialled Emma's number. Quentin listened as she spoke to Colin's daughter.

'Emma? Hello, it's Wanda … Fine, thanks, how are you? … Good. Emma, your dad's been in to collect the wedding dress, but it's still here. He's taken my friend's bag by mistake. There are some important papers in it that he needs by tomorrow. Is it all right if we drive over and get it, and bring the dress at the same time? I'd like to see it on you.'

She broke off and grimaced at Quentin before continuing, 'No, I don't want to make your dad have to come back here. I could do with a drive out anyway … OK thanks. See you in – say, about an hour and a half then. Bye now.'

She hung up and looked at Quentin steadily. 'There we are, sorted. I'm going to get ready, and you can go home and get what you need.'

'OK,' Quentin said reluctantly. 'Don't be too long though.'

In his own house he had a quick shower, cleaned his teeth and changed his T-shirt. Then he put fresh food and some cat milk out for Magpie, who watched disdainfully as though disapproving of his imminent departure.

'It's all right, boy,' Quentin said fondly. 'I shouldn't be too long.'

As he collected his car keys his gaze fell on the telephone. He would miss his weekly call from his mother. It was an unwritten rule that she rang every Sunday morning from Australia. Sometimes he rang her in the week, or sent an email via his sister, Shelagh, who lived a few miles from his parents, but the Sunday morning call had turned into a ritual. He'd ring her this evening, he decided. It would be Monday morning in Australia by then, but she would worry if he didn't call. Although he never admitted it, two years after her emigration he still missed her. Apart from the natural mother-and-son bond, she had always taken his side in his conflict with his belligerent father. After her visit to the UK the previous year, their relationship had been strengthened even more.

Wanda's familiar knock at his door told him she was waiting for him. When he'd locked up, he joined her by the gate and they set off. The wind was still chilly and Quentin was glad he'd put a waterproof over his jacket. It flapped in the breeze as they walked along. Before they got to the end of the street the figure of a man appeared ahead of them, emerging from one of the alleys that separated the blocks of terraced houses. He looked first one way and then the other as if deciding which way to turn. As they drew nearer, Quentin blinked, looked at the man again, then clutched at Wanda's arm and turned her round, forcing her to go back the way they had come.

'Don't look back,' he hissed, almost pulling her along.

'Why? What's the matter?'

'That bloke, the one by the alley. I'm sure it's the bloke from the station.'

Looking confused, Wanda took two steps to his one. 'The station? You mean the bloke who stole our bag or the one who collapsed?'

'The one who stole our bag. Keep going.'

Wanda's pace slowed when they came to her house, but Quentin tugged at her arm.

'Keep walking. We'll go the other way.'

When they'd rounded the corner at the far end of the road, Wanda said, 'Why didn't we just go indoors if you didn't want him to see us?'

'Because if he spotted us, he'll know exactly where we live. He already knows we live in this street.'

'How?' Wanda panted, still trying to keep up with him. 'How could he know?'

'I don't know, but it makes one thing perfectly clear.'

'Does it? Can't we slow down a bit now?'

They'd emerged onto the main road, and in front of them was a mini supermarket. Quentin steered her in through the door, then stood back so that he could see passers-by through the glass frontage.

'We'll wait here a while,' he said. 'If he's followed us, we should be able to lose him now.'

Pulling her arm free, Wanda asked, 'Are you sure it was him?'

'Pretty sure.'

'But you said you couldn't describe him.'

'Not in detail, but this guy was the same height, with dark hair, and– and he looked like him. He looked suspicious, didn't you think so?'

'Suspicious?'

Not taking his gaze from the pavement, Quentin continued, 'Why would anyone stand there looking up and down the road like that?'

Wanda shrugged. 'He was lost? Or he was looking for someone?'

'Yep. He was looking for us. And that means he knew what was in that holdall and he means to get it back.'

'Right.' Wanda frowned, then looked at him as if he'd tried to explain the theory behind quantum mechanics. 'So you've deduced all this on a mere glimpse of some guy who just happened to be in the same street as us? It's ridiculous. How could he possibly have found out who we are?'

'I haven't worked that out yet, but I'm sure it was him.'

A woman came in and squeezed by them, the wire basket she had picked up at the door catching Quentin's hand and grazing it. 'Sorry,' she said. 'Not much room, is there?'

'Come on, Quentin,' Wanda urged. 'We're in the way here. If he was following us he'd have gone past by now.'

'Probably. Unless he thought we'd turned the other way.'

'We don't even know if he saw us. If he did, he may not have recognized us.'

'Not you, maybe, he didn't really see you at the station. But he'd recognize me, that's for sure. And I'm carrying a holdall. If he spotted that, he'll be after us. He'll think we've got the money with us.'

'But this holdall's navy-blue–'

'As you said, navy looks black at a glance. Colin got it wrong and it was right next to him.'

Wanda sighed. 'Well, we can't stand here indefinitely. I'll go and buy a bottle of water. After that, we'll go. OK?'

'OK.'

Five minutes later, Quentin peered cautiously out of the shop doorway, looking left and right alternately. 'Can't see him,' he said, stepping onto the pavement.

'Thank goodness,' Wanda said. 'Can we go now?'

They walked on, glancing back from time to time in case the man was in sight. After a few hundred yards, they slackened their pace a little. The parade of shops was interrupted by a petrol station, and Wanda guided Quentin to a sheltered spot by the wall of the garage building.

'Before we go any further,' she said, 'I need to get my head straight. There's no point hurrying now – we'll never catch up with Colin, so we'll just have to hope he picks up my message and doesn't open the holdall. If he does, we'll have to tell him what's going on.'

'But–'

'But nothing. How could this bloke from the station know where we live? Think. Was there anything in that bag with your name on? An old travel label or anything?'

Quentin shook his head. 'No, nothing. I haven't used it much, and I haven't been away since I moved to Greenwich, so there's no need for my name or address to be in it. Even if it were, it would be my old address, and no one there knows where I live now.'

'So there was nothing in the bag except Lucky and the blanket? What about the blanket?'

'What about it? I stopped putting my name on things when I left school.'

As he waited for Wanda's response a thought struck Quentin. 'Lucky!' he shouted. Glancing round to make sure he hadn't drawn attention to himself, he lowered his voice. 'That's it. Mrs Freeman was worried he might try to go back to his old house, so she had a collar made with his address on. That's how the thief knew which street we live in. He'd assume the cat's mine, and the address on the collar is mine too.'

Wanda was looking worried now. 'So you think he was trying to see where number fifty-two is? That's where Mrs Freeman lives, isn't it?'

'Yes, but more likely he'd already sussed that there was no one in at number fifty-two, and was waiting to see if we came home.'

'Or,' said Wanda, looking even more worried, 'perhaps he'll wait till tonight and break into Mrs Freeman's to look for the money.'

Quentin frowned. Wanda's suggestion was a distinct possibility. Having suffered a break-in himself, he wouldn't wish it on anyone.

'He might, but he won't bother doing that if he's seen the holdall now and thinks the money's in it.' He glanced at his watch. 'There's plenty of time to get to Emma's and back before it gets dark anyway. It's only eleven-thirty.'

Shaking her head, Wanda said, 'If you're sure it was him, maybe we should go to the police now.'

'No, we'll get the money first. This is all going to sound pretty far-fetched to Philmore if we don't even have the money. Hold this a minute, could you, while I do this thing up.'

He handed the holdall to Wanda while he pulled his waterproof together and zipped it up. 'Come on,' he urged when he'd finished. 'Let's get a move on.'

They began walking past the garage, Wanda now carrying the holdall. Suddenly she stopped and clutched at Quentin's arm with her free hand.

'The man you saw just now, was he in motorbike gear?'

'He was all in black. Why?'

'Is that him, on the other side of the road?'

Quentin looked across to see a tall, dark-haired man in black trousers and a black leather jacket sliding into a shop doorway. 'Bloody hell! He must have followed us after all.'

'In here, quick,' Wanda said, turning into the forecourt. 'Go over behind the pumps. He won't try anything here.'

Quentin stared across the road, but the man had disappeared. They stayed near the pumps, ready to dart into the garage shop if they saw him approaching. After five minutes Quentin ventured to the front of the forecourt and looked around. Seeing no one who looked like their pursuer, he beckoned for Wanda to join him. Still clutching the holdall, she came up beside him, looked over his shoulder, gasped and drew back. He followed her gaze across the road and spotted the tall, dark-haired figure peering out from behind a payphone box.

'Bugger it!' Quentin muttered as the man ducked out of sight. He gazed desperately about him to see if there was any other route they could take other than along the road. There wasn't. A short distance ahead a set of traffic lights changed colour, and a line of vehicles formed a barrier between them and the opposite side of the street.

'Run!' he barked, propelling Wanda from the forecourt along the pavement to the nearest corner junction. 'Down here.'

They ran pell-mell down the side street and around the next corner, then stopped and paused for breath.

'With any luck we've lost him,' Wanda said, holding her side. 'I hope so. I've got a stitch. Can we get to the lock-up this way?'

'Yeah, we're nearly there. We've been round in a square. We'll need to go back onto the main road first to get to it. Let's hope he doesn't spot us, if he's still hanging about.'

They came to a junction further along the same road where they had seen their pursuer. Edging out cautiously, Quentin looked left and right. Traffic whizzed by and the pavements were crowded, even though it was Sunday. A little further along, the shops gave way to several blocks of houses.

'We'll have to risk it,' he called, beckoning to Wanda.

Together they ran up to the houses and into the gap that separated the first block from the second.

'Made it!' Quentin puffed. 'I'll go ahead and get the garage door open.'

He sprinted away, but as he reached the alley where the lock-up was, he heard a cry. Whirling round, he saw Wanda slumped against the wall, while the tall dark figure was making off with the holdall. Heart thumping, he dashed back to where Wanda was struggling to stand upright.

'Wanda! Are you all right?'

She gulped and grabbed his arm. 'I think so. Let's get to the car before he realizes he hasn't got the money.'

Minutes later they were at the lock-up. Quentin swung the door up and they ducked in, bringing the door down behind them. The unit was windowless, and in the near-dark Quentin felt his way round the car, avoiding the leads that connected the battery to the charger and whispering to Wanda to follow him. He fumbled to locate the car door, then wrenched at the handle. They tumbled in and sat catching their breath for a moment. Then Quentin switched on the interior light.

'I'm sorry, Wanda. I don't know what I was thinking of, leaving you behind when he was after us.'

'Well, we thought we'd shaken him off, didn't we?' Wanda said, her voice quavering. 'Don't talk too loudly. If he's opened the bag, he might come back and look for us.'

'Unlikely,' Quentin countered. 'After all, he doesn't know I've got a car here. As far as he's concerned, we just turned down the alley to get away from him. He might have a quick look round, but for all he knows we could have climbed a wall or gone through one of the back gates.'

Wanda chewed at her bottom lip. 'He'll still thinks we've got the money though,' she said after a few moments. 'He won't give up. I'm surprised he spotted us after we came out of the mini-market.'

Quentin gave her a quizzical look. 'Really? You don't think you would have made it easy for him?'

Even in the dim light inside the car, Wanda's red coat was as bright as a post box in a snow scene.

'I see what you mean,' she said, glancing down at the coat. 'I should have taken it off. I didn't think.'

'Neither did I. Too late now and you've lost your wedding dress.'

Wanda grimaced. 'And my satin shoes, tiara and some wedding magazines. It doesn't matter about the magazines, but the other things… Oh well, I've only kept them for sentimental reasons. The dress is probably too old-fashioned for Emma anyway.'

He put a sympathetic hand on her arm. 'Sorry,' he said. 'Still, you've got to see the funny side. First he steals a holdall and finds a dead cat, then he nicks one and gets a wedding dress! He's not going to be a happy bunny.'

Wanda laughed. 'I'd love to see his face when he opens it. At least a wedding dress is better than a dead cat.'

Quentin caught her mood and laughed with her. 'I don't think he'll see it that way,' he said, throwing up his arm and banging it down on the steering wheel. His fist caught the horn, filling the enclosed space with its raucous noise.

'Bugger!' he said, laughter deserting him. 'Let's hope he's not poking around outside or he'll guess we're in here.'

'Well, we can't sit here all day, we'll have to do something.'

'We'll give it a bit longer, then we'll go. After all, we're in a car and he's on foot. He can't do anything even if he sees us.'

'He could break into Mrs Freeman's,' Wanda reminded him.

'Like I said, we'll be back before dark. I'll disconnect the charger, then check outside.'

After climbing out of the car he unhooked the charger from the battery, closed the bonnet and pulled open the garage door. Then he peered into the alley. It was empty.

'All clear,' he said, sliding into the driver's seat. 'You close the door when I've driven out.'

Two minutes later, Wanda banged the garage door down while Quentin manoeuvred the BMW into position. When she had scrambled in beside him Quentin eased the car forward and around the corner into the opening that led to the road. As they waited to pull out into the stream of traffic, a tall figure with a navy-blue holdall ran along the pavement towards them. Seeing a gap in the traffic, Quentin hit the accelerator and sent the car screaming past him.

'He's totally lost it!' Wanda shouted, looking behind her. Unable to resist, Quentin slowed down and looked in the off-side mirror to see their adversary staring after them with a raised fist.

‘That’ll teach him,’ Quentin chuckled as they sped away. ‘He must have noticed it wasn’t the bag I took from him and checked inside.’

Wanda nodded. ‘Yes and now he knows for sure we’ve got the money, otherwise why would we run from him? He also knows what car we drive, and unless he’s blind, he knows our registration number as well.’

Chapter Six

‘Come on, come on!’ Quentin muttered when they’d rounded the corner and were stopped at traffic lights. ‘Are these things out of order or what?’

‘No, but there’s road works up ahead,’ Wanda said, craning her neck to see beyond the queue in front. ‘Ah, here we go.’

As they inched towards the lights they changed again. After what seemed like an age, Quentin drummed his fingers on the dashboard. ‘This is ridiculous. It’s lucky our man’s on foot or he’d have caught up with us by now.’

‘He might not be on foot. He was in motorbike gear, or it looked like it, so he could be on a motorcycle. Anyway, we’re off again now.’

‘Where are we going?’ Quentin asked when they’d crawled past the road works and turned east on to the A102 out of Greenwich.

‘Emma lives in Westerham. Westerham, Kent, that is.’

‘That’s helpful. I mean where am I going now? Which is the quickest way?’

‘Straight down the A2212, I should think, then the A233, but they’ve got a lane closed off near Bromley. When I went down the other day there were queues a mile long.’

'Typical!' Quentin grunted. 'We'll carry on to the A2 and take the M25. It'll be quicker in the long run.'

Wanda pursed her lips. 'As long as there are no hold ups. They don't call it the biggest car park in Europe for nothing. All right, go on. We're heading that way anyway.'

When they'd joined the motorway Quentin was pleased to see the traffic moving steadily. He slipped into the nearside lane, nudged the gear stick into drive and relaxed a little.

'Ring Colin again,' he said, not relishing the thought of Colin discovering the money and having to explain how they'd come by it.

'There's no point,' Wanda told him. 'I've left a message, and I've spoken to Emma. He's more likely to nose inside if we make a big thing of it.'

'Yeah, I suppose so,' Quentin conceded. 'How far is it?'

'I don't know. I've only ever gone with Colin, so I didn't pay much attention.'

'Look at the map, see what exit number it is.'

'OK. Where is it?'

Quentin cursed under his breath. 'In the boot. Just look for the signs.'

Feeling increasingly impatient, Quentin pulled out into the next lane and increased his speed. 'This isn't exactly how I intended to spend my Sunday,' he complained. 'Chasing around the M25 because some idiot took the wrong bag.'

'Hark who's talking! You didn't bring the wrong bag from the railway station, then? Colin's no more an idiot than you are.'

Quentin gave her a sidelong look. Wanda always seemed to stick up for Colin, no matter what. They fell silent until Wanda said, 'There's a lot of motorbikes out today.' Then, as a sign came into view, 'Oh, here we are – Westerham, exit five.'

They travelled on, the traffic growing heavier as the M26 merged into the M25. As they neared the Westerham exit, Quentin pulled into the inside lane ready to turn off. He indicated left and was about to steer the BMW across when the roar of a powerful motorbike engine filled his ears. He heard Wanda's sharp intake of breath as the motorbike drew level on their inside. Instead of dropping back or going forward, the motorcycle kept pace with them, swerving dangerously near and blocking their exit, forcing them to carry on ahead.

'Bloody road hog!' Quentin yelled, his stomach lurching at the near collision. 'What the hell is he playing at?'

He felt for the horn and pressed it hard. The motorcycle, ahead of them now, slowed down enough to stay just in front. Checking his mirror and indicating, Quentin swung the car out to overtake the bike, intending to beep at him again. His hand stayed fixed to the wheel as they passed him when Wanda grabbed his arm.

'It's him!' she cried. 'Quentin, it's him.'

'What?' Quentin glanced in his offside mirror at the shiny black bike – a Suzuki, he decided, though he couldn't name the model. Its rider was helmeted, but the visor was up. The visible part of the face bore a strong resemblance to that of the man who had snatched the holdall from Wanda.

'How could it be him?' Quentin said, his pulse quickening. 'We left him standing on the pavement.'

'I don't know, but it's him, I'm sure of it.'

Trying to pull his thoughts together, Quentin said, 'We've missed the turning so we'll just carry on and outrun him.'

'Outrun him? He's got a motorbike, not a mobility scooter.'

'Yes, and we've got a BMW. It's about time I took it to top speed.'

'Right. Well, don't kill us in the process.'

Putting his foot further down on the accelerator, Quentin moved over into the outside lane and drove as fast as the preceding traffic allowed. The motorcycle followed. With his visor down now, the rider changed lanes every time Quentin did, not leaving enough space to allow another vehicle to come between them.

'Blast it!' Quentin shouted when he thought he'd out-manoeuvred the bike, then caught sight of it overtaking a car on the inside and coming up behind him. 'He'll cause an accident if he goes on like this.'

'Maybe that's what he's hoping,' Wanda said. 'We'll never get rid of him like this.'

'You could be right. OK, there's a sign coming up. See how far the next services are.'

'That'll be Clacket Lane,' Wanda said with an air of authority. 'It's not too far. Why? What are you thinking?'

Flicking the indicator lever, Quentin switched lanes. 'I'll try and pull into the service area at the last minute. Hold tight.'

The motorcycle followed as they moved across again, ready to exit at the services. Instead of signalling and slowing down, Quentin sped up, wrenching the wheel round at the last moment and narrowly missing the slip road barrier. Brakes squealing, he glanced in the mirror and grinned.

'It worked. He's shot on ahead. He'll have to go to the next exit before he can turn round and come after us.'

Driving into the car park, he pulled up and cut the engine. 'How the devil did he get here? We left him in Greenwich.'

'Yes, but he would have seen which way we turned, and we were held up at that first set of traffic lights for ages. If he had his bike nearby he could have picked up our trail there.

Quentin scratched his chin. 'Even so, I'm surprised we didn't notice him before.'

'Well, there were other bikes on the road. Why do you think he had his visor up? It's as if he wanted us to recognize him.'

‘Perhaps he did. After all, we know what he looks like. He wants us to know he means business.’

‘We know that all right,’ Wanda said with a shudder.

‘Yep. Any ideas on what our next move should be?’

Wanda moistened her lips. ‘Only one: get out of here before he has a chance to double back and find us. We can get to Westerham from the next junction, I’m sure. Just a minute, I’ll get the map. About time you got a new satnav. You’ve been saying you would since you broke the old one.’

She got out, went to the boot and returned with road map. ‘Yes,’ she said when she’d found the appropriate page. ‘The A22 south from Junction 6, then east on the A25. It won’t take long.’

Quentin nodded. ‘Keep your eyes peeled, though, Wanda. We wouldn’t want to lead him to the money. Even if he got the money, he wouldn’t leave it at that. We can identify him. He can identify us too. He knows what street we live in, plus our car registration, and he sure as hell won’t be working alone. The higher-ups will want to be certain we don’t report the whole thing to the police.’

Lowering her gaze, Wanda said, ‘How do we know there are any higher-ups? Don’t answer that. Big money means big business, so he wouldn’t be working alone. But how do they know we haven’t already been to the police?’

‘Because if we had we would have gone straight to a police station when we spotted our man in Greenwich, not gone off on a jaunt on the M25.’

‘That doesn’t mean we won’t report it now,’ Wanda pointed out.

There was a moment’s silence. Cars came and left the car park, and people walked to and from the service building. Quentin gazed through the window, seeing but not registering the outside activity. He knew it was probably foolhardy to try to deal with this on their own. It wasn’t like following an errant husband or trying to catch a persistent shop lifter. A hundred and fifty thousand pounds was serious money, serious enough for someone to kill for.

That thought sent a frisson of excitement through him, edged with fear. Things could get dangerous.

'Do you want to report it now?' he asked. 'I mean what could they do at the moment? Only send traffic cops to look for the biker and arrest him for dangerous driving or something. Still, it would get him off our backs if they got him.'

'It would,' Wanda conceded, 'but if we call them everything might come out, then we'll be back to the boring cases we're supposed to be working on.'

They shared a look of understanding, and Quentin knew that Wanda was also caught up in the thrill of solving this mystery together.

'Let's get out of here,' he said as he started the engine. 'Did you get his registration?'

Wanda reddened. 'No, I was too busy worrying about him not hitting us. I think it was LR something.'

Quentin was about to back out of the parking space when a shiny black motorcycle drove into the car park. At the sound of its engine, they both looked round, eyes wide as it approached. Almost unconsciously, Quentin pressed the electric switch to lock the doors. He held his breath as the bike passed them and parked in the bay reserved for bikes. Seconds later, the air was filled with the sound of motorcycles, and five or six more appeared to join the first one. Soon there were thirty or so piling in looking for parking spaces.

'There must be a rally on somewhere,' Quentin groaned. 'There might be hundreds of them on the motorway soon. Just as well we didn't phone the police. They'd never find our friend in that lot.'

'You're probably right. I wish I'd got his registration number.'

'Well, it's no good worrying about that now. We've lost him, thank goodness. If he comes off at the next exit to double back here, he'll be out of luck.'

'Let's get going then,' Wanda said. 'I thought that first bike was him.'

'So did I. Stupid really. I mean what can he do on his own in a public place?' Slipping the car into reverse, Quentin eased the BMW backwards, then moved towards the exit. 'What are you doing?'

'I've dropped my phone. I think it went under the seat.' She leaned over, scrabbling about trying to reach her mobile, her elbow digging Quentin in the ribs. Taking his foot off the accelerator, he slowed down, intending to locate the phone himself.

'Never mind that, Quentin, just drive,' Wanda said, pulling herself upright. 'I think I've just seen him come in.'

Quentin straightened up and looked in the rear-view mirror. Another bike, black and shiny, was approaching the parking area. Putting his foot to the floor Quentin drove to the exit as quickly as he could.

'Why do you think it's him? How can you possibly tell?'

'I don't know. Just a feeling. Do you think he spotted us?'

'Highly unlikely, if it *was* him, but he couldn't have got back here that soon. I think you're being paranoid.'

'You'd be paranoid if he'd grabbed you from behind and snatched your bag. He's not following us though.' Wanda swivelled round in her seat. 'It couldn't have been him. I wish we were in my car.'

'Why?' Quentin patted the steering wheel fondly. He loved his car, with its sleek, silver lines and distinctive badge, even though it was seven years old now. 'Your car's nowhere near as fast as this.'

'It's nowhere near as noticeable either. My little Toyota isn't as conspicuous as this.'

Back on the motorway more motorcycles were in evidence. 'Definitely a rally,' Quentin concluded. 'Not long till the next junction.'

They fell silent until the sign for junction six came into view. 'Here we are,' Wanda said.

Quentin grunted and signalled to turn off. As he exited he checked his mirrors. Several vehicles had followed, but no bikes. The roar of their engines grew fainter when they left the busy motorway behind. When they were safely on the road towards Westerham, Quentin gave Wanda a sideways glance.

'Why the long face?' he asked. 'We'll be all right now.'

'I'm just thinking of what I'm going to say to Emma. About why I haven't got the dress, I mean.'

'Tell the truth. You were mugged and your bag was taken. No mugger knows what's in a bag until after they've taken it, do they? She'll think they were after money or a mobile phone.'

Wanda thought for a moment. 'Yes, but money and phones are usually in handbags, and I've still got my handbag.'

Swerving to avoid a football that came bouncing from the pavement, Quentin cursed. 'Kids! Haven't they got gardens to play in?'

'Perhaps they haven't.'

'Parks, then. Anyway, stop worrying about Emma. It doesn't matter what we tell her. Getting the money back is more important.'

'Hmm…'

Quentin looked at her again. 'What does that mean?'

'Stop looking at me and watch where you're going,' she said as the car veered slightly. 'It's just – what are we going to do with the money when we get it? It's too dangerous to take it home – when Motorbike Man can't find us he's bound to go back to Greenwich to wait for us.'

'He'll be waiting outside the wrong house then, if he goes to Mrs Freeman's. Still, you're right. He could easily see us.'

'He can't stay there all day and night,' Wanda reasoned. 'He'll have to sleep sometime.'

'Like we said, he won't be working alone. You can bet your life that someone will take his place when he goes. He only has to give them our description.'

They fell silent, this thought hanging between them.

'We don't have to go home,' Quentin said eventually. 'Once we've got the money we could check into a B and B for the night.'

'We could, but I'll have to go home. I can't leave Mozart indefinitely.'

'No, I suppose not. Magpie will be all right – he's got food and water, and the freedom of the garden since I've had the cat flap put in.'

'Right. We're nearly there.'

They cruised past a sign welcoming them to Westerham. 'Straight on,' Wanda instructed. 'Left at the traffic lights, then – I'm not sure. I think it's a turning on the right somewhere along there.'

Ten minutes later they found the place, helped by the sight of Colin's white Honda, and pulled up outside a modern semi-detached house with latticed windows.

'Bit smart for first-time buyers,' Quentin commented.

'I don't think Emma's fiancé's parents are poor,' Wanda told him.

Quentin pulled a face. 'It's all right for some.'

'Hey!' Wanda rounded on him. 'You didn't have a nice little house provided for you then, no deposit or rent?'

Quentin flushed. 'That's different,' he said. 'Mum inherited the house, she didn't buy it for me. Anyway, I don't have to justify my circumstances.'

'Of course you don't. Neither does Emma.'

His flush deepening, Quentin opened the car door. 'Point taken,' he said, climbing out.

As they left the car and walked up the path, he tried to compose himself. He'd thought he and Wanda were on an equal footing, that the gap in their ages made no difference to their relationship, yet she still had the ability to make him feel like a little boy. Oh well, he thought sighing, there's one good thing about little boys: they grow up.

Chapter Seven

Emma was a pretty brunette with brown eyes and a good figure. Not bad, Quentin thought when she opened the door to them. She must have got her looks from her mother. She obviously didn't get them from Colin.

'Wanda!' she said, ushering them inside. 'Nice to see you again. And this must be Quentin. Pleased to meet you, Quentin.'

'Hello, Emma. Good to meet you too.' Quentin followed her and Wanda into an airy sitting room where Colin was lounging in an armchair, a Sunday newspaper covering his lap. He stood up when he saw them, the paper slipping to the floor.

'There you are. I was beginning to wonder where you'd got to.' He moved forward and pecked Wanda on the cheek, then nodded curtly to Quentin before scooping up the fallen paper.

'Cup of tea?' Emma asked, looking from Wanda to Quentin.

'Yes please,' Wanda said. 'But I've got some bad news I'm afraid. I haven't got the dress.'

Emma looked disappointed. 'Really? Why not?'

Wanda looked at Quentin. 'Well–'

'She was mugged,' Quentin interrupted. 'On the way here.'

Emma gasped. 'Oh, you poor thing! Did they hurt you?'

'Mugged?' Colin was all concern. 'What happened?'

'We were on the way to pick up Quentin's car. He went ahead to open the garage door and this bloke appeared from nowhere and snatched the bag the dress was in.'

Colin glared at Quentin as if to say, you again!

'She was only on her own for a minute,' Quentin said hastily. 'I heard her cry out and ran back to her, and the bloke ran off.'

'Lucky he did,' Wanda said. 'Otherwise he might have got my handbag as well.'

'Have you reported it?' Colin asked.

'No,' said Wanda before Quentin could answer. 'It didn't seem worth it. After all, I wasn't hurt. I didn't see him properly, and I don't think the police would consider a fourteen-year-old wedding dress valuable.'

Colin frowned. 'Maybe not, but it would alert them to the fact that there are muggers in the area. Still, as long as you're all right.'

'Yes, that's all that matters,' Emma said. 'I've seen a few dresses I like anyway. To be honest, Martin isn't keen on me wearing a second-hand dress, or least his mother isn't. She wants to come and choose one with me.'

Wanda nodded. 'I can understand that. Where is Martin, by the way?'

'Football practice. He plays for the local team. He just rang and said he is having a few beers with the boys. I'll get the tea.'

When she'd gone into the kitchen, Colin turned to Wanda. 'Why did you come if you didn't have the dress? You must have been shaken up. Quentin should have taken you home and looked after you.'

Quentin opened his mouth to defend himself, but Wanda forestalled him. 'I wanted to come, Colin. I wanted to take my mind off it. If I'd gone home I'd have only sat brooding.'

Colin looked at Quentin, as though for confirmation.

'That's right,' Quentin said. 'She insisted on coming.'

'I suppose I should take some of the blame,' Colin said. 'Sorry, Wanda. If I hadn't taken the wrong bag, you wouldn't have had to bring the dress over. Not that you had to. There's no rush – the wedding's not till December.'

'Talking of bags, where's mine?' Quentin asked, hoping he sounded nonchalant.

'In my car. When I got your message I left it there. Not much point bringing it in.'

Quentin felt a stab of panic. Colin's car was on the road in front of his – anyone could steal it or break into it. He fought back the urge to suggest that he went to get it now. If he made a fuss, Colin would suspect something.

'Don't know why you had to drive all this way to get it anyway,' Colin continued.

Quentin's mouth tightened. 'I've told you. Wanda wanted to come.'

'And on the phone, she told Emma there were some papers you needed?'

Quentin cursed under his breath. He wasn't fond of Colin but he had to give him some credit. The man wasn't stupid. They had lost one of the two reasons for coming here, but they had come anyway. Colin was obviously suspicious of Wanda's assurance that she merely wanted to take her mind off the so-called mugging.

'It's a case we're working on,' he said at last. 'We need the documents for work tomorrow.'

He was saved from further explanation by Emma returning with the tea. 'So, you're a private detective, Quentin,' she said brightly as she handed out the mugs. 'I bet that's exciting.'

'Sometimes,' Quentin murmured.

'Well, it was last year, wasn't it?' Emma babbled. 'That case Dad helped you on? I think he enjoyed that. Perhaps he could help you again if you get a big case. He needs something else to do instead of worrying about me all the time.'

Not trusting himself to speak, Quentin smiled. Over my dead body, he thought, and shook his head when he realized that if they weren't extremely careful it probably would be.

As if sensing the hostility between him and her father, Emma turned her attention to Wanda. Quentin listened to their small talk for the next half an hour, wishing they could retrieve their holdall and leave. He was anxious to get started on the case properly. Colin's unannounced visit this morning had held things up.

After fidgeting away another twenty-five minutes listening to Emma's talk of the forthcoming wedding and her plans for the house, he stood up. 'We'd better be going, Wanda.'

'Yes,' Wanda agreed. 'Thanks for the tea, Emma.'

'I should be going too, Em,' Colin said. 'I'll just see Wanda off.'

When they'd said goodbye to Emma, Quentin and Wanda followed Colin to his car.

'Thanks,' Quentin said as Colin unlocked the Honda and took out the holdall. He reached out to take it, his hand brushing Colin's fist on the handle. He waited for Colin to release it. Instead, Colin held on.

'This case you're on,' Colin said. 'It must be quite big if you're so keen to get these papers back.'

Resisting the urge to tell him to mind his own business, Quentin smiled politely. 'That's confidential.'

A triumphant grin appeared on Colin's thin face. 'That means it is. Anything you can tell me about?'

The smug look on Colin's face irritated Quentin. 'No,' he said, wrenching the holdall from Colin's grip.

Colin's grey eyes narrowed. 'Please yourself. But if anything happens to Wanda… I'm not silly, Quentin. I don't buy that random mugging story. If someone's taken

Wanda's bag it's got something to do with a case you're working on. Right, Wanda?'

Wanda sighed. 'It's all right, Colin. I can look after myself. Bye for now. I'll ring you.'

With a snort of frustration, Colin whirled round and walked back to the house. Quentin unlocked the BMW, put the holdall on the back seat and got in. When Wanda was sitting beside him he started the engine and reached for the gear stick. Her restraining hand on his stopped him from pushing it into the drive position.

'What's up?' he asked, turning to her.

Wanda didn't answer straight away. Instead she stared through the windscreen as though trying to work something out.

'Well?'

'I've had an idea.'

'If it involves Colin, I'm not interested.'

'Don't be childish,' Wanda said with a toss of her head. 'It's no good cutting off your nose to spite your face.'

Quentin sighed. 'All right. Let's hear it.'

'It's simple really. You know what we said about not going home?'

'Yes, and you said you had to because of Mozart.'

'So I did. But we don't have to go.'

'Don't we?'

'No. Colin could go. Motorbike Man still thinks we live at number fifty-two, so if he sees us going into either of our houses then we've blown it. But he doesn't know Colin. If he goes to mine, collects a few things and brings Mozart, Motorbike Man will have no idea that Colin doesn't live there.'

Quentin raised his eyebrows. As much as he hated to admit it, he knew it was far safer to stay away from home until they were certain they weren't being watched.

'Will he do it?' he asked, knowing the answer. Colin would do anything for Wanda, and his daughter was right: he did need something to occupy him. 'I'll need some things as well,' he added. 'He can't be seen going into two houses.'

'He can go in your back door, over the wall. You've done it often enough.'

'But we can't expect him to help and keep him in the dark,' Quentin pointed out. 'We'll have to tell him why.'

'Of course we will but we can trust Colin. You know that.'

Sheepishly, Quentin murmured, 'I know. It's just…'

Wanda put her hand on his knee. 'I've told you, there's no need to be jealous of Colin.'

'I can't help it. Remind me again why his wife left him.'

'You know very well. She led him a merry dance then went off to work in Greece.'

Quentin stopped himself from saying what he thought; that Colin had probably bored his wife into leaving. Still, whatever the reason there was no excuse for her to leave their daughter with no explanation or subsequent contact.

'What's that got to do with anything?' Wanda was saying.

'Nothing. He winds me up, that's all.'

Wanda withdrew her hand. 'Well, get over it. I'm going back to ask him to help.'

'In front of Emma?'

Wanda slumped back in her seat. 'No. We don't want her getting involved. The fewer people that know the better. We'll drive to Colin's and wait for him to get back, then ask him. He won't mind going out again.'

'Drive to Wanstead? But Colin will practically have to pass our door to get home.'

'I know, but there's no alternative unless we go in now and explain in front of Emma, and we don't want to be discussing it over the phone. Suppose they can listen in? We shouldn't take any chances after what happened last year.'

'You're right. OK, if you're sure.'

'I am.'

I'm not, Quentin thought as he signalled to pull out. A motorbike came from a side road and he heard Wanda gasp. He stiffened until it had sped past them and roared ahead. He let out a long breath and wondered if they would react in the same way every time a motorcycle came into sight.

'Here we go, then,' he muttered. Swivelling round in his seat he glanced at the holdall. A hundred and fifty thousand pounds. Despite the possible danger, he couldn't help a thrill running though him. Yes, he thought as he started on their journey to Wanstead, here we go. Again.

Chapter Eight

As soon as Colin's car drew up outside his house Quentin took the holdall and he and Wanda went to greet him. He looked surprised to see them but a broad smile lit his face when Wanda said, 'We've changed our minds, Colin. We've talked it over and we'd like you to help. Can we come in?'

When they were safely ensconced in his lounge, Colin listened in amazement to their revelation about the money. He stared at Quentin as if he'd said the holdall contained rocks from Mars.

'A hundred and fifty thousand quid?' he choked. 'Are you sure?'

Unzipping the holdall, Quentin held it open. Colin peered in, his eyes threatening to pop out of their sockets and his mouth agape.

'Oh my God! You weren't joking!' Putting his hand inside, he lifted out a bundle of notes and flicked through them. 'I've never seen this much money all at once. And you're going to investigate it? You should hand it over to the police. Look what happened last time.'

'We solved that case and the gang was caught,' Wanda reminded him.

'Some of the gang,' Colin said. 'And you had to involve the police then.'

'I know, but they couldn't have done it without us, and we couldn't have done it without your help. Isn't that right, Quentin?'

Quentin tried to think of anything constructive Colin had done to help in their previous brush with crime and couldn't. Despite their best efforts and those of the police, the mastermind of the gang had escaped. Nevertheless, he nodded. 'We will hand it in of course, but we want to have a go at investigating it ourselves. We are detectives, after all.'

Colin snorted. 'Yeah, right. It sounds dangerous to me, and anyway what's the point? No one's going to pay you for finding out where the money came from.'

Quentin and Wanda exchanged glances. 'The point is,' Quentin said patiently, 'that this bloke on the motorbike knows we have the money, and that we can identify him, so we're in danger whether we give the money to the police or not. Anyway, it's the satisfaction of… of…' Getting one over on the criminals and knowing we can do it was what he wanted to say, but didn't.

'Oh, admit it, Quentin, it's just the thrill of the chase you want,' Colin said, then shifted under Wanda's resentful gaze.

'We think what we do has some value, Colin,' she said coldly. 'You said you wanted to help.'

'Yes, well, I do, but like I said, it's dangerous. I'm only thinking of your safety.'

'So will you help or not?' Quentin demanded.

'Only if you promise to keep me fully informed this time.' Colin looked at Wanda, who nodded. 'Right, so…

you want me to go over to your house, Wanda, and get you some things? And Mozart?'

'Yes please, Colin. Just shove some clothes and toiletries in a bag. My make-up's on the dressing table, and can you bring my phone charger, address book and camera?'

Colin returned the money to the holdall. 'OK. I suppose you'll want things too, Quentin?'

'Yes,' Quentin said as Colin got up to go. 'Can you feed Magpie and put some fresh water down? There's food in the cupboard. Put some dried stuff in the automatic feeder too, in case we don't get back there for a few days. Wanda's got a key to my back door on her keyring.'

This earned him one of Colin's hostile glares.

'Make sure the cat flap's not stuck again,' Quentin continued, 'and don't forget to turn off the alarm and reset it. I'll give you the code.' He tore a piece of paper from the edge of a magazine and scribbled on it. 'Thanks.'

'I'll cook dinner while you're gone, Colin,' Wanda offered.

'If you like. There's chicken in the fridge. Not too much for me – I had lunch with Emma.'

When he'd left, Wanda sent Quentin a triumphant smile. 'There. That wasn't too difficult, was it? I told you he'd do it.'

Quentin flopped back in his chair. 'You did. The thing is, we've got the money back but we're no closer to knowing where it came from. Now we've finished chasing after it we need to get on with deciding the best way forward. And I think we should start with the taxi driver.'

'Yes, we've lost a whole day. We should go down to Eltham now, really. At least we could find out which taxi driver it was, even if he's not there.'

Quentin looked at his watch. Six o'clock. He didn't fancy the idea of driving anywhere. He'd done enough driving for one day, and his earlier enthusiasm to get going on the case had surrendered to hunger and tiredness.

'There's no need. We're safe here and a few more hours won't make any difference. I don't suppose you saw him, did you?'

Wanda wrinkled her forehead. 'Not clearly. He was bald, I know that much. Anyway, I'm with you. Tomorrow will do. I'm going to raid Colin's fridge. Put the TV on. Let's lighten up a bit.'

Quentin fiddled with the remote, switched the television on and slid further down in his chair. Soon the smell of food cooking wafted in from the kitchen, making him feel even hungrier. As if by some magical thought transference, Wanda reappeared with a can of beer and three cracker biscuits.

'I can't find any vegetables,' she told him, 'so I'm doing rice.'

'Fine,' Quentin said, yawning. 'Need any help?'

She shook her head and went back to the kitchen. Quentin munched the crackers and drank a few sips of beer. His tiredness grew. He wished he was at home lounging on his own settee in his dressing gown with the promise of a fun filled evening with Wanda. Or just curled up in front of his own TV with Magpie on his lap. Magpie…

He was shaken awake by Wanda. 'Hey,' she was saying. 'Dinner's ready.'

Quentin sat upright and rubbed his eyes. He glanced around, feeling disorientated. 'Aren't we waiting for Colin?'

'You didn't hear the phone then, obviously. He left his lights on and now he's got a flat battery. He's waiting for the RAC.'

'Where is he?'

'In the parking bay near my house.'

'That's a nuisance. There's a charger in my lock-up but he'd have to get there first.'

Hunger pangs clawed at Quentin's stomach. 'Has he seen anyone hanging around?'

'He says not, and he says we should have dinner without him. He knows we haven't eaten.'

His antagonism towards Colin slipping a little, Quentin stood up. 'Good, I'm starving. Where's this food?'

Halfway through their meal the phone rang. Wanda went into the hall to answer it while Quentin finished eating. He tried to make sense of the conversation he could hear through the doorway.

'… Oh, Colin, how annoying … It's up to you … if it's late …'

'What was that all about?' he asked as she reappeared.

'The RAC can't get there for another two hours. He offered to stay at mine tonight.'

A silence hung between them as Quentin digested this. Suddenly Colin didn't seem such a bad sort after all. It wasn't so long ago that Colin had insisted on spending the night at Wanda's so she wouldn't be alone with Quentin.

'That's sensible,' he admitted grudgingly. A grin spread over his face. 'And it's a great idea.'

'No, Quentin.'

'Why? He'll be perfectly comfortable at yours. Why would he want to drive all the way back here? Just think, a nice quiet evening to ourselves and…'

Wanda eyed him over her uplifted fork. 'And nothing. I couldn't, not in Colin's house. You know how he feels about me.'

Quentin gazed at her, knowing she wouldn't change her mind. 'Oh well,' he said shrugging. 'If he stays, he could keep an eye on Mrs Freeman's. Hold on though. I've just remembered something. I think Mrs Freeman said she was leaving the lights on a timer, you know, to make it look like somebody's at home. Come think of it, that might make things worse. They think we live there, and they're obviously desperate to get the money back. They've already mugged you in broad daylight, and if they think we're there with the money–'

'They might break in,' Wanda interrupted.

Quentin fingered the mole by his ear. 'Except they won't know if we've got the money or not. We could have handed it over to the police or hidden it somewhere else, for all they know.'

He saw the worry on Wanda's face. 'Then again, they might abandon the whole thing until the morning,' he added. 'They'll need to get some sleep.'

'Yes, but you said yourself Motorbike Man's not working alone. If it's not him, it could be one of his associates. I'm not happy, Quentin. We can't risk Mrs Freeman's house being turned over. Maybe we should go back.'

'But it was your idea not to go home in the first place – that's why we came here.'

'That was before I knew about the lights. If they think we're there anything could happen.'

Quentin grimaced. After a pause he said, 'Well, if they break in they'll want to have a good look around for the money. It could take a while, and the longer it takes the more chance there is of them being caught.'

'Yes, there is that,' Wanda agreed. 'After all, they know we're on to them. They'll know we'll be on our guard.'

Quentin didn't voice the other thought that had come to him – that for a hundred and fifty thousand pounds the criminals might hold them at gunpoint or knifepoint if they intervened during any burglary.

'Even so,' Wanda went on, 'the more I think about it the more I think we've made a mistake coming here. If there's the slightest danger of Mrs Freeman's being broken into we should stop it if we can. After all, it's nothing to do with her, is it? It's not her fault her cat died and got snatched. And if we go now, while it's dark, there's less chance we'll be seen.'

Quentin couldn't argue with that. 'I agree. It'll be bad enough coming home to find her cat's dead without being burgled as well. But… If Motorbike Man sees us… I'll tell you what, I'll go and keep watch. You stay here with the money. You'll be safer here, so will the money.'

'No thanks,' Wanda said immediately. 'If you go, we both go. We'll take turns. You can't stay awake all night.'

'I'll be all right,' Quentin said, warming to the idea of mounting surveillance. 'If things get out of hand, I'll call the police and say there's a robbery in progress. I'll give them an anonymous tip-off!'

Wanda rolled her eyes. 'We might be too late anyway,' she told him. 'Not all robberies take place at night, as you know very well.'

Don't I just, Quentin thought, the events of their first case coming back to him.

'I'm calling Colin to let him know we're coming,' Wanda said, her tone decisive. 'But you're right about the money being safer here. We'll leave it and come back for it when we need to.'

Finding his jacket, Quentin fished out his keys and waited while Wanda stepped into her shoes and collected her coat and bag. She straightened up and flicked her hair behind her ears. A lick of desire coursed through Quentin. As she brushed past him to get through the door he caught her to him and nuzzled her neck. 'Ring him again,' he said hoarsely. 'Say we've changed our minds.'

For a moment she melted into him and his pulse quickened. Then she pushed him away. 'I'd like to, but I can't,' she whispered. 'How would you feel if I slept with him in your house?'

Defeated, Quentin followed her out and closed the door.

Chapter Nine

To be on the safe side, Quentin parked the BMW in the lock-up so it wouldn't be seen on the street. Wanda left her red coat in the car and, after rummaging in her bag, pulled out an elastic hairband and piled her hair on top of her head. Among the various items littering the back seat, Quentin found a baseball cap and put it on. Not a very thorough disguise, he thought, but if they were seen in the streetlamps at least they would look different from the way Motorbike Man had seen them that morning. Looking out for anyone acting suspiciously, they hurried as far as the alley that gave access to the rear of the houses, then turned into it.

'I feel like a burglar now,' Wanda said when Quentin helped her scramble over her back wall. 'I don't know why our houses haven't got back gates like the ones over the road.'

Quentin hauled himself up, glad that his running machine and the circuits around the park had made him fitter and more agile.

When they got indoors, Mozart bounded up to them. 'Hello, Mozart,' Wanda murmured, bending down to pat him. 'It's all right, I'm home now. 'Hello, Colin,' she went on as he appeared. 'Sorry about your battery.'

Colin indicated two bulging carrier bags. 'I only left the lights on while I was looking for your things. I think the battery must be on the way out. Seems pointless you coming back here, though, when I've driven all the way over so you can stay out of sight.'

'Like I said on the phone, we're really worried about Mrs Freeman's house,' Wanda said.

Colin looked bemused. 'And you're really going to stay up all night and watch it?'

'I don't know about you two, but I could do with a drink,' Quentin said, trying to avoid a lecture from Colin about the police being better equipped to tackle burglars.

'Good idea,' Wanda agreed. 'Have a look in the kitchen, Quentin. I think there's some whisky left. If not, there's brandy. No beer though, sorry, Colin.'

'Whisky will do,' Colin conceded. 'I need it after this fiasco.'

Wanda pouted. 'Oh, come on, Colin. At least you're not at home on your own in front of the telly.'

'No, unfortunately.'

At that moment Wanda's landline rang.

'That could be the RAC,' Colin said, reaching for the phone. 'I called them from here.'

Seconds later he replaced the handset. 'They'll be here in ten minutes.'

'Quicker than they thought, then,' Quentin said. 'If we're going to keep an eye on Mrs Freeman's, one of us needs to be at the upstairs front window; unless you could keep a lookout while you're outside, Colin?'

'Why not?' Colin replied. 'I'll be out there anyway. Not for long though, and once the car's going, I'll have to drive around a bit to charge the battery.'

'That's OK,' Wanda said. 'Tell us when you're going.'

Thirty-five minutes later Colin re-entered the house. 'All done,' he told them. 'There wasn't anyone hanging around and, from what I could see, Mrs Freeman's looked all right. I'll take the car for a short spin now, and get a new battery in the morning. I don't want to get caught like that again.'

While Colin was gone, Quentin went up to the front bedroom and positioned a chair so he could see Mrs Freeman's. He asked Wanda for some paper and, in between glances into the street, jotted down everything that had happened since their holdall had been snatched at Eltham station.

'It'll help me remember things,' he said.

'Will it? I don't need reminding about being mugged,' Wanda answered grimly. 'I won't forget that in a hurry.'

When Colin returned, Wanda made him some cheese on toast, poured them a second drink each and carried them upstairs. After some discussion and several yawns from Wanda, it was decided that Quentin would keep watch from his own window, and that Colin would go with him to take over after four hours, leaving Wanda to have a good night's sleep.

Though Quentin didn't relish the idea of spending the night with Colin, he collected the carrier bag Colin had filled earlier and went the back way home. Twenty minutes later, while Colin sat in his lounge watching the news, Quentin pulled out the new fold down bed in his front bedroom and flung on a quilt and some pillows, muttering his antipathy towards Colin before realizing he needn't have bothered. While one of them was sitting at the window, the other would be sleeping in Quentin's room.

He should be more gracious towards Colin, he knew. He had been willing to let him and Wanda stay over at his house, and really, there was nothing wrong with the man. But it was evident to Quentin that Colin had no intention of giving up the fight for Wanda, and that she had no intention of giving up Colin's friendship.

Magpie came into the room and rubbed against his legs. 'Hello, boy,' he said softly. 'Thank goodness I can be sure of you. What a weekend, eh?'

His landline rang, and he fetched the handset from his bedroom.

'Quentin?' His mother's voice sounded anxious. 'Are you all right? You didn't answer yesterday.'

Yesterday? For a moment Quentin was thrown. Then he remembered it was already Monday morning in Australia.

‘Hello, Mum,’ he said. ‘Sorry, I had to go out. How are you?’

After the usual time delay, his mother replied, ‘Fine, Quentin dear. And I’ve got some news. You’re going to be an uncle again – Shelagh’s pregnant.’

Although his parents had visited last year, Quentin hadn’t seen his sister since she and her Australian husband had returned to Sydney four years before. He pictured her now, slim like their mother but taller, with eyes much the same as his own caramel-coloured ones. ‘That’s great news, Mum. I bet she’s over the moon.’

‘She is. I think your father’s pleased too.’

Nice to know the old man’s pleased about something, Quentin thought. But then Shelagh had always been his favourite – she’d never disappointed him.

‘How is Father?’ he felt compelled to ask.

‘He’s fine, dear. He sends his love.’

Quentin thought love was the last thing his father felt for him, but he said nothing.

‘I think he’d like it to be a girl,’ his mother went on. ‘It would be nice if it was, but we’ll love it whatever it is. Perhaps you can come over after it’s born – you promised you would.’

‘I will, Mum, but I want to come for at least a month, so I’ll need to plan ahead.’

‘I suppose it’s difficult with work. Have you got a case on at the moment?’

‘Yes, as it happens. Quite a big one.’

Suddenly the TV blared from downstairs.

‘Have you got someone there, dear? Is it Wanda?’

No such luck, Quentin wanted to say. ‘No, Mum, it’s a friend. He’s staying the night.’

‘Oh. Well, I won’t keep you, Quentin. Have a good week.’

‘And you, Mum, and congratulate Shelagh and Howard for me. I’ll give them a ring later in the week, and I’m thinking of getting Skype, so I'll be able to keep in touch with them more.'

'That would be wonderful. I wish your father would get a computer, but he's still living in the dark ages.'

'There's no reason why you can't get one, though, Mum. He doesn't have to use it.'

'That's what Shelagh said. I might just do that. Well, bye, Quentin.'

'Bye, Mum. Thanks for ringing.'

He hung up, wondering what his mother would think if she knew he had a hundred and fifty thousand pounds in a holdall. Or rather, didn't have, because it was still at Colin's. Was he being overzealous, staying awake just in case there was a break-in at somebody else's house? He knew Colin thought so, even though he'd agreed to take the second watch. And was Colin really keen to be part of the investigation, or was it a ploy to keep close to Wanda?

It doesn't matter, he thought as the TV shut down and he heard Colin's footsteps on the stairs. It's our case and we'll handle it in our own way.

It must have been almost three o'clock when Wanda appeared, gliding up to him in a diaphanous dress that revealed her shapely curves. With the lift of an eyebrow and the beckoning of a finger, she drew him to her like a magnet to metal. But she wasn't metal; she was smooth flesh and hot blood, and she was enticing him onto the bed with all the charm she possessed.

He awoke with a start when Colin's voice cut through his dream. Colin, here, seeing him and Wanda in bed?

'Quentin! You were supposed to wake me up, not sleep all night!'

'What?' Quentin rubbed the sleep from his eyes. He was in his own house and Wanda wasn't with him. But Colin was, and from the look on his face Quentin guessed it would be a long time before Colin let him forget it.

Chapter Ten

The railway station at Eltham seemed different without the hordes of football fans they'd seen on Saturday. After leaving Colin in Greenwich, Quentin and Wanda had driven to the station. Although busy, it was far easier to move about, and they stood for a few minutes trying to recall exactly where they'd been when the man with the green scarf had collapsed.

'It was about here,' Wanda said, moving along a few yards. 'Not far from the taxi rank.'

Quentin glanced over at the line of taxis. Some of the drivers stood outside their cabs smoking. Others sat in their vehicles, waiting for passengers from the next train to come onto the concourse. Quentin approached one of the drivers standing by his cab.

'Taxi, sir?' the man said, stubbing out his cigarette.

'I only want some information,' Quentin said.

The man looked annoyed at having put out his cigarette and not getting a fare, but nodded to Wanda as she came up beside him and smiled.

'We're looking for a cabbie who was here Saturday lunchtime,' she said sweetly. 'He picked up a man at about twelve-thirty.'

'Could have been any one of us,' the cabbie said. 'Need more to go on than that,'

'I couldn't see the driver clearly,' Wanda continued, 'but he was bald.'

The cabbie screwed up his face. 'Might be Joe. I think he was here Saturday. What d'you want him for?'

'The man he picked up was sick, he collapsed here outside the station and we called an ambulance, but he wouldn't wait. He went off in a taxi. I just want to make sure he got home all right, that's all.'

The cabbie grunted and pointed to a cab at the front of the taxi rank. 'Tash knows Joe more than me. She'll know if he was here Saturday.'

Thanking him, they walked to the taxi at the front of the line. A youngish woman leaned through the open window and looked up expectantly.

'Hello,' Quentin said. 'Are you Tash?' When she nodded, he repeated their enquiry.

'Yeah,' she answered. 'Joe was here Saturday. He's not in till later though.'

'Do you know his phone number?' Quentin asked.

The woman cast him a distrustful look. 'No.'

'Couldn't you find out?' Wanda cajoled. 'It's important.'

Quentin pulled out his wallet and extracted a twenty-pound note. 'Very important,' he said. The cabbie's gaze fixed on the money.

'That's all you want?' she said. 'To ask where he took this bloke?'

'That's all, yes.' Quentin could see she was weakening. He took out a ten-pound note and added it to the twenty.

'All right,' she said. 'I don't suppose it will hurt. I do know his home number.'

Wanda produced a pen and an envelope from her handbag. 'Can you write it down for me?' she asked, turning the envelope over to the blank side.

The cabbie scribbled a name and number down and held out her hand for the money before passing it over. Quentin gave it to her and took the envelope just as a crowd of people emerged onto the concourse from the platform.

'Well,' said Wanda as they stood back and watched five of the six taxis pick up fares and pull away, 'that was the quickest I've ever seen you lose thirty quid. It's right what they say. Money talks.'

'It certainly does. Let's hope this Joe's the right driver. There could be dozens of bald cabbies working the station.'

Back in the car park, in the relative quiet of the car, Quentin unfolded the envelope the cabbie had written on and took out his mobile.

'Perhaps we should wait a bit. If he was working late he won't take kindly to being woken up.'

'It's gone nine. Let me do it.' Wanda took the phone and the paper from him, stabbed at the keys and lifted the phone to her ear. Nothing happened, and Quentin was about to tell her to try later when she spoke.

'Is that Joe Brady? … I wonder if you can help me. Someone at the railway station gave me your number. I hope you don't mind but it's very important. I'm worried about my brother. He gets these fits and he rang me from the station on Saturday to say he wasn't feeling well. The thing is, he never finished the call and now I can't get hold of him. I understand you picked him up. Can you remember where you took him? Only he's just come back from abroad, and he wasn't on the phone long enough to tell me where he's staying.' She paused. 'Yes. It was lunchtime … Luggage? Well, he would have had something … A holdall? Yes, that's right.'

Another pause. Quentin gazed at her in astonishment. She should have been an actress, he thought as she spoke again.

'Ditchling Street, Catford. Do you know what number? You turned in from Watford Street and dropped him just inside Ditchling Street. Well, that's a great help. I should hate anything to happen to him. Thank you so much. Goodbye.'

'Ditchling Street, Catford,' she said, handing the phone back to Quentin.

'How do you do that? Make things up on the spot?'

Wanda laughed. 'It worked, didn't it? And a woman's got a perfect right to know if her brother's all right, hasn't she?'

Shaking his head, Quentin rummaged in the glove compartment for a pen, then wrote the name of the street on the envelope.

'What now?' he said, turning to Wanda. 'Catford?'

'Yes.'

'OK. Let's find out exactly where we're going.' He reached behind to the back seat for the map, then changed his mind. 'The A-Z will be better,' he said, getting it from the glove compartment.

Wanda raised her eyebrows. 'The sooner you get a satnav the better. You can get maps on Google now, and apparently we'll be able to get them on mobile phones soon. Bring it on, I say.'

As they drove Quentin wondered what they would do when they got there. We'll have to mount surveillance, he mused, smiling to himself. He recalled all the terminology his father had used when Quentin had set up the agency: Surveillance, undercover, incognito, safe houses. It made Quentin sound like a secret agent, and he knew his father was trying to mask the fact that his son didn't have a "proper job". A retired army officer, he had never been afraid to show his constant disappointment in Quentin. Although this had affected Quentin greatly and made him rebellious, he no longer cared what this boorish man thought of him. Since finding his niche as a detective, Quentin thought he would make a very good secret agent.

Wanda interrupted his thoughts. 'We can't knock on doors to find him,' she said. 'He'll recognize me, I'm sure. He won't recognize you though. He was unconscious all the time you were there.'

'True, but if he's the one Motorbike Man was going to give the money to, then Motorbike Man could have given him my description. We could do with an invisible cloak.'

'A cloak of invisibility, you mean.'

'Whatever. Is this the road the cabbie mentioned?'

Wanda peered at the sign on the corner of the road. 'Watford Street. Yes, he said he turned into Ditchling Street from here and dropped our sick friend just inside. We can park up and wait for a bit.'

'Easier said than done,' Quentin said when he'd driven the length of Ditchling Street without finding a parking space. 'I'll go round again.'

The street was lined with rows of early twentieth-century terraced houses with small front gardens and no evidence of garages. When he entered the road the second time, a car was pulling out from the left-hand side. Quentin slipped the BMW into the vacated space.

'We could be here all day,' Wanda pointed out. 'Our friend may have gone out already and he may not come home till tonight.'

'You're right. We need to find out exactly which house it is.'

'And how do you propose we do that?'

'We'll ask someone,' Quentin said, spotting a woman and a child coming out of a house ahead. 'You stay here.'

Leaping from the car, he ran up to the woman. 'Excuse me,' he said, putting on his best smile. 'I'm trying to find an old friend. I know he lives in this road somewhere, but I can't remember what number.'

'What's his name?' the woman asked amiably.

Quentin searched for a suitable name. Grey Coat or Green Scarf didn't seem adequate. 'Johnson,' he said glibly. 'Robert Johnson, when I knew him, but he may have changed it.'

The woman shook her head.

'He was an actor,' Quentin added.

'Don't know anyone called Johnson round here,' the woman replied. 'What does he look like?'

Picturing the man as he lay on the ground, Quentin said, 'About my height, quite slim, brown wavy hair. I heard he'd been ill, so I thought I'd try and find him, cheer him up.'

'Has he got any kids?'

Stumped, Quentin answered, 'Not that I know of.'

'Can't help you then. Sorry.' She made to leave, then turned back. 'He's been ill, you say? You could try the corner house there.' She pointed across the road. 'Mrs Page used to live there. She couldn't sell so she lets it out. I saw a paramedic outside a couple of weeks ago.'

'Thank you, that's a great help.' Quentin smiled at the boy who tugged impatiently at his mother's arm, and went back to Wanda.

'Anything?' she asked.

'Maybe.'

'Nothing definite then,' Wanda said when she heard what Quentin had learned. 'It could be that corner house. How do we make sure?'

'Don't know yet. I'll think of something.'

'Right. Well don't think too long. I could do with a coffee.'

Quentin drummed his fingers on the steering wheel, random thoughts chasing themselves round in his mind. An idea came to him, but he dismissed it as too risky.

'Ring Colin,' he said at last. 'See if he's still at yours and if he's seen anyone who looks like Motorbike Man.'

'What if he has?'

'Then we'll know not to go home, or at least make sure we're not seen. That's if Colin's still there.'

'I should think he would be. I asked him to ring before he left in case we wanted him to do anything. We might be out all day and I'm not leaving Mozart on his own for too long.'

'Right,' Quentin said absently, still racking his brain for something positive to do. A movement outside caught his attention: a man, walking along the pavement on the opposite side of the road. His breath snagged in his throat as the man drew nearer. He put his hand over Wanda's to stop her making the call. 'Don't bother,' he said. 'Motorbike Man won't be there.'

Wanda looked mystified. 'How do you know?'

'Because,' Quentin told her, his eyes following the approaching figure, 'he's here.'

Chapter Eleven

Looking up, Wanda gasped, then slid down in her seat. Quentin did the same, praying that Motorbike Man wouldn't notice them or recognize his car. Unlikely, he assured himself, with the car being wedged in between others.

He wriggled up enough to peer out. The man was striding towards the corner house, his gaze focused directly ahead. Wearing the same black trousers and leather jacket as the day before, he reached the gate of the house and stopped. That's when Quentin noticed the holdall he was carrying.

'Not another bloody holdall,' he groaned, staring at it. Black, though it could have been navy-blue, like the one he'd taken from Wanda the day before. After glancing around as though making sure no one was watching, Motorbike Man went up to the door and rang the bell. The door remained shut. He stood there for a while, then looking about him again, walked round to the side of the house.

'He's gone round the back,' Quentin told Wanda.

'What shall we do?'

'We'll sit tight, maybe follow him when he comes out.'

'He might not come out,' Wanda said. 'He could live here for all we know.'

Quentin started. Could Motorbike Man live here? 'No,' he said. 'If he lived here, he'd have a key.'

'He could have forgotten it, or lost it, but… No, you're right. And he's in motorbike gear. If he lived here, he'd park outside, or in the garden if there wasn't a space. Where *is* he parked?'

Quentin craned to see if the bike was in sight, but couldn't see it. 'Might be tucked in behind a car. I didn't hear it though. Perhaps it's round the corner. There weren't any empty spaces when we came.'

'I'm getting backache,' Wanda complained. She sat up and flexed her spine. 'I hope he's not too long.'

'Well, we can't go anywhere while he's here. We need to find out what he's doing.' The idea he'd had earlier came to him again. 'I'm going over there.'

'What for?' Wanda asked in alarm. 'You can't go skulking around in broad daylight.'

'Why not? He did.'

'Suppose he sees you?'

'Then I'll dash back here. Move over to the driver's seat and get the engine running. Be prepared to go as soon as you see me coming.'

'No, Quentin, that's stupid. Let's just wait.'

Ignoring her words, Quentin got out and strode over to the house. Being on the corner, and the first house in the street, there were only houses on one side. The other side was fenced in by a hedge, with a pathway leading to the rear. Slipping swiftly through the gate, Quentin went around the side of the house where he'd seen Motorbike Man go. At the end of the path, at the entrance to the back garden, was a shed. Alleluia, he thought, diving behind it, the gods are with me. From that position he had a good view of the house and saw that the back door was slightly ajar. Blessing his luck and ensuring that no one was looking through the back windows, he darted forward, flattening himself against the wall. He felt like a TV detective as he put his ear to the door. The buzz of voices came to him, but it was indistinct. He edged along until he was nearer the gap.

An agitated voice that Quentin took to be Green Scarf's was saying, 'I forgot my pills, that's all. Don't worry, it won't happen again.'

Motorbike Man's voice was raised. 'Too right it won't. You nearly cocked up the whole operation. The boss wasn't happy, I can tell you. If that statue had been found at the station the bloody lot would have been blown.'

'Well, it wasn't, was it? Who is the boss anyway?'

Motorbike Man's reply was scornful. 'You think I'm going to tell you? You know the rules – we operate on a need-to-know basis only.'

'I don't believe you know who the boss is any more than I do,' Green Scarf replied.

There was a pause, as though Green Scarf expected the other man to contradict him. When he didn't, he went on. 'Whatever, the system's worked so far. I rang the person I get my instructions from to let them know the handover would have to be rearranged and you turned up, so someone knows what's happening, otherwise you wouldn't be here.'

'I don't know what goes on between the powers that be, and I don't care,' Motorbike Man snarled. 'All I know is the client's getting impatient and when the person I report to found out what had happened, I was given your address and told to come here to pick up the goods. I'm not coming here again, though. A public place is much less risky – at least it would be if people did what they were supposed to.'

'I couldn't help–'

'Never mind the bleeding hearts. I'm not dealing with you again. They'll have to find a new carrier before I take on any more assignments.'

Quentin moved along and risked a peek through the window. A few feet from the back door, the window gave onto the kitchen. The connecting door into the living room stood open, and though Quentin couldn't see Motorbike Man he had a side view of Green Scarf. Without his scarf and coat he looked thinner, but his grey pallor hadn't changed since his collapse on Saturday. He spoke, but Quentin couldn't hear what he said so he moved back to the door.

'Of course I've got the money,' Motorbike Man was saying. 'Just give me the statue – I haven't got all day.'

Quentin blinked. Motorbike Man had the money? Had the client shelled out another hundred and fifty grand, or was Motorbike Man bluffing? He had to be bluffing – who would trust someone who'd lost a small fortune and got nothing but a dead cat in return? He pictured the bag being opened to reveal poor Lucky in his last repose.

'Let's see it,' Green Scarf said.

'What for? You think I've spent it over the weekend? Give me the statue.'

The talking ceased and Quentin heard a shuffling noise. Instinctively he went back to the window. Green Scarf had stepped back from the doorway and stood by a table. He bent and lifted a black holdall onto it.

Now Motorbike Man came into view, the handles of the holdall he'd been carrying still over his arm. He set it on the table next to the first one. They were making the exchange, Quentin realized. Whipping out his mobile, he selected the camera function, held it up to the glass pane and clicked the button. Guessing that Motorbike Man would be leaving any minute, Quentin slid the phone into his pocket and turned to head back behind the shed. Raised voices then a cry made him swing round, and through the window he saw Motorbike Man staring down at the floor. Quentin soon saw why. Green Scarf lay on the floor, motionless. Motorbike Man hovered for a moment, then snatched a holdall from the table.

It was at that moment that Quentin's mobile rang. Not just rang. In the quiet of the garden, it shrieked. Quentin jumped and pushed his hand down in a desperate effort to stop the noise. Pulse racing, he darted behind the shed, knowing that, with the back door ajar, the ringing would have been heard inside the house. He crouched down just as a sound came from the doorway. A second's silence, then the whoosh of someone running. Spurred into action, Quentin shot out from his hiding place and ran after the fleeing man.

As his quarry sped along the side path towards the front of the house, someone came round the corner. Going too fast to stop, Motorbike Man careered into Wanda, who fell backwards with a cry. Motorbike Man teetered, falling against the hedge, arms flailing, the holdall slipping from his grip. Making a grab for it, Quentin pulled it out of his reach. Recovering, Motorbike Man leapt forward, lunged at Quentin and tried to snatch back the bag.

'Call the police, Wanda!' Quentin yelled. 'Say there's been a murder.'

He gave an almighty shove and his assailant tottered sideways. Whether the sight of the phone at Wanda's ear as she sat on the ground or the thought that he could be charged with murder made Motorbike Man run, Quentin couldn't be sure. All he knew was that he turned, made a hurdle jump over Wanda, kicking the phone from her hand as he did so, and was gone.

When he'd recovered from the tussle, Quentin stood for a moment, wondering if they had attracted attention from neighbours or passers-by. Perhaps that thought had occurred to his adversary too. Although the hedge would have obscured any onlooker's view on that side, the commotion could have easily been heard. All seemed quiet, though, and nobody approached the house or called out from beyond the bushes.

'Are you all right, Wanda?' he asked anxiously, helping her up.

'I think so,' she said, putting a hand to the opposite elbow. 'I'll have a nice bruise, though. Shouldn't you go after him?'

'He'll be on his bike and away before I catch him. Anyway, we've got this.' He held up the holdall.

Retrieving her phone Wanda asked, 'Is Green Scarf really dead?'

'Don't know, but that's another reason I'm not chasing Motorbike Man. Green Scarf was on the floor the last I saw of him.'

'We can't just leave him, then,' Wanda said, starting to walk along the path.

'Not so fast,' Quentin told her. 'He could be up like he was last time.'

Catching her arm and putting his finger to his lips, Quentin ducked down and crept towards the kitchen window. Seeing no shadow nor hearing any sign of movement, he peered cautiously over the sill. The man was still on the floor. Next to him, half under the table, a black holdall lay on its side.

He straightened up and beckoned to Wanda. She came up behind him, following him into the house. Together they stood over the fallen man. He lay by the table, one arm flung out to the side as though he'd tried to grasp it as he fell. The other was across his chest, and a thin trickle of blood oozed from a gash on his temple.

'His lips are blue,' Wanda said, kneeling down and feeling for a pulse. 'There's a pulse but it's weak. Phone for an ambulance.'

'This is getting to be a habit,' Quentin muttered as he punched 999 into his phone. While Wanda brought a coat from the hall and placed it over the man's upper body, he gave the address, answered routine questions and was assured that an ambulance was on its way.

The call ended and he glanced round the room. It was minimalist and tidy. He longed to search the place, hoping to find some clue as to who this man was or who he was working for, but he hesitated. Entering a house to help a sick person was one thing. His fingerprints all over the place was another. If the police came here, he might be implicated in whatever was going on.

Get a grip Quentin, he thought. Your prints aren't on record, and you're a detective. You're entitled to follow up a case. Except strictly speaking it wasn't his case. And why didn't he have gloves and a proper camera? A true professional would have come prepared. Still, it was stupid not to look, and he didn't have much time. Going into the kitchen, he took two tea towels and wrapped them round his hands like gloves.

'Just a precaution,' he said when Wanda turned an enquiring gaze on him. 'You never know.'

'I thought we were the good guys,' Wanda said. 'The paramedics will know we were here anyway. Our prints are bound to be here.'

'Not on every surface. We're supposed to be helping a sick man, not searching his house. And put those holdalls out of sight before the ambulance gets here.'

He opened drawers and cupboards but, apart from cutlery and table mats, found nothing except a rent book, which he couldn't open through the tea towels, and an electricity bill addressed to Mr A Walberg. At least that gives us his name, he thought.

He was upstairs when Wanda cried, 'Quentin!'

He rushed down to see her pumping rhythmically at the man's chest with the heel of her hand. 'He's stopped breathing,' she said without looking up.

A blue light pulsed outside and Quentin hurried to the front door to let the medics in. 'In here,' he said, leading them into the living room where Wanda was still pumping the man's chest.

'OK, love, we'll take it from here,' one of the paramedics told them. To his female colleague, he said, 'Defibrillator.'

Quentin watched as she handed a box-like piece of equipment to him, then prepared a syringe.

'Stand clear,' she warned when the equipment was in place. 'What's his name?'

'Walberg,' Quentin said.

'First name?'

Quentin said the only name beginning with A that came to him. 'Anthony.'

Wanda sent him a look that said *now who's making things up,* then looked back at the stricken man. Quentin followed her gaze. Come on, come on, he thought. For God's sake don't die on us. He gave a sigh of relief when the man's body convulsed and his eyelids twitched.

'I've got a pulse,' the female paramedic said. 'Let's get him in the ambulance.'

'Where will you take him?' Wanda asked. 'The Queen Elizabeth?'

The male paramedic nodded while he and his partner expertly lifted their patient onto a stretcher. When they started to make their way to the ambulance, the female paramedic turned back to them. 'Will one of you be going with him?'

'We're not family,' Quentin explained as they followed them out. 'He's an old friend. I haven't seen him for years but we were in the area so we thought we'd call in. This is how we found him.'

'Has he got any family?'

At a loss, Quentin shrugged. 'Not that I know of. As I said, I haven't seen him for years.'

The paramedics manoeuvred the patient into the ambulance and began work with various tubes and medical paraphernalia. 'Lucky you called when you did,' the woman said. 'You probably saved his life.'

Quentin's mobile rang, and he pulled it out and answered it, glad for an excuse not to have to answer any more questions. It was Colin.

'Quentin? Why didn't you answer my call–'

Talking over him, Quentin said loudly, 'What did you say? … OK. Yes, yes, I'll be there. Bye.'

'Sorry,' he said, snapping the lid down, 'urgent business call. We need to go. I'll call the hospital tomorrow; see how he's doing.'

He saw a flicker of surprise on Wanda's face, but as usual she rose to the occasion. 'We'll just close the house up,' she said.

Fully occupied with their task, the paramedics seemed not to hear. Quentin followed Wanda back into the house, praying that the ambulance would leave soon. He wanted a chance to finish looking round the place. He was rewarded when, just a few minutes later, the ambulance moved off, blue light flashing. The screech of the siren filled the air for what seemed an age, then faded into the distance.

Wanda closed the back door, picked up the holdall they'd rescued from Motorbike Man as well as the one he'd left in the house and carried them into the hall. Quentin continued his search upstairs. It wasn't difficult. The few pieces of furniture were devoid of ornament, the drawers practically empty and the wardrobe housed only a few pairs of trousers, some shirts, one pair of shoes and a jacket. A dressing gown lay across the bed. Checking all the pockets for clues proved fruitless. The bathroom yielded nothing but toiletries and two blister packs of tablets, presumably Walberg's medication. Quentin cursed silently. If the tablets had still been in their original packaging, he could have at least confirmed Walberg's name and the pharmacy where the pills had come from, then he would know if they were dispensed locally or further afield. He checked the waste bin, which contained nothing but a broken toothbrush and the wrapping from a bar of soap. Either Mr Walberg was very tidy or he left nothing to chance.

'Hurry up,' Wanda called. 'We're not supposed to be here, and there're a couple of people across the road looking over.'

'There would be,' Quentin called back. 'Nothing like an emergency vehicle to draw attention.' Hurriedly he pulled opened the last drawer. Surely Mr Walberg had a passport? Birth certificate? National insurance number? If he did, they weren't here. In fact, Mr A Walberg had the least paperwork of anyone he'd ever known.

When he was satisfied he'd made a thorough search he went downstairs. After a last glance round, he picked up one of the holdalls and handed the other to Wanda.

'Come on,' he said, opening the front door. 'Let's get out of here.'

Chapter Twelve

'Well,' Quentin said, as they drove away from Catford, 'what's in the bags? Don't tell me you didn't look while I was upstairs.'

'I might have done.'

'OK, *I'll* tell *you*. A statue, in one.'

'You're right. And the other one?'

'Supposed to be money.'

'Yes.'

'Yes?'

'Some money, yes.'

'A hundred and fifty grand?'

'Not quite.'

Quentin looked sideways at Wanda, who was smirking. 'All right, I give up. What *is* in the other bag?'

'Wait and see.'

'Wanda–' He broke off as Wanda pulled her mobile from her handbag.

'Out of battery,' she groaned. 'Where's yours? I need to ring Colin, see if he's still at my house.'

'I shouldn't bother. He's probably lost the will to live by now,' Quentin said, feeling a measure of sympathy for Colin. 'He got a flat battery, probably because we asked him to go out last night, and he's rung me twice and been cut off.'

'Mmm. Poor Colin, he always draws the short straw. I'll ring him anyway, let him know we're on the way.'

Quentin drew his mobile from his jacket pocket and handed it to her. During the conversation that followed he gathered that a new battery had been fitted on Colin's car and that he'd gone home.

'He got fed up with waiting for us,' Wanda recounted when the call ended. 'He's taken Mozart, and the two overnight bags he packed for us yesterday, in case we decided not to go back. Perhaps we shouldn't. I don't fancy Motorbike Man spotting us. He'll be fuming now. I'll have to collect Mozart anyway, so we might as well go straight to Colin's.'

'I suppose so, though I'm sure Motorbike Man won't go back to Greenwich yet. He knows we've got the statue with us, and even he won't think we're stupid enough to take it straight home. He'll have to think of a plan, or…'

'Or get some help,' Wanda finished. 'Things are getting a bit out of hand for him, aren't they? After all, as far as he knows, his contact could be dead. Shows what sort of bloke he is, running off and leaving a man in that state.'

Pulling up at traffic lights, Quentin relaxed for a moment. 'Yes, well, I don't think he had a lot of choice. My mobile rang – he must have heard it. That's why he legged it so fast.'

'Why didn't he leg it out the front door?'

'I told you, he heard my phone. Otherwise I guess he'd either have taken the other holdall as well or waited to see if Walberg came round. When he heard my phone, he just rushed out the way he came in.'

'Oh. So we're going to Colin's then?'

Quentin raised his eyebrows. 'Unless you can think of a better idea?'

'Only the same one you've had.'

Quentin didn't answer. If they had any sense, they would head for the nearest police station. At last he said, 'We'll go to Colin's, have a think and make a note of everything we've found out. I suppose I'd better call Philmore this afternoon. We've got the statue and the money, and whatever's in the other bag you're being so mysterious about.'

'How do you know about the statue?' Wanda queried.

'I heard Motorbike Man mention it. He was supposed to hand over money in exchange for the statue. He must have rustled up some more from somewhere, seeing as we've got the original one hundred and fifty grand.'

As the traffic lights changed to green, an idea came to Quentin. 'When will your car be ready? They must have fitted those brake pads by now.'

'I only took it in on Friday afternoon. They said they'd do it Saturday if they could fit it in, if not then today. I should have rung them, but I've been a bit busy, or perhaps you didn't notice.'

'Right,' Quentin said, ignoring her sarcasm. 'Ring them now. If it's ready, you can collect it before we go to Colin's.'

'Good idea,' Wanda said. 'Then we can leave yours in the lock-up and use mine. I won't ring, we'll just go and see if mine's done. It's more or less on the way.'

As the built-up area gave way to a stretch of greenery, Quentin glanced in the rear-view mirror and caught his breath at the sight of black motorcycle.

'Bloody hell!' he exclaimed as the bike gained on them, the sound of its engine reverberating through the air.

Wanda swivelled round. 'What? Is it him?'

'Don't know,' Quentin said, pushing his foot down on the accelerator. 'Let's find out.'

He drove as fast as the speed limit allowed, overtaking other vehicles then slowing to see if the bike would pass him. It didn't. It followed them, slowing and picking up speed when they did, then looked about to overtake but fell back when the road narrowed to single file traffic.

'You'd have thought he'd had enough for one day, wouldn't you?' Quentin muttered. 'Time to lose him.'

Deciding to use the same tactics as the last time, he sped up and, without indicating, hurled the car round the next corner. Jamming on the brakes, he pulled into the kerb.

'That'll do it,' he said, grinning, then gasped as the bike thundered round the corner and screeched to a halt in front of them.

The rider dismounted and began to approach them, the black leathers and space-like helmet giving the tall figure a sinister appearance.

Quentin started to back the car away.

'Wait,' Wanda said, laying her hand on his arm.

Pushing the gearstick into neutral, Quentin secured the door locks, wild thoughts invading his mind. Why were they running away? Motorbike Man was the criminal. Surely he was the one who should run, just as he had in Catford. They should challenge him, make a citizen's arrest–

It was then that he saw why Wanda had told him to wait. The motorcyclist had lifted the helmet's visor. The face it revealed was young and feminine, with mascaraed eyelashes and gold studs piercing the brows.

Quentin wound down the window as the girl spoke.

'Thought I should tell you your back number plate's almost falling off,' she said. 'Only you'll get done if a cop spots it. My dad did.'

'Is it?' Quentin said. 'OK, thanks. We'll get it sorted.'

The girl returned to her bike leaving Quentin feeling somewhat abashed. The bike wasn't even the same make as Motorbike Man's. He went to look at his number plate.

One side was drooping, and it shifted under his touch. Tutting, he recalled backing into a low wall a few weeks earlier. The dent wasn't too deep, and he hadn't bothered getting it repaired.

'Must have loosened the bolts when I had that crunch,' he told Wanda. 'It'll be all right for a bit.'

Wanda gave him a tight smile. 'Remind me never to wear motorbike kit,' she said. 'Everyone thinks you're a Hell's Angel or a criminal. Come on, let's get going.'

Wanda's blue Toyota was ready and on the forecourt when they reached the garage. After she'd paid the bill, and Quentin had arranged to have his number plate fixed the following week, he transferred the two holdalls to her boot, then drove the BMW to the lock-up garage in Greenwich. Wanda followed, waited until he had put his car away and they set off for Wanstead in the Toyota. On the way, Quentin told Wanda everything he'd heard and seen at the house in Catford before Walberg had collapsed.

It was just after one o'clock when they reached Wanstead. Colin's eyebrows lifted when they carried the two holdalls in.

'Not more bags,' he grumbled. 'This place is turning into a left luggage depot.'

His next words were drowned out by Mozart, who bounded into the hall barking excitedly. He jumped at Wanda and licked her hand. After he'd quietened, Wanda went straight to the kitchen.

'Can I put the kettle on, Colin?' she said, switching it on without waiting for a reply. 'We're gasping.'

'Let's look at this statue first,' Quentin said. 'I can't wait any longer to see what's so special about it.'

'Statue?' Colin repeated.

'We'll tell you everything in a minute, Colin,' Quentin said, lifting a holdall onto the worktop.

When he'd unzipped it, he frowned when all he could see was white material. Then he realized it was wrapped around something solid. After carefully lifting the object out, he unwound the protective covering to reveal a statue. About a foot high, it was of a woman, her hair piled on her head in elaborate curls and the folds of a long garment falling from her shoulders in ancient style. Roman or Greek, Quentin guessed. He wasn't sure what it was made from – possibly bronze, he decided.

'She's beautiful,' Wanda said, gazing at the statue in awe.

Quentin knew nothing about sculpture, but he had to agree with her. 'She looks like a goddess,' he said, passing it to her.

Wanda placed the statue gently on the worktop and ran her hands over it. 'She probably is. I'm not up on goddesses, or ancient artefacts.'

'Is it ancient, then? Not a copy?'

'How would I know?'

'You're the one who was married to an antiques dealer.'

'Gerry sold mainly furniture,' Wanda reminded him. 'Mostly Victoriana.'

'That's right,' Colin chipped in. 'He never had anything like this, did he, Wanda?'

'Not that I saw,' Wanda admitted. 'It looks old. There're a few marks here and there, and the base is chipped, so…'

'It could be made to look old,' Quentin pointed out. 'They can make anything look old these days.'

'I wouldn't think it was a genuine Roman or Greek treasure,' Wanda said. 'It's more likely to be of the Renaissance period. Ancient art and sculpture was admired and often copied, I believe. Only an expert could tell.'

'Or it could be a modern copy,' Colin suggested. 'There must be thousands of fakes in the world.'

'Yeah, but someone thought it was valuable, unless…' Quentin picked up the statue, turning it upside down and examining it intently.

'What are you looking for?' Wanda asked. 'Oh no. Don't tell me it's got *Made in China* stamped on the bottom.'

Quentin clicked his tongue. 'I just thought, you know, perhaps it was hollow or came apart somehow.'

Wanda stared at him. 'You mean to hide something?'

'Just a thought, but no go. There's no way it will come apart, and it feels solid, but there's a crack under the base.'

'Well, if it's really old you'd expect it to have some damage,' Wanda said. 'What do you make of it, Colin?'

Colin shrugged. 'It's not something I'd pay a fortune for. It would look a bit out of place on my sideboard. It is beautiful, though. I can see why a collector might want it. I'm glad you had the wit not to take it to your house, Quentin, and that you brought Wanda here out of danger.'

Never mind me being in danger then, Quentin thought, but kept quiet.

Steam curled its way from the kettle and Wanda turned her attention to making coffee. Colin cleared his throat noisily. 'I don't mind you swanning in here and taking over my kitchen, but can you please tell me how you got this statue?'

'We will,' said Quentin. 'But first I want to see what's in the other bag.' Lifting the second holdall, he rested it further along the worktop and stared at it. Black with brass tags, just like his own, the one he'd put poor Lucky in. He paused before opening it, trying to guess what it held if it wasn't full of money. Surely it wasn't…

Yanking at the zip, he peered inside and found himself looking at bundles of notes.

Fifty-pound notes. Giving a low whistle, he reached in and pulled a bundle out. It was loosely packed, secured with an elastic band. As he handled it, he felt a difference in the top and bottom notes. Flicking the notes apart, he saw why. Blank pieces of paper were covered with a genuine banknote. It would fool anyone looking into the bag. Pulling out another bundle, he frowned. There appeared to be two layers of phoney money, but it didn't look like the same amount as he had seen in the original money bag. He tipped the holdall upside down. Bundle after bundle thudded onto the worktop. When no more came, he put his hand inside. A piece of cardboard was wedged between the canvas sides. He prodded it, and it gave under his fingers. A premonition coming to him, he held his breath as he slid a finger under the false cardboard base and lifted it out, allowing the last items in the bag to fall free.

'Voila!' he grinned.

'Oh my God!' Wanda gasped. 'My wedding dress!'

Chapter Thirteen

'Fancy putting it in the bag with fake money,' Wanda said when she recovered. 'Why would he hand it over to Walberg?'

'Probably got sick of cutting up bits of paper,' Quentin chuckled. 'He had to make the bag look and feel how Walberg would have expected it to. Your shoes and tiara are here, too. The cardboard covered them and the fake money was laid on top. That's why he was so against Walberg having a proper look at it. Motorbike Man was planning on getting the statue for next to nothing, and he almost did. I'm sure this is my holdall. He needed a bag the same colour as the one the real money was in – he couldn't use your navy one in case Walberg noticed. My guess is they use identical bags to make a switch. He must have dumped poor Lucky somewhere and used this. The fasteners are different colours, but no one would notice that straight away.'

'Well, I'm pleased to have my dress back. I thought I'd never see it again. I wonder why this bag was on the floor. I suppose Walberg had just picked it up when he fell.'

'Fell, or was pushed,' Quentin said. 'Motorbike Man was pretty riled up. Walberg had already asked to see the money, so perhaps he was going to take it out and look at it properly. Motorbike Man could have taken a swing at him.'

'You didn't see him do that?'

'No. I'd turned away. I didn't want to be seen and I knew Motorbike Man would be leaving soon. But he raised his voice. I think they were arguing, and there was that gash on Walberg's head.'

'He could have hit it on the table as he fell, if he just collapsed,' Wanda speculated.

During this exchange Colin looked at each of them alternately. 'For God's sake!' he exploded. 'It's worse than being at Wimbledon, watching you two. Are you going to tell me what happened or not?'

'Sorry, Colin,' Wanda said, hanging the wedding dress over the back of a kitchen chair. 'Take these mugs into the lounge. Quentin can fill you in and I'll make us some lunch, if you don't mind. Oh, and can you find my phone charger for me? It should be in that bag you brought from my house.'

* * *

After coffee and sandwiches, Quentin felt better. 'I needed that,' he said, chasing crumbs around his plate with his finger. 'Of course Walberg might not be Green Scarf's real name. It could be a false name he gave when he rented the place. My guess is he's not there all the time. I think he only uses it as a cover. Perhaps he only goes there when he's got some sort of job on.'

A snigger escaped Colin. 'You sound like Inspector Morse. You're only a one-man band who's solved one case.'

‘A big case, Colin,’ Wanda said. ‘And it’s a two-person band, in case you’ve forgotten. I thought I was the reason you wanted to help.’

Colin looked abashed but said nothing.

‘Surely,’ Wanda went on, ‘when Walberg collapsed at the station he’d have wanted to go back to his real home. If he felt as ill as he looked, he’d have gone where he felt the most comfortable, perhaps where someone could look after him.’

Quentin had been thinking about that. ‘Not if he doesn’t live in London. He could live anywhere, and only come to London when he has to.’

‘Mmm, I suppose,’ Wanda agreed.

Quentin sat back in his chair and sighed. Colin’s disparaging remarks had hit a nerve. Apart from the previous year’s adventure, their cases to date had included finding a missing husband who wanted to stay missing, spying on errant housewives, and lying in wait for a bunch of kids whose main source of enjoyment seemed to be letting the air out of every car tyre they came across. Today, though, he had tracked down a central character in the mystery of the money, discovered what the money was being exchanged for, learned a little about the criminals involved, stopped a crook from getting away with the goods and possibly saved a man’s life. Colin could say what he liked. Today, Quentin felt like a real detective.

Wanda’s voice brought him back to earth. ‘So when are you going to call DI Philmore?’

‘Let’s make some notes first, see what we can piece together.’

‘We can do that after you’ve called him. I’m not spending long with that statue, Quentin. It’s too dangerous. Motorbike Man will be desperate now. He’ll be under fire from whoever wants the statue, and he’s likely to go to extremes to get it and the money back. He won’t run away again – he can’t afford to. He’ll come armed, bring reinforcements – or both.’

'He'll have to find us first,' Quentin said grimly. 'OK, we'll call Philmore and take the money and the statue to him.'

Wanda looked relieved. 'Good. Look, I know you'd like to see the whole thing through and present it to the police as a fait accompli, but we can't. We shouldn't put ourselves in any more danger – I like the thrill and excitement as much as you do, but I'm not prepared to die for it.'

Quentin sighed. 'Nor am I. We could check into a hotel for a few days to be on the safe side.'

'We could.' Wanda sounded doubtful. 'I know we've got the money from that last job but we're not exactly flush, are we?'

'You don't have to go to a hotel, Wanda love,' Colin said. 'You know you're welcome to stay with me, and no one knows you're here.'

'Does that go for me as well?' Quentin asked sharply.

Before Colin could reply Wanda said, 'I know, Colin, thanks, but it could be a while before we can go home.'

'I don't mind. You'd have to leave Mozart here anyway. You can't take him to a hotel.'

Wanda hesitated, and Quentin could see she was weakening. 'All right,' she said. 'We'll stay tonight, but if things go on too long–'

'We'll cross that bridge when we have to,' Colin said. He gave a triumphant smile, and Quentin gave a silent groan. He just wants to get his own back on me for coming between him and Wanda, he thought. Glancing at Wanda, he felt a stirring of desire. Though it had been only the day before yesterday, it seemed an age since they'd made love.

'What about watching Mrs Freeman's?' he asked, still reluctant to relinquish his hold on the case.

A titter of laughter escaped Colin. 'Philmore can arrange that when you ring him. He'll make a proper job of it.'

'Right,' Quentin said, trying to draw the conversation away from last night's failed vigil. 'I'm guessing Motorbike Man works for someone who gave him the money to exchange for the statue. Then it would be sold on, either to someone who's ordered it or someone he knows will be in the market for it.' He paused, remembering Motorbike Man's words. *The client's getting impatient.* 'There's a client ready and waiting for this statue. That's what Motorbike Man told Walberg.'

'OK, so that's what we'll tell the police,' Wanda said. 'We've practically done their job for them. We can give them descriptions of two of the criminals, the address and whereabouts of one, and the money and the statue as evidence. All they need to do is catch Motorbike Man and find out who's behind the operation. Piece of cake.'

Quentin looked sideways at her. 'In that case, why don't we just carry on ourselves? No need to look like that, Colin. You're right, it's too dangerous. I'll ring him now.'

Colin nodded approval and looked surprised when Quentin produced his mobile and began scrolling through his contacts. 'You've got his number in your contacts?'

'Direct line to his office,' Quentin said. 'Kept it just in case.'

He didn't mention his second mobile, currently in a drawer in his bureau, bought at Philmore's request and used during their big case last year as a sole contact for Philmore. Ignoring Colin's disbelieving look, he gazed at the number for a long moment, wondering exactly what he should say. What if Philmore didn't believe him, told him he should have come to him sooner or said he couldn't handle the case? He knew he was procrastinating. Now was the right time to involve the police, but with everything they'd found out since Saturday, would it be wrong to spend just a little longer trying to flush out other members of the gang? Solve the case completely on their own?

No, his common sense told him. He didn't relish the idea of his life being cut short, or of his ribs being caved in. Sighing, he placed the call. He was almost relieved when the engaged tone sounded.

'Engaged,' he said. 'I'll call later.'

'Didn't you have his mobile number?' Wanda asked.

Colin looked incredulous at Wanda's words. Turning to Quentin he said, 'You've got a detective inspector's mobile phone number?'

'That's right, but I'm only supposed to use it if the brains behind last year's case contacts me.'

'Well, this case is just as big,' Wanda insisted.

'I know.' Strictly, Quentin was only meant to use his second mobile to call Philmore, but he kept the number in his contacts on his main mobile as well. 'I'll give it half an hour, then ring his mobile.'

'Give it ten minutes,' Colin said. 'I don't think my house insurance covers stolen property.'

Exasperated, Quentin snapped, 'What's up with you, Colin? Nothing's going missing from here. No one knows we're here.'

'Just as well,' Wanda said. 'If Motorbike Man calls in reinforcements anything could happen. Mind you, that would mean him admitting he's lost the money and the statue. His life won't be worth living. In fact, if he's got any sense he'll do a runner.'

Quentin gave a low whistle. 'That's a thought. I would, that's for sure. Unless–'

'Unless what?'

'Unless he doesn't admit it, not yet anyway. I got the impression he already had, from what he said to Walberg, but he could just have been spinning him a line. I mean, I expect he told whoever he's supposed to hand the goods to about not being able to get the statue from Walberg, but maybe he didn't admit to losing the money. The more I think about it, the more I think he might be keeping it to himself until he's had another go at trying to get the money back.'

'How do you think he'll do that?' Colin asked.

Quentin made a face. 'He must know some unsavoury characters. He might hire his own guys to track us down. Still,' he added, noticing Wanda's alarmed expression, 'he'll take a bit of time to think about it, and deciding who to call. We should be all right for a bit, and as I said, he doesn't know where we are. *And* we've changed cars.'

'But he could still break into Mrs Freeman's,' Wanda said.

'He won't do that if we're not there.'

'Except he might think you're there,' Colin pointed out. 'The lights are on a timer, remember.'

'Yes,' Quentin said, 'but he thinks we live there, and he knows we know that, so why would we risk taking the statue there? What he might do is break in to make us tell him where the goods are.'

Wanda shivered. 'Or just to rough us up for causing him so much trouble?'

'That's possible,' Colin agreed.

'But if we tell the police that, they could put a watch on the place.' There was a note of excitement in Wanda's voice now. 'Thinking about it, they probably will. That would be a good way to catch Motorbike Man or any heavies he sends round there.'

'It would be, if you ever get round to telling them what's going on,' Colin said. 'And something else. This bloke, the one who went to hospital.'

Quentin frowned. 'Walberg? What about him?'

'You're the detective, I should have thought you'd have worked it out. OK, so you scared off his motorbike friend when your phone rang, and you've got the goods, but he's bound to find out what's happened to Walberg. If he thinks you've gone to the police, he'll know they'll visit the hospital, because Walberg can identify him and maybe identify whoever arranged the handover of the statue.'

'Bloody hell,' Quentin groaned. 'I hadn't thought of that.'

Wanda looked stricken. 'You mean Motorbike Man or some other thug might try to get to Walberg to stop him talking? We have to get him protection then, and quickly. We didn't save his life just to get him killed.'

'All the more reason to call the police,' Colin put in. 'I wouldn't wait any longer. Call someone else if you can't get hold of Philmore.'

'Go on then, Quentin,' Wanda urged. 'Ring now.'

'All right, all right,' Quentin said, annoyed that Colin had thought of something he should have thought of himself. Walberg may be a crook, but he didn't want to be responsible for his death. With a resigned sigh, he did what he knew he should have done as soon as they'd left Catford. He rang the only person he hoped would take action immediately.

When the ring tone stopped and Philmore spoke, Quentin felt a quiver of apprehension. Then, impelled by the importance of his call, he answered, 'Hello Inspector. Quentin Cadbury here. I've got something you might like to have a look at. Can I come and see you?'

Chapter Fourteen

Quentin was surprised when Philmore agreed at once to arrange protection for Walberg without hearing the full details of the case, then invited him to come to his office as soon as possible. Apart from his initial greeting, all he'd told Philmore was that they'd accidentally come across what they thought was a criminal operation, and that a member of it could be in danger. He'd given Walberg's name and the hospital he'd been taken to, but nothing else.

He had secretly feared that despite their collusion in their previous encounter, the Detective Inspector – Detective *Chief* Inspector now, Philmore had advised him – wouldn't take him seriously until he'd seen some proof. But a senior member of the Metropolitan Police trusted him enough to act on his word. That would give the bullish man who called himself his father something to think about.

'I'm coming with you,' Wanda said when she knew Quentin was going to see Philmore.

'So am I,' said Colin.

Quentin tossed his head. 'Don't be daft, Colin. It doesn't take three of us to explain what's going on.'

'I don't see why you should get to do everything,' Colin said through stiff lips. 'You asked me to help, the holdalls are in my house, so why shouldn't I share in some of the glory?'

'I'd hardly call it glory,' Wanda interrupted. 'It's good of you to help, Colin, but Quentin's right. We can't all troop in to see Philmore. We won't be long. You stay here with Mozart.'

Colin's mouth tightened further and he cleaned his glasses with the hem of his shirt. 'Right. Well, do something useful before you go. Take those overnight things upstairs, can you, Quentin.'

'I'll do it,' Wanda offered. 'I need the loo anyway.'

'So do I,' Quentin said. 'After you, Wanda.'

'We've upset him,' Wanda whispered to Quentin upstairs.

Quentin shrugged. 'He'll get over it.'

By the time they'd got downstairs again Colin had two black holdalls in the hall ready for them to take. 'There we are,' he said. 'The money and the statue.'

'What about the other one?' Wanda asked. 'We ought to take that as well.'

'What on earth for?' Colin asked. 'They're not going to want bundles of blank paper, are they? I've taken off the top banknotes and put them in with the rest of the money.'

'They might need it for fingerprints,' Quentin told him.

Colin raised his eyes heavenwards. 'They'll get those from these bags, won't they?'

'Come on, Quentin,' Wanda urged. 'Let's go,'

'All right. See you later, Colin.'

'Yeah. And if you don't come straight back, let me know what you're doing.'

'We will,' Wanda promised, kissing his cheek before following Quentin along the front path.

'You'd better,' Colin barked, and closed the door after them.

* * *

DCI Philmore, a slim, dark-eyed man of medium height, looked the same as Quentin remembered except for his hair, now more grey than brown. His tie matched the blue stripe in his shirt and his suit jacket hung on the back of his chair.

After accepting Quentin's congratulations on his promotion, he introduced a colleague as Detective Sergeant Debbie Francis and asked her to note down their conversation. Francis, plain-featured but with startling green eyes, had a look about her that suggested to Quentin that she took her job seriously and meant to get on. Her light brown hair was pulled back from her face in a tight bun and she wore a long-sleeved blouse over a calf-length skirt. Her shoes, black and flat, were what Quentin often heard described as sensible. She produced a pen and a notepad, which she balanced on her knee.

Philmore sat back and listened carefully to everything Quentin told him without interrupting, with Wanda filling in any gaps in their story. There was a silence when they'd finished.

From the other side of his desk Philmore looked at each of them in turn.

‘So,’ he said, picking up a pencil and twirling it round in his fingers. ‘You were on the way to take this dead cat to the vet’s, and it was stolen.’

DS Francis giggled, and tried to cover it up by coughing. Quentin and Wanda exchanged glances.

‘I know it sounds unlikely,’ Wanda offered, ‘but it’s true.’

‘And you ran after him,’ Philmore went on. ‘You tackled him as he got on a train and managed to get the bag back.’

‘That’s right,’ Quentin said, ‘only it wasn’t the same bag.’

Philmore caught DS Francis’s eye, and Quentin saw a muscle twitch in his cheek before he swallowed and said, ‘And you didn’t notice until you got home? You didn’t check?’

‘There was no need,’ Wanda said. ‘It looked the same, and as far as we were concerned there was a dead cat inside.’

‘I offered to open it and show the guard at the station,’ Quentin explained. ‘He didn’t seem keen when I told him what was in the bag. He took a peep but that was all. There was a blanket on top of the money, a fleecy one. It probably looked like cat fur on first sight.’

Another cough from DS Francis.

‘Why did you agree to see us if you didn’t believe me when I rang?’ Quentin said, beginning to feel that his apprehension in calling Philmore had been justified.

‘I took notice of what you said, Quentin, but you didn’t mention a dead cat.’

‘Poor moggie,’ DS Francis said. ‘I expect you’ll miss him.’

‘It wasn’t mine,’ Quentin admitted. ‘I was looking after it for a neighbour.’

This time the detective sergeant didn’t even try to cough. She just burst into peals of laughter.

'That'll do, Debbie.' Philmore's voice was strained, as though he was trying not to laugh himself. 'Right, show me the money and this statue.'

Scooping up the nearest holdall, Quentin dropped it onto the desk and shoved it towards him. Calm down, he told himself. After all, we laughed when we realized that the thief only got poor Lucky for his pains.

Philmore waited until DS Francis provided him with a pair of latex gloves and eased them on before standing up, unzipping the holdall and peeking in. 'There's no blanket here now,' he said, in a reproving tone.

Quentin and Wanda exchanged glances. 'Must have left it behind,' Wanda murmured.

After pulling out several bundles of notes Philmore flicked through each one in turn. DS Francis's jaw dropped as she watched.

'Wow!' she said. 'How much did you say was there?'

'A hundred and fifty thousand, plus what we took from the other bag, the one the bundles of paper were in.'

'Why didn't you bring that as well?' Philmore demanded. 'Tampering with evidence could compromise an investigation.'

Quentin was tempted to blurt out that it was Colin who'd stopped them bringing the third bag, but stopped himself when Wanda gave an almost imperceptible shake of her head.

After Philmore had returned the money to the holdall, Quentin handed him the second one, then sat down and waited for him to lift out the statue.

'There's a cloth round it,' Wanda told him. 'To protect it.'

Philmore nodded, unzipped the bag, looked inside and then up at Quentin. 'A statue?' he asked, sounding puzzled. 'There is some sort of cloth, but…'

He held up something long and white.

Wanda's disbelieving gasp turned to a groan. 'Oh my God,' she said for the second time that day. 'My wedding dress!'

DS Francis looked as though she couldn't take any more entertainment. She gaped at Wanda, who flushed in embarrassment.

Philmore tipped the bag up. A tiara and two satin shoes thudded onto the desk, as well as bundle after bundle of banknote-sized paper.

'Stupid bloody Colin,' Quentin ranted. 'Can't he get anything right?'

'You've brought the wrong bag?' Philmore asked, managing to keep a straight face.

'No,' said Wanda, studying the tags on the zips. 'Right bag, wrong contents. We took the statue out at our friend's house, and emptied out the other one, the one Motorbike Man took to Walberg. Colin must have put the statue in the other bag, which means it's still at his house.'

Any amusement Philmore had shown was replaced by a thunderous look. 'You shouldn't have touched anything. You should have brought it straight to us.'

'We have now,' Wanda said defiantly. 'And we only got the first bag two days ago.'

Francis found her voice. 'This guy, the one from the station, you reckon he went to make the swap at Catford with fake money and a wedding dress? Didn't he think the other bloke would at least check inside?'

'The dress and shoes where at the bottom, under a piece of cardboard,' Wanda explained. 'The fake money was on top.'

This earned her another dark look from Philmore.

'And Motorbike Man was pretty nasty to him,' Quentin added. 'The more I think about it, the more I think he probably pushed Walberg down somehow. He just wanted to take the statue and run. He knew Walberg was ill – it would have taken a while before he sussed out the fake money and by the time Walberg was fit enough to do anything he'd be well away.'

'Anyway,' Wanda said, 'the statue's at our friend's.'

'Right,' Philmore said, gathering up the bundles. 'We'll soon have it back, though it won't really do us much good.'

Quentin jerked his head up. 'What do you mean? Surely–' He stopped and growled with impatience as Wanda's mobile trilled.

'Sorry.' She fumbled in her handbag and located the phone. 'It's only Colin. I'll call him later.'

The ringing stopped and Philmore suddenly seemed agitated. 'Colin, your friend with the statue?' he asked. 'Ring him now.'

Wanda looked surprised but did as she was told. Quentin drummed his fingers on his knee, annoyed that Colin had interrupted the proceedings. Lucky he didn't ring me, he thought. I'll give him a piece of my mind when I see him, putting the stuff in the wrong bags. Wanda's change of tone made him turn to look at her. 'What is it?' he asked as she lowered the phone.

'It's Colin. He's been arrested.'

Chapter Fifteen

'Arrested!' Quentin was jolted out of his internal ravings against Colin. 'What do mean, arrested?'

'The police went to his house. They were after the statue.'

'But how did they know it was there?' Quentin tried to think if he'd spotted anyone following them on the way to Colin's. He hadn't.

Philmore cleared his throat. 'I think I can answer that. I'd better tell you, I suppose.'

Quentin cast a suspicious look at the DCI. 'Hold on a moment. Am I being set up here?'

Philmore spread his hands. 'Not at all. I had no idea you were involved until your phone call. I'll tell you as much as I can – you've probably worked some of it out already. This operation you've stumbled on – we've been aware of it for some time. Minor works of art have been going missing from various galleries and museums, and sold either to collectors or to dealers who pass them on for inflated prices–'

'That's what we thought,' Wanda interrupted. 'But I wouldn't call the statue a minor work of art. Not many people would pay a hundred and fifty grand for something to decorate their living room.'

'The stolen items are usually worth a lot more than that. This money,' Philmore indicated towards the holdall, 'is payment for the people who steal the goods and deliver them. We think they're sold on to the highest bidder or someone who's agreed a price beforehand. Not always millions, but a steady stream of smaller items mounts up money-wise, and it's less risky than trying to deal in really valuable items. I mean, how could anyone sell the *Mona Lisa* or *The Fighting Temeraire*?'

'I see that,' Quentin said, 'but they still have to be stolen. Surely all museums and galleries have security?'

'Yes, that's what puzzled us, until we received some information.' Philmore paused, as though trying to decide how much he should reveal. He took up his pencil and tapped it on the desk.

Information. Cogs whirred round in Quentin's brain. He'd phoned Philmore, told him very little except…

'Walberg,' he said excitedly. 'The information you received must have involved Walberg. Either you were told he was part of the gang, or– or Walberg is your informant. That's why you've arranged protection for him so quickly and why you agreed to see us.'

Wanda followed his train of thought. 'Yes, that makes sense, but it doesn't explain how you traced the statue to Colin's house.'

Philmore turned to DS Francis. 'Debbie, can you get someone to take this lot over to SOCO then rustle us up a cup of tea? Thanks.'

'Scene of Crime Office?' Quentin queried, pleased at remembering what the acronym stood for.

Philmore gave a tolerant half-smile. 'It's evidence, so it has to be treated as part of a crime scene. So will the statue, or will be if you haven't compromised that as well.' Waiting while DS Francis put on some white rubber gloves, Philmore picked up both holdalls.

'Can I at least keep my wedding things?' Wanda asked. 'Surely you can get any DNA from the holdalls and the money?'

Debbie Francis looked at her boss. When he nodded, she put the holdalls down again and pulled out the dress and accessories from one of them. She held them out and Wanda took them, then turned appealing eyes to Philmore.

'Can't I keep them in the bag?' she asked. 'I'll let you have it back.'

'No. Put Mrs Merrydrew's things in an evidence bag, Debbie.'

DS Francis hesitated, as though unsure whether to question Philmore's decision. She did as she was told when he said impatiently, 'It's all right, Debbie. I'm sure Mrs Merrydrew will return her things if we need them.'

Wanda gave him an alluring smile. 'You know you can trust me, Inspector.'

With a look at her boss that said he ought to know better, Debbie Francis took both holdalls and left the room.

When she had gone Philmore said, 'I shouldn't be telling you this, but you *have* brought the money in and told us about the statue, and–'

'And we are detectives,' Wanda finished. 'You might need our help.'

Philmore pursed his lips as though to stop himself from issuing another reprimand. Then he looked at Wanda for a long moment, and Quentin saw the flicker of appreciation in his expression as he took in her blonde hair, cornflower-blue eyes and slender figure accentuated by a clinging cream-coloured top. Her deep, melodious voice hadn't escaped his notice either, Quentin was sure.

'You're right about Walberg,' he said quietly. 'We suspected him and pulled him in for questioning. I don't think he'd have admitted anything but for the fact he's ill. He doesn't think he can go on much longer in this racket and he's worried about his family. We did a deal and after he took possession of the statue a microchip was fitted inside it.'

A light went on in Quentin's head. 'A microchip? Underneath the base?' When Philmore nodded he went on, 'The base was cracked, but I never thought– how on earth did you do that?'

'*I* didn't do anything, but we have our ways, experts and specialists.'

'So that's how you traced the statue to Colin's?'

'Yes.'

'And if we'd still been there, we'd have been arrested too?' Wanda asked.

'Probably, until you'd proved your story.'

'Right,' Wanda said, giving Philmore a cool look. 'Well, hadn't you better get our friend released?'

Quentin had an image of Colin trying to convince several policemen that he wasn't the receiver of stolen goods. Normally it would have made him smile, but he was beginning to understand that their heroic action of flooring Motorbike Man and snatching the statue hadn't been such a good idea. Not in Philmore's eyes anyway.

'Yes, we'll get him released of course, but quite frankly that's not my main concern.'

Wanda bridled, and Quentin put his hand on her arm to stop what he knew would be a cutting reply.

'I think what the chief inspector means is that we've foiled their plans,' he said, looking at Philmore and knowing he was right. 'I'm guessing that the microchip was meant to lead you to whoever Motorbike Man passed it on to.'

'That's about it. But now the statue isn't even in their hands.'

'Oh!' Wanda sounded disappointed. 'You mean our gallant efforts were all for nothing?'

'Not entirely,' Philmore said. 'You warned us about Walberg. We don't want anybody getting at him. I'm sure he'll be grateful to you for calling an ambulance.'

'Twice,' Quentin reminded him. 'Though he didn't make use of it the first time.'

'No,' said Philmore. 'His illness is making him pretty unreliable. If he'd handed the statue over at the train station as he was meant to, we might have the top man by now, or at least someone who could tell us who he is.'

'Yes,' Wanda agreed. 'If he hadn't collapsed none of this would have happened. He'd have made the exchange and we would have gone off to the vet's and been none the wiser.'

Quentin sat upright, seizing the chance to prove they had done something useful. 'The exchange. That reminds me.' He took out his mobile and scrolled through to the photo he'd taken in Catford. 'I took it through glass so it's not very clear,' he said, handing it to Philmore.

'And I took photos of the original money bag,' Wanda said. 'They're still on my camera. I don't suppose you'll need them now though. You'll have all three bags soon.'

DS Francis returned bearing a tray with four mugs and handed them round.

'I can see the holdalls, but the faces aren't really discernible,' Philmore said, gazing at the picture on Quentin's phone. 'It wouldn't prove anything in a court of law. We might be able to enhance it. I'll get someone to upload it to our computer.'

'There's one of Walberg on the floor at his house too,' Quentin told him. 'And a couple of the inside of the house, but there's not much to see.'

'This man, the one on the motorbike, do you know what model the bike was?'

'I couldn't say what model, but it was a Suzuki,' Quentin said. He saw Philmore nod, as though he'd just confirmed something he already knew.

Quiet descended on the room. Everyone sipped their tea, but Quentin knew they were all thinking the same thing. A carefully laid plan to catch the criminals had been thwarted. So how could they get it back on track?

Chapter Sixteen

It was nearly seven o'clock before they were reunited with a disgruntled Colin. He emerged from an interview room at Wanstead police station after DCI Philmore had explained the situation to the arresting officer and taken charge of the statue.

'You can all go now,' he said to Quentin. 'I'll be in touch.'

'Will you?' Quentin said doubtfully. 'I hope so. I'd like to help, you know, be part of a scheme to catch this gang, especially Motorbike Man. Any idea who he is, by the way?'

Philmore shook his head but avoided Quentin's eyes. He knows but he's not going to tell me, after all we've been through, Quentin thought, frustrated. His frustration wilted when he realized how things must seem to Philmore. However accidental, they'd disrupted a police operation that might have taken months to plan, told an unlikely story about a dead cat and presented a wedding dress as evidence. He had to admit it didn't look very professional.

'Well,' he said, swallowing his frustration, 'he knows me, and I should think he's pretty upset at the aggro I've caused him. What if he comes looking for me?'

'He doesn't know your friend, does he? Can you stay with him for a few nights? Keep away from where he's seen you and you should be all right. Any problems, though, ring me direct at any time, and I'll get something sorted.'

'Can't we, you know, help in some way?'

Philmore shook his head. 'Not at the moment. Keep a low profile and if I need you, I'll call.'

'What about Walberg?'

'We've got it covered.'

'Right. Well, keep us informed.'

Philmore extended his hand. 'I will. Goodbye, Quentin. Bye, Mrs Merrydrew, Mr Ward.'

On the way home, Colin's mood alternated from fury at having his house invaded and being arrested to chagrin at having put the statue in the wrong bag.

'You left your wedding things in the kitchen,' he explained. 'When you were upstairs I nearly spilt coffee on them, so I put them back where they came from, or I thought I did. I didn't think the police would want them, or the bundles of blank paper. I was only trying to help. I wish I hadn't bothered.'

'Never mind, Colin,' Quentin said, recalling the rollicking they'd had about tampering with evidence. 'The statue's in safe hands now.'

Grunting, Colin shot him a look of exasperation tinged with gratitude. 'Yes, well, I could use a drink,' he said.

'Good idea,' Wanda said. 'We'll go to that pub near you. We can get something to eat there too.'

The pub was busy but not overcrowded. Although it wasn't really cold, a log fire burned in an inglenook fireplace, giving the place a cosy ambiance. The buzz of voices and the aroma of food cooking were cheering, and Quentin felt himself relaxing. They had a drink each before they ordered their meal, making small talk and not mentioning the day's events.

They had almost finished eating when Wanda said, 'You know what we didn't say to Philmore, Quentin?'

'No, what?'

'Mrs Freeman's. We didn't ask if he was going to put a watch on the place.'

'Oh. Well, I meant to, but after Colin's call–'

'So I'm to blame for something you didn't say now!' Colin snapped.

'I didn't mean that. I could call him, ask him if he's going to send someone over there.'

'I'm sure he'll think of that,' Colin said. 'That's what he's paid for.'

Wanda looked uncertain. 'Yes, it's just… it would be awful if someone broke in and made a mess of the place.'

Laying down his knife, Colin said, 'We've been through this. They know you wouldn't take either the money or the goods there – it's too obvious. Why would you make it that easy for them?'

'Which is what I said before,' Quentin agreed.

'The police will work that out,' Colin continued, 'so they won't bother sending anyone round there, and I shouldn't think they've got the manpower anyway.'

'No,' said Wanda. 'But we have.'

Quentin and Colin both stared at her. 'You mean go back to your house and keep a midnight vigil?' Colin asked. 'But we've just said they won't break in.'

'Not to get the statue or the money, but as Quentin said before, they might try to get at us to tell them where they are.'

Colin gulped down the last of his food. 'Highly unlikely,' he said. 'They probably think you've done exactly what you have done – gone to the police. In which case they'll have to drop the whole thing.'

Quentin compressed his lips. He pictured Motorbike Man struggling to stop him taking back his holdall at the station, during the chase on the M25 and again when they'd left him with nothing but a wedding dress, accessories and magazines. After the ignominy of being brought down as he fled from a crime scene and having the goods snatched from him – no, there was no way Motorbike Man would let that pass.

'They won't drop it,' he said slowly. 'Motorbike Man will have to do something. He's cost the organisation a hundred and fifty grand plus whatever the statue's worth.'

Colin looked thoughtful. 'Yes. I don't suppose he's very happy, but what can he do? He can call in the big boys, but they won't bother with Mrs Freeman's if they think the police have already got the statue, and–'

'They don't know that for sure,' Wanda interrupted. 'And like Quentin said, they might want to take revenge for us spoiling their plans.'

Colin looked at Quentin. 'Do you really think they might?'

'It's a possibility.'

'So is winning the lottery,' Colin jibed. 'And if you really think they'd do that, all the more reason to keep away from the place.'

Having finished her salmon, Wanda pushed the few remaining chips to the side of her plate and put her fork down. 'Yes, but even if it's a remote possibility, surely it's our responsibility to make sure Mrs Freeman's house isn't trashed? Because that's what they'll do if we're not there, either as a warning or just out of spite. And she's the innocent party in all of this.'

Background noises invaded the lull in their conversation. Quentin was only vaguely aware of them as he mulled over Wanda's words. He could see her point of view, but he could guess at Colin's opinion too – that it was all well and good taking a moral standpoint, but putting themselves in danger to protect an empty property seemed foolhardy.

'The other thing is,' he said, picking up his fork and stabbing at one of Wanda's leftover chips, 'if we keep a watch on the place, we stand a chance of catching them.'

Colin leaned back in his seat. 'Them?'

'Motorbike Man or whoever he sends. Could be just him, or he could send someone else or he could even bring someone with him. Or he could just do a runner, as you said.'

'Right.' Colin eyed Quentin with incredulity. 'So, after all that baloney about keeping away from home in case you're spotted, sending me over there like an errand boy, going to the police because things were getting dangerous, you now decide to go back there just in case one of those blokes turns up?'

Quentin raised his hands in a meaningless gesture. He didn't really have an answer to that, except he felt he'd left something unfinished. They'd foiled the gang's plans, but they'd interrupted a police investigation as well. He liked to think that despite the mix-up with the bags and his remonstrations, Philmore appreciated their efforts; or more likely, appreciated the fact that Quentin had agreed to cooperate with him if he were ever contacted again by the international criminal, known to the UK police as Whitelaw, the man Quentin had nicknamed Cultured Voice. It had been nearly a year since Quentin had heard that voice, but Philmore seemed to think contact was still possible. Quentin had foiled Whitelaw's plans, and although he'd escaped capture, he hadn't taken kindly to having his operation disrupted.

'Let's get this straight in our minds before we decide anything,' he said, signalling to the waitress. 'I don't think we should talk about it here. We'll go back to yours, Colin.'

He paid the bill and they walked the short distance to Colin's house, where they had parked the car earlier. Wanda made coffee and carried it into the lounge, then sat on the settee next to Colin with Mozart at her feet.

She looked at Quentin over the rim of her cup. 'So where were we?'

'Well, like I said before, Motorbike Man may not have owned up to losing the statue yet,' Quentin said. 'He might not even have told them about losing the money. So let's think. He was supposed to make the exchange at the station on Saturday. He sees Walberg on the ground, takes our holdall thinking it's the statue, and when I tackle him, I get the money bag but he gets away with what he thinks is the statue. We don't know when he was supposed to hand it over, but probably quite quickly. He wouldn't want to be caught with it – he'd want to hand it over and collect his payment.

'When he realized he didn't have the statue and that we had the money, he spent most of Sunday chasing after us trying to get it back. Somewhere along the line he must have contacted Walberg and arranged to go to his house.'

Quentin paused, trying to recall what he'd overheard in Catford. 'He told Walberg that when his boss found out the exchange hadn't taken place, he was given Walberg's address and told to make the exchange there. We don't know if this boss found out from Motorbike Man or from someone on Walberg's side of the game. Even if Motorbike Man did tell him that the exchange hadn't taken place, he needn't have admitted to not having the money. He could have just said he'd hang on to it until the exchange could be made.'

Wanda flicked a strand of hair from her forehead, her features set in concentration. 'The switch would have to be made quickly. I can't see anyone trusting Motorbike Man with that much money for long. I mean, it's a bit risky, leaving a small fortune in the hands of a hardened criminal like him.'

'He must have worked for these people for quite a while for them to use him for such a big job,' Colin suggested. 'But hardened criminal or not, I'm sure he's very aware of the consequences if he gets any ideas about running off with the money.'

'Yep, of course,' Quentin said. 'Which is what makes me think he wouldn't have told them he'd lost the money and the statue, and why he's desperate to get them back before they find out.'

'He'll have to be quick, though,' Wanda pointed out. 'If he was meant to hand over the statue sometime today, he hasn't got much leeway. He can probably make an excuse, get away with it for a day, but no longer. His employer will smell a rat.'

Quentin took up the narrative. 'That means he's got three options. Disappear, though he knows they'll try to hunt him down, tell them the truth or make a last-ditch attempt to recover either the money or the statue. Both, if he can. And we're the only people who can tell him where they are.'

Quentin's last sentence hung in the air. He could almost hear his companions weighing up the possibilities. When they said nothing he went on, 'Mrs Freeman aside, what do we think is Motorbike Man's most likely course of action?'

Colin shrugged. 'I'd get as far away as I could. Can't see the point of staying around to get beaten up, or worse.'

'I wouldn't.' Wanda spoke slowly, with her eyes closed as though she was trying to picture the situation. 'I'd want to try to recover what I'd lost before I gave up, and I'd want to get paid.'

'And if Motorbike Man could recover both holdalls by tomorrow, and as far as he knows we've still got them, he'd be able to hold his head up and still get paid. If he only recovered one, he wouldn't get paid for doing half the job, but he might escape having his head bashed in.'

'My thoughts exactly,' Quentin admitted. 'So… where does that leave us?'

'We have to go back and watch Mrs Freeman's,' Wanda said at once. 'We must.'

Colin gave an impatient toss of his head. 'That's ridiculous. You heard what the DCI said – keep a low profile. We can't put ourselves in danger to protect the house of a woman we hardly know, even if she is your neighbour. As for catching this bloke, how do you propose to clobber him if he does turn up?'

Quentin noted that Colin had said *we* can't put ourselves in danger. Wanda obviously picked up on this because she smiled at him and said, 'We'll think of something, with your help of course, Colin.'

A resigned look came over Colin's face and he sighed. 'What do you want me to do?'

Wanda shot a triumphant glance at Quentin. 'Well,' she said, 'if we go back to mine or Quentin's we can take turns at keeping watch and alert each other if anything happens.'

'And if it doesn't?'

'At least we'll have covered the possibility with no harm done,' Wanda answered. 'It's a pity Mrs Freeman didn't give you a key to go in and feed Lucky, Quentin, instead of leaving him with you.'

'Why is it?' Colin demanded. 'Don't tell me you'd want us to stay in her house tonight?'

'No,' Quentin said, excitement stirring in his stomach. 'But as Wanda said, he's desperate now. He'll try anything if he doesn't want to end up floating down the Thames.'

'All right,' said Colin, 'but if we're going to do it, we'll have to tell Philmore.'

'No!' said Quentin, remembering the DCI's refusal to his offer of help.

'He'd try to stop us,' Wanda added. 'We'll ring him as soon as anything happens. I'm going to get my things.'

Quentin stood up. 'So am I. Are you coming, Colin?'

Chapter Seventeen

They arrived back in Greenwich in separate cars, Colin opting to drive his own. It was ten o'clock and the road was quiet. Keeping their heads down and Wanda covering her hair with a scarf in case Motorbike Man was watching from some concealed place, they made straight for Wanda's, Quentin and Wanda going the back way as they'd done before. As Motorbike Man hadn't yet seen Mozart, Colin took him the front way, using Wanda's keys as previously.

'The lights are on at number fifty-two,' Colin told them when they were inside.

'The timer's still working then,' Quentin said. 'I wonder when they go off. Eleven or twelve, probably. Nothing will happen before twelve, I shouldn't think.'

'Nothing'll happen anyway,' Colin grunted. 'We're wasting our time.'

'In that case we don't need to worry,' Quentin answered. 'No action, no danger.'

Mozart, seemingly pleased to be home, trotted from room to room as if ensuring nothing had changed, eventually curling up under the dining table.

His movements reminded Quentin of his own pet. 'I ought to go and check on Magpie as we're here. We can see Mrs Freeman's better from my window anyway. I'm closer, though there's not much in it.' Hardly anything, he knew, given the width of these terraced properties. 'How are we going to work these shifts?'

'I'll take the first watch,' Colin offered.

'Thanks, but I didn't mean that. I don't think just watching out the window will be enough this time. He's hardly likely to break in at the front. He'll go in from the back, through the alley.'

'Not necessarily,' Colin countered. 'If he does turn up, he won't expect anyone to be looking through their window in the dead of night.'

'I suppose we should really cover the back and the front,' Wanda put in. 'It's a shame the yellow lines go up as far as Mrs Freeman's, but the parking bay starts just past it, you know, almost opposite.'

'You mean keep watch from the car, which is what I was thinking,' Quentin said. 'We could go round the back every so often, then we would see any flashes of torchlight.'

'You must be joking,' Colin objected. 'We'll freeze to death.'

'It's not that cold,' Quentin said. 'We can wrap up well. We'll take a flask of coffee, keep us awake.'

'Yes,' said Wanda. 'I've got a couple of those insulated mugs.'

Colin's expression showed his disapproval. 'I can't see any advantage in doing that. We can just as easily go out and round the back from here.'

'Except if he does come and makes a run for it, it would be better to be in or near the car to go after him.' Wanda looked at Colin as though she expected him to agree with her logic. 'I don't mind going first. I'll call you as soon as I see anything.'

'No!' said Quentin and Colin together. Catching Quentin's eye, Colin made a face. Quentin waited for his characteristic gesture – cleaning his glasses with his shirt – but it didn't happen.

'All right,' Colin conceded. 'I suppose it is a bit nearer. I'll go first, but you'd bloody well better wake up if I call you, not sleep through the night like last time.'

'I will,' Quentin promised. 'I'll keep my mobile next to me. Ring when your shift's up, and I'll relieve you.'

'Too right you will. I'll wait till her lights go off, then I'll take up my position.' Colin gave a humourless chuckle. 'I'm getting to sound like a hit man myself.'

* * *

Mrs Freeman's lights went off at eleven-thirty, though a dim glow still filtered through the upstairs window – a landing light, timed to be left on all night, they decided. When Colin had been duly despatched with thermos mug, blanket and torch, Quentin went the back way home to check on Magpie. The cat lifted his tail and tossed his head when he saw him.

'Sorry, boy,' Quentin said fondly. 'Couldn't be helped.'

Magpie fixed green eyes on him, as though deciding whether to forgive him for his increasingly long absences, then padded across and rubbed against his legs. Quentin refilled his water and food bowls, then wandered into the lounge. He was tired, but he knew he wouldn't sleep. He should have taken the first watch. Perhaps he should go to bed in the hope that sleep would come. He'd be fit for nothing tomorrow if he didn't rest before spending half the night in the car. A sudden feeling of hopelessness came over him. What were they doing, waiting up all night for something to happen? Just that, he supposed. This case was big, and it had started so promisingly. He wanted something to happen. It wasn't right that involving the police should be the end of it.

He glanced at the clock. Nearly twelve. Was Wanda asleep? He was willing to bet she wasn't. What did it matter where he slept? Colin could ring him wherever he was. Pocketing his mobile and picking up his keys, which included Wanda's as well as his own, he left through the back door and went over the wall to Wanda's.

* * *

It was one-thirty when the shrill of his mobile woke him from a satisfied sleep. Jerking awake, he unwound himself from Wanda's arms and felt for the phone.

'Colin?' he croaked. Stupid question. Who else would ring him at this time of night? 'Anything up?'

Colin's voice came in hushed tones.

'Speak up,' Quentin said, 'I can't hear you.'

'I can't speak up,' Colin whispered. 'I'm at the end of the alley. I came round the back to check and saw a light flash in Mrs Freeman's garden.'

'A torch, you mean? Hold on, Colin, I'll be right with you.'

He switched on the bedside lamp and reached for his clothes. Wanda sat up and looked at him enquiringly. He repeated what Colin had said while he thrust his legs into his jeans, then started down the stairs.

'Quentin!' called Wanda, rushing down after him. 'For goodness' sake be careful. Motorbike Man's a nasty piece of work.'

'I will,' Quentin said, snatching up a heavy doorstop. 'If we're not back in ten minutes, ring Philmore or dial 999.'

Not waiting to find his shoes he pushed his feet into Wanda's mules, soft and pink and two sizes too small. In just his jeans and the jacket he'd left over the banister, he slipped quietly out of the house, hurrying along the pavement in the soft-soled slippers, something he regretted as soon as he'd crossed the road and entered the passageway between the houses. Sharp stones and grit pricked his feet; he winced but didn't slow down. As he neared the corner where the alley met another that ran across the backs of the houses, he heard scuffling noises.

'Aah!' a voice cried. Unmistakably Colin's. 'Let me go. I'm not who you think I am.'

Torch beams flickered crazily into the night sky like a laser show. Quentin pressed himself against the wall of the garden that ran to the end of the alley and risked a peek round the corner. He saw three shapes. Motorbike Man hadn't come alone. He'd brought reinforcements.

His thoughts were interrupted by another voice, and he froze. A woman's voice, one he'd heard before, though he couldn't think where.

'Give it up, mate. Do you deny you were trying to break into this house?'

'Of course I do. I was trying to stop it being broken into.'

Another voice came, male this time. 'Really? So what were you doing skulking about in the middle of the night?'

'I can explain,' Colin began.

'Don't bother,' came the female voice. 'You can explain down at the station.'

Understanding swamped Quentin, and he recognized the voice: DS Francis.

Prising himself away from the wall, he rounded the corner and approached the three figures. 'It's all right, Detective Sergeant, I can vouch for this man.'

A ray of light fell on him, and he heard the DS gasp. 'Mr Cadbury! What are you doing here?'

'About bloody time,' Colin snorted, wrenching himself free from her colleague's grip.

Quentin looked at the figure on the other side of Colin. It wasn't Philmore. 'A bit mean of your DCI, sending you to stand guard all night,' he said.

'I volunteered,' she told him. 'So did PC Walters. Are you going to tell me what you're doing here?'

'The same as you – waiting to see if anyone breaks in.'

'And what were you planning to do if they did?'

'Call you of course. The police, I mean.'

The police constable pointed to Quentin's hand. 'What's that? I hope you're not carrying an offensive weapon.'

Quentin raised the doorstop for him to see and the constable blinked. He looked at DS Francis as though uncertain how to proceed.

'We'll pretend we didn't see that,' she said, 'but I've a good mind to take you in for wasting police time.'

'We were only trying to help,' Quentin snapped. Tiredness was creeping up and he felt irritable. It was their own time they'd wasted. 'If you'd told us you were going to be here, we wouldn't have bothered.'

'I don't think DCI Philmore will see it that way,' the DS said. 'And you still haven't told us who this is.'

'He's the friend I told you about. He's helping us.'

'The one who got arrested earlier?'

'Yes,' shouted Colin, 'and now I'm in bloody handcuffs, so can you please take them off?'

DS Francis glared at him. 'Quiet. We don't want to wake the whole neighbourhood.'

'I think it's a bit late for that,' Quentin muttered as a light snapped on in one of the houses and a bedroom window opened.

'What's going on down there?' a gruff voice called.

'It's all right, sir,' PC Walters called back. 'Nothing to worry about.'

'Well, keep the noise down or I'll call the police.'

The window slammed shut. Sighing, DS Francis turned to the police constable. 'Stay here, Dave, in case anyone turns up later, though if our man was in hearing distance he won't come near the place after this fiasco.'

'What about these?' Colin bleated, holding up his cuffed hands.

After a nod from DS Francis, the constable produced a key and removed the handcuffs.

'Let's go and talk in our car,' DS Francis said, starting to walk back along the alley. Quentin and Colin followed, Colin rubbing his wrists and Quentin treading carefully in his slippered feet.

Oh well, Quentin thought as he went, it's not a complete disaster. Motorbike Man could still turn up. But as they turned from the back alley into the side passage that led to the road, the roar of a motorbike engine throbbed through the air, then grew fainter. The three of them ran to the mouth of the passageway just in time to see the shape of a motorbike and its rider disappear at speed round the corner of the street.

Chapter Eighteen

It was Wanda who explained why they hadn't heard Motorbike Man approaching. She met them on the pavement a little along from Mrs Freeman's and suggested they talked back at her house.

'I was watching from the upstairs window,' she told them when Quentin, Colin and DS Francis were seated in her lounge. 'I thought I heard an engine, but it cut out. Then I saw someone pushing a motorbike along. He got to the front of Mrs Freeman's then stopped. I came down, opened the front door and heard shouting. I thought maybe one of the gang was breaking in and Motorbike Man was just the getaway driver, although that's daft now I think about it – he would have been in place earlier. Anyway, I was worried, so I called 999, gave the address and said someone was trying to break in.'

'Great,' groaned DS Francis, her green eyes darkening. 'So now we'll have a patrol car at the house. We might as well have lit a bonfire and spelled out "the stakeout's here" in fireworks.'

'So you think I should have tackled Motorbike Man myself, or just left these two to their fate?' Wanda said, a sardonic note creeping into her voice.

DS Francis raised her eyebrows. 'You did the right thing, of course, but if you had just left it to us in the first place, we might have our man by now. This is a police matter.' She looked at Quentin pointedly.

Quentin bridled. 'DCI Philmore promised to keep us informed, and if it hadn't been for us your informant might be dead and you wouldn't have the money or… or…' He stopped short of saying they wouldn't have the statue, because they didn't want the statue – not until it had led them to the criminals.

The DS's radio sounded, and she raised it to her mouth. 'What's up, Dave? OK, I'll be there.'

She looked at the three of them in turn. 'The patrol car's arrived,' she said. 'I need to go and have a word with them.' She turned to go. 'I think you can expect a call from my boss tomorrow,' she called as a parting shot.

* * *

After two whiskies and half an hour of enduring Colin's complaints that he was always either left out or the one who came off the worst, Quentin sank gratefully into his own bed while Colin snored on the put-you-up. He lay staring into the darkness, imagining the rollicking Steve Philmore was going to give him in the morning. He knew he deserved it, but if Philmore or Francis had let him know they were going to watch Mrs Freeman's then he, Colin and Wanda wouldn't have wasted their time doing it themselves.

Once again Quentin had the feeling of incompleteness. He wasn't just a member of the public who'd stumbled across something accidentally. Well, he was, but he was more than that. He was a detective with his own detective agency who had helped the police break up a dangerous gang of criminals. Philmore hadn't forgotten that, he was sure. No – when he realized his oversight he would thank Quentin for doing the right thing, even if things hadn't worked out as they intended.

Anyway, Quentin mused as his eyes closed, I'm not being left in the dark. As a detective it's my job to investigate when there's a need, and there's definitely a need now.

* * *

The following morning, Tuesday, Wanda said, 'I was thinking…'

They were at her house eating breakfast. When she didn't continue, Quentin exchanged glances with Colin.

'Go on,' Quentin said. 'You were thinking what?'

'About Green Scarf.'

'Walberg? What about him?'

Wanda twiddled her knife around in her fingers. 'Well, I was wondering if I should go and see him.'

Quentin and Colin both stared at her.

'But he's in hospital, under police protection,' Colin said. 'You can't just walk in there.'

'And he might be in the ICU,' Quentin added.

Wanda's features set into a determined mask that told them she had already made up her mind, she went on, 'I could ring and find out, say I'm his sister or something.'

'They won't tell you if he's under police protection,' Colin said. 'They won't give information to anyone.'

'I'll just turn up then. I might be lucky, get someone on reception who doesn't know the situation.'

'How do you propose to get past the copper on duty?' Quentin asked.

'And why do you want to see him anyway?' Colin demanded. 'What good would it do?'

'He might tell me something, something useful.'

Colin looked incredulous. 'Why on earth would he? He's part of the gang. OK, so he's a police informant – that means he informs the police, not every Tom, Dick and Harry. And you've disrupted his plans, taken the money and the statue he was responsible for–'

'He may not know that yet,' Quentin interrupted. 'If he's been out of it for a while the police may not have had a chance to tell him. They might not want him to know yet anyway. The copper on guard won't know anything – probably just been told not to let anyone in except medical staff.'

'There will be more than one, surely,' Colin said. 'They've got to have a break sometime. Makes no difference, and the question was – why would he talk to us?'

'Because we saved his life, and because wc helped him at the station.'

Colin frowned. 'I thought you said he was unconscious when you found him at home. He won't know it was you who called the ambulance.'

'He should remember me from the station, though. It was only a few days ago, and he saw me plainly enough when he came round. If I can get to him…' Wanda shrugged. 'I think it's worth a try.'

'So do I,' Quentin said, warming to the idea. 'Even if he tells you Motorbike Man's name it would be a start. That's if he knows it.'

'Well, I think it's a stupid idea,' Colin snorted. 'I thought you had more sense, Wanda. It's dangerous, you'll upset Philmore even more and gain nothing in return.'

He took a bite of his toast and chewed furiously, as though taking his anger out on the innocent bread. Crunching sounds filled the silence.

Quentin tapped his fingers on the table. Philmore would be cross, there was no argument there. But would they gain anything? And suppose the gang had already tried to get at Walberg?

'No,' he said, 'they won't have.'

'Who won't have what?' Colin asked.

'No one in the gang will have got to Walberg yet, because I don't believe Motorbike Man's told his boss what's happened. I think he's stalled them, trying to get the goods before he has to own up. He was on his own last night as far as we know. You didn't see anyone else, did you Wanda?' When she shook her head, he carried on. 'And we didn't see anyone else at the back, so I think your theory is right, Wanda. He's trying to make a last-ditch attempt to save face.'

'The thing is,' Wanda said slowly, 'that the game's going to be up soon. Motorbike Man will have to admit what's happened or do a runner. If they think we've gone to the police the higher-ups will want to get at Walberg to stop him talking, or if Motorbike Man runs they'll want to know if he's got the statue or just taken the money. After all, unless the police have told him, Walberg doesn't know we intercepted Motorbike Man and took the statue. He doesn't even know we had the money. We should get to him first.'

Quentin's mobile rang, and he grimaced when he recognized the number. He considered not answering, but decided against it. Why prolong the agony?

'What the hell do you think you're playing at?' Quentin winced at Philmore's sharp tone. 'Just because you told us about Walberg doesn't give you carte blanche to take matters into your own hands. You've probably cost us the whole operation – six months' work.'

'I didn't think you would cover the place.' Quentin knew his explanation sounded feeble.

'What, you thought I wouldn't work out that he'd try to get in there if there was the remotest chance of his getting what he wanted?'

Quentin racked his brain for a line of defence. 'I thought you would have mentioned it. We could have worked together – he thinks I live there. You must have means of entry into people's properties – I could have been inside, waiting for him, and you could have nabbed him.'

Crackling noises sounded in Quentin's ear. At last Philmore spoke, his tone calmer. 'Look, Quentin, I know you want to help, but I can't put members of the public at risk when there's no need.'

'That's not what you said last year. I thought we had an agreement.'

Quentin heard Philmore's sigh, and guessed at his frustration. 'Our agreement was that you contact me if you hear anything from our friend.' Quentin wondered why he didn't mention Whitelaw by name. Perhaps he didn't like discussing things on the phone. Or perhaps it was his police training. 'Did you hear that? I said contact me, not handle things yourself.'

Determined not to back down, Quentin said, 'How's our mate at the hospital?'

Philmore tutted. Quentin imagined the DCI's pleasant face creased into a frown, his fingers twirling the pen on his desk. The pause lengthened, as though Philmore was wondering what to say.

'Obviously much better,' he said at last. 'Recovered enough to give us the slip and disappear.'

Taken aback, Quentin gasped. 'Disappear? You mean he just walked out?'

'Apparently so, about five o'clock this morning.'

'So did you get a chance to speak to him?'

'No. Now, do I have your word that you'll do nothing else without checking with me first?'

'All right,' Quentin said reluctantly. 'But what if Motorbike Man comes after me? I'll have to defend myself.'

'If anyone comes anywhere near you, let me know.'

'OK, but–'

'But nothing. I've got to go. I've got work to do.'

The call ended and Quentin lowered his phone. 'Never mind about going to see Walberg. He's gone.'

'Gone?' Wanda sounded amazed. 'But he was at death's door yesterday.'

Quentin shrugged. 'Well, whatever they did for him at the hospital it worked. He just walked out.'

'With nobody noticing?' Colin asked.

'Not until it was too late.'

'He won't last long in his state,' Wanda decided. 'He'll be weak, and if he doesn't get his medication or he's in a stressful situation he'll keel over again, maybe for good next time. Do you think he's gone back to Catford?'

'I suppose he might go back to see if the money's still there. He doesn't know what happened after he blacked out,' Quentin answered. 'On the other hand, he might think Motorbike Man's taken it.'

'He's more likely to go back for his medication,' Wanda said. 'Quentin said there were some tablets in the bathroom. Unless he took some from the hospital.'

'It's all speculation,' Colin said. 'We don't know where he is or why he decided to up sticks and leave hospital when he was half dead.'

'Yeah,' Quentin agreed, 'but if we're going to follow this up, we need to start somewhere, and Catford is as good a place as any.'

'I agree,' Wanda said. 'We can't sit around doing nothing.'

Colin looked doubtful. 'Should we be interfering with a police case? I mean I can't believe Philmore exactly begged for your help when you spoke to him.'

Not meeting his gaze, Quentin said, 'He didn't, but I'm sure he won't turn down any information we can give him.'

'Right,' Colin said, bringing his fist down on the table and making the cutlery rattle and the crockery chink together. 'If you're going to Catford then so am I. I'm fed up with being left out of things. You asked me to help and so far all I've done is look after Mozart and get arrested. I want to do something useful.'

Surprised, Quentin said, 'That's good of you, Colin, but three of us going might attract attention. Really, it only needs one of us to go in with another one nearby for backup, just in case.'

'In case of what? Motorbike Man's not going to go there, is he? He knows Walberg hasn't got either the money or the statue, and he didn't care enough to stick around when he collapsed.'

'Well, they weren't exactly best mates,' Quentin pointed out. 'It was no skin off Motorbike Man's nose if Walberg died, as long as he didn't have the statue or the money in the house. In fact, at that point it was probably better for him if Walberg was dead. No chance of him discovering the money was fake and alerting whoever he was working for, and it would give him more time to try and recover the goods.'

With a disgruntled bark, Mozart jumped up and put his front paws on Wanda's lap. 'All right, Mozart,' she responded, standing up. 'I'll get your breakfast.'

'You do that,' Colin said. 'In fact, why don't you stay here with him and I'll go with Quentin.'

Quentin exchanged a wary glance with Wanda, which Colin evidently noticed because he snapped, 'Give me one good reason why I shouldn't come with you.'

Wanda cleared her throat. 'No specific reason, but a minute ago you were trying to stop us from doing anything.'

Colin pulled a face. 'In for a penny, in for a pound. At least I won't be sitting about wondering what's going on.'

'Thanks, Colin,' Quentin said, not relishing the idea of Colin on the scene, 'but we asked you to help, not take unnecessary risks.'

'Ha!' Colin looked triumphant. 'Then you admit it's an unnecessary risk? I rest my case.'

'I didn't mean unnecessary, but it is a risk, yes.'

'In that case why go– no, don't bother, you're going anyway, I can see that.' Colin made a show of pushing back his chair and standing up. 'Either I go with Quentin, or you can count me out of the whole thing. I'm sure Detective Chief Inspector Philmore would be very interested in what you're planning.'

'Colin!' Wanda sounded shocked. 'You wouldn't!'

'Why not? I thought one of the back-up plans was that I should call him if you're in danger.'

'But we're not in danger,' Wanda began.

'All right,' Quentin said irritably. 'All the time we're bickering nothing's getting done. Come then, Colin, if you want to. Wanda can stay here on call, if it's all right with her.'

Wanda looked about to protest, but instead looked from one to the other before beginning to clear away the breakfast things. 'Mozart could do with a nice long walk,' she called as she went to the kitchen.

Colin raised his eyebrows, and Quentin guessed he was surprised that she hadn't put up more of an argument. 'We'll go in your car Colin,' he said, starting to walk out of the room. 'I'll go and get some things, feed Magpie and lock up.'

At home, Quentin cleaned his teeth and checked his jacket, making sure he had his wallet, mobile and notebook and pen. He was annoyed that he'd agreed to Colin coming with him.

'It probably won't matter,' he said to Magpie as he squeezed a gelatinous mess into his dish. 'I don't suppose we'll find anything, but I'll have to put up with Colin going on instead of having Wanda for company. Not a fair exchange, do you reckon, boy?'

The cat mewed, rubbed against his legs, sniffed at his food, took a delicate bite and then sat looking at it.

'Is that all the thanks I get? I thought you liked that flavour. You'll eat it when you're hungry enough. Now, I've got to go.'

Quentin fondled Magpie's ear before stepping back and picking up his keys. As an afterthought, he located his Swiss army knife and decided to take it with him. It might prove more helpful than a doorstop.

'Bye then, boy,' he said when he was ready. 'Don't look so hard-done-by. I'll be back soon.'

As if dismissing this farewell, Magpie rose to his feet, stuck his tail in the air and stalked off.

'Please yourself,' Quentin muttered. 'But think yourself lucky – you could be lying in a holdall or dead on a rubbish dump somewhere.'

Chapter Nineteen

The journey to Catford was uneventful. Colin hardly said a word, concentrating on the directions Quentin gave him and hunting for a parking space. When he found one, he cut the engine and turned to Quentin.

'What now?'

Good question, Quentin thought. He'd gone over some possible scenarios on the journey, but had only come up with one that seemed feasible.

'We need to establish whether Walberg's there,' he said. 'It's pointless just going round the house if he isn't.'

'I can't imagine he will be,' Colin said. 'Once he realized neither the money nor the statue were here, he'd have taken his medication and scarpered.'

Quentin looked at the house, which was three cars along, half expecting to see Philmore or DS Francis outside. 'I don't think he's in a fit state to scarper anywhere. I should think getting from the hospital to wherever he went would have knackered him. That's if he even made it.'

'What are you looking at?' Colin asked, craning his neck to follow Quentin's gaze.

'I just wondered if the police would come here. Still, I can't see anyone hanging around. Maybe they've been and gone. They might have taken him back to hospital, or he might have contacted them himself since we spoke to Philmore, told them he was all right, for all we know.'

'Maybe,' Colin said, screwing up his face. 'Why would he run away from hospital anyway? He'd be far safer there with a police guard.'

'Yes, but if he thought any of the gang might trace him there and the police were standing guard, they'd know he was an informant. Why else would he warrant police protection?'

'Hmm, there is that. Well, come on then genius. What's the plan? And don't tell me to sit here while you swan off.'

'Oh no, I won't do that this time. I don't know if Walberg will recognize me from the station – I don't think so – but a neighbour saw me here yesterday, when I was looking for Walberg's house. Nobody knows you though, so you could knock, see if he's there. If he answers, just pretend to be a double-glazing salesman or something. Walk slowly, see if you can see any movement through the window.'

'And then what?'

'Come back and tell me.'

'And what will you do?'

'I don't know,' Quentin admitted, weary of Colin's apparent need to have every detail spelled out for him. 'We'll have to think on our feet. Just do it.'

Colin's look of incredulity told Quentin he wasn't impressed with his haphazard method of detection. Gut feeling and intuition didn't seem to figure in his make-up. Neither did grasping at straws, which, Quentin realized, was what they were doing now.

He flinched as Colin got out and banged the car door shut, then watched as he walked up to the corner house. He saw him hesitate at the gate, then push it open and stroll up the path. Colin raised his hand and knocked on the door, then repeated the action several minutes later. Then he walked back to the gate, turning and looking towards the window. Slowly he retraced his steps to the car and got in.

'Nothing?' Quentin asked.

'Oh yes,' Colin said, looking pleased with himself. 'Someone's in there all right. I heard movement, and I think I saw something, just a shadow or a reflection maybe, but something, through the window.'

Quentin grinned. 'Good man. So we haven't come on a wild goose chase after all.' An unpleasant thought came to him. Suppose it was a police officer inside, posted there in case Walberg returned? No, he told himself. If Walberg had gone missing at five that morning and they wanted to check his house they would have done it by now. Still, they could have left someone there, but if they had wouldn't they come to the door? There was only one way to find out.

'Right,' he said. 'Now I know someone's there, I'll see what I can do.'

'What can you do when he won't open the door? Break in?'

'I'll think of something. I'm going round the back, like I did last time.'

'Suppose a nosy neighbour challenges you?'

'I'll just say I'm an old friend. That's what we said last time. I'll say he's gone AWOL from hospital and that I'm making sure he's all right.'

Saying this allayed Quentin's misgivings. Even if there were a police officer inside, it would be a regular copper, not someone who'd seen him before. He could give the same story to them if necessary. Emboldened by this thought, he got out.

'Keep hold of your phone,' he called over his shoulder, 'but don't ring me.' As an afterthought he leaned into the car and added, 'Take Philmore's number, too, just in case, but for heaven's sake don't ring him unless you really have to. I'm already in his bad books. If I'm not back in fifteen minutes…'

'Don't worry, I won't leave you to get battered to death.'

As he walked away Quentin wondered what Colin would do. He wished Wanda was here, with her calm common sense and quick thinking. He reached the gate but carried on walking past in case anyone was watching through the window. On the corner of the road he waited, so that if he'd been seen from the house they would think he was just a passer-by. A woman with a dog on a lead rounded the corner and passed him. He waited until she'd walked by the car and crossed over before going back to the gate. By approaching it from this side, he avoided walking in front of the main ground floor window where there was no hedge.

Slipping through the gate and making sure it didn't bang shut, he went round the side of the house as he had previously. There were no windows until he reached the one in the kitchen on the near side of the back door, with a bigger one on the far side. Unlike yesterday, the door was firmly closed. He flattened himself against the wall, his ear close to the kitchen window. He heard nothing, so he ducked down and peeked over the sill. As before, the door to the sitting room stood open, but he could see no sign of anyone. Was Colin mistaken?

Knees aching, he risked standing up and peering in from the edge of the window. As he looked, he frowned. Something was different. The place had been tidy, almost bare, with its meagre furnishings. Today, an upturned drawer sat on the table, its contents spilled on the wooden surface and on the floor. Someone must have been searching for something. The shadow of a figure fell across the space in the doorframe, causing Quentin to draw back. Pulse quickening, he wondered what to do. Ducking down again, he crawled under the window to the door and, very gently, depressed the handle. It wouldn't budge. Well, of course it won't, Quentin thought, remembering he had locked the door himself after Walberg had been taken to hospital. If only it were open, he could rush in and confront Walberg before he had a chance to escape. Was that even Walberg in there? Pursing his lips, he came to a decision. Time to employ some tricks of the trade. He might not be particularly organised or methodical, but he hadn't been a detective for almost a year without picking up some necessary, if questionable, means of entry.

Slipping his hand into his pocket, he felt for his Swiss army knife. He held it in his palm, along with several other gadgets on the same chain. Hmm, he thought, gazing at them. They would do the job but would make a noise. The front door would be quieter. Pocketing the knife, he crept back to the front and drew out his credit card. To his relief he saw there was only one regular-looking lock. Feeling like a burglar, he cast a furtive glance around him, and seeing no one close by, he slid the credit card into the gap between the lock and the doorframe, knowing that any noise would have to travel through the hall to the sitting room. Quickly and quietly the card did its work. Quentin pushed against the door and it swung inwards. He stepped into the hall and pushed the door to but didn't shut it. Sounds came to him, like someone scrabbling inside drawers and cupboards. Whatever Walberg, or whoever it was, was looking for, he obviously hadn't found it.

Feeling more like a burglar than ever, he tiptoed across the hall and stood against the wall next to the sitting room door. This door, half open, was almost opposite the one that led into the kitchen. From this angle, Quentin could see one half of the room, the half that housed the sideboard he'd gone through yesterday and the settee. His eyes widened when they focused on the settee. Walberg was slumped against the backrest, his face grey, his eyes hooded and dark in their sockets. The rasp of his breath made it clear that he was having trouble breathing. Quentin's mind went into overdrive as the scrabbling sounds continued. If Walberg was on the settee, seemingly incapable of doing anything, who was making those sounds?

He moved a fraction, trying to see further into the room, but his movement must have caught Walberg's attention because his head jerked up and he gasped, lifting a hand in a feeble gesture.

Quentin froze, his thoughts in chaos. He'd been prepared to confront Walberg on his own. He hadn't expected anyone to be with him, except possibly the police, but they wouldn't be hunting around the place while Walberg was so obviously in need of medical attention.

Too late, he lurched for the front door, only to collide with someone who flew from the sitting room and felled him with a rugby tackle. A searing pain shot through his knee as it cracked on the un-carpeted floor. Twisting round, he stared up his attacker.

It was Motorbike Man.

Chapter Twenty

Quentin's arm was nearly jerked from its socket as Motorbike Man yanked it towards him and planted a weighty foot on his hip.

'You!' snarled Motorbike Man. 'You interfering arsehole of a bastard – I'll kill you!'

Face red with fury and veins standing out on his forehead and neck, Motorbike Man drew back one arm and balled his hand as though to smash it into Quentin's jaw. An indistinct squawk from Walberg caused his fist to falter in its trajectory, and it hit Quentin with a forcible blow on the side of his cheek. His head reeling and ears ringing, Quentin heard Walberg speak again but couldn't make out what he said. Whatever he said it was enough to stop Motorbike Man from taking another swing at him. Instead, he pulled Quentin to his feet and shoved him into the sitting room.

Trying to wrench himself from his assailant's vice-like grip, Quentin made a half twist and kicked out at Motorbike Man's shins. He was rewarded with a knee in his side and another bout of abuse. Still dazed from the unexpected punch, he felt his knees buckle as he was forced against the wall and a large hand closed round his throat. When he struggled, the hand tightened on his windpipe.

'I'll kill you,' his captor hissed, his face a grotesque mask of hatred. 'After you've told me what you've done with the money and the statue.'

Quentin tried to talk but the pressure on his windpipe made it impossible. He gave a few choking gasps, and for a moment he thought they would be his last. Then the pressure eased as he heard Walberg's voice, still weak but clearer now he was closer.

'Give him a chance to speak. You'll never find out if he's dead.'

At that moment Quentin thought that helping to save Walberg's life was the best thing he'd ever done. As he drew in lungful after lungful of life-giving air, he was pushed onto an upright ladder-backed dining chair. The edge of the wooden seat bit into his thighs and the top rung came just above his shoulders. He sat panting, trying to take stock of his situation. Motorbike Man's tall frame hovered in front of him for a nanosecond before it moved in again and Quentin felt a hand round his neck, pulling his head forward against the metal of a belt buckle; and something sharper, something that dug into his throat and threatened to pierce his skin.

Panicking, he thought: Bloody hell! He's really going to kill me. He felt sweat form on his forehead and trickle onto his eyelid. Keeping absolutely still so as not to cause the knife at his throat to cut him, he attempted to marshal his thoughts. One thing overlaid everything else – he mustn't admit that the police had the bags or that would be the end. If they didn't think he could lead them to what they wanted they wouldn't hesitate to kill him.

'Where are they?'

Quentin gulped, and the knife pricked him. He sat motionless, not even daring to speak. He thought of his own knife nestling in his pocket, could feel its hardness against his thigh, but knew it was useless. Any attempt to reach it would be curtailed in the deadliest possible way.

'Last chance,' Motorbike Man growled.

'Let's be civilized about this,' Walberg croaked. 'Stand back and let him speak.'

'Civilized bollocks,' snapped Motorbike Man, not moving. 'I've had all I can take from this bastard. If we don't get that stuff back we're done for, the pair of us. Not that it matters to you, you're likely to be dead before we see the goods again, but I'm alive and I intend to stay that way.'

Quentin couldn't see Walberg's face, but guessed he wouldn't take kindly to those words, even though they might be true.

'All the more reason to let him speak,' Walberg croaked. 'He can do that better without a knife at his throat.'

'Whose bleeding side are you on?' Motorbike Man spat.

'Yours, but I can't think why. I could have died here yesterday, for all the help you were.'

'Stop whinging. How was I to know you wouldn't get up again? You shouldn't be in this game if you're not up to it. And why you had to keep a bloody record of our transactions, God only knows. Does your illness affect your brain or what? And where the hell is that notebook? I know I picked it up yesterday.'

As if talking had tired him, Walberg let his head loll back against the settee. 'I've told you, it's not here,' he said, his voice almost a whisper.

Recovering a little from his attack and the shock of the knife threat, Quentin thought quickly. Walberg had kept a notebook. Why? Because he was a police informant who traded information for the safety of his family? Had he become alarmed at his declining health and kept a record for the police to find, which he hoped would ensure his family's security after his death?

Quentin didn't know if Motorbike Man saw the sense in Walberg's words or if he couldn't be bothered to argue about it. Whichever it was, he moved aside slightly, pulled the knife away from Quentin's throat and slapped him hard around the face with his free hand. The weapon once more against Quentin's neck, Motorbike Man fumbled one-handed with the buckle, pulled the belt free and was behind the chair before Quentin had time to realize that the knife was no longer pressing into him. Instantly his arms were wrenched behind the back of the chair and his hands held securely. Too late, he realized that Motorbike Man must have let go of the knife because he was using both hands to wind the belt round his wrists and through the rungs of the chair back. While he bent down to fasten the buckle Quentin felt his breath on his neck, smelled the faint odour of stale after-shave and sweat that hinted at his adversary's late-night activities and sleepless hours. Breathing hard, Motorbike Man straightened up and came round to face him.

'OK,' he said, darting a look at Walberg. 'Happy now? If you're so concerned for his welfare, why don't you ask him where the stuff is? But be quick about it. If the powers that be don't hear from me by this afternoon, they'll be sending out a search party.'

Quentin wondered why a search party hadn't been launched already. Motorbike Man must have spun quite a story for them to wait this long.

Walberg nodded wearily. 'I know, but killing him won't help if you're caught. You'll be done for murder.'

Motorbike Man snorted. 'Won't make any difference will it, if they get to me first, or if that notebook falls into the wrong hands.'

'You shouldn't have taken it, then,' Walberg wheezed.

'What was I supposed to do when you were laid out on the deck, leave it for anyone to find?' Motorbike Man's face relaxed for a moment, as though something had just occurred to him. Then it contorted, and Quentin flinched as he swung back towards him and waved the knife menacingly before his face. 'You, you've got it.'

'N- no!' Quentin yelled. 'I haven't seen any notebook–' He shrank back as the knife was held to his throat again.

'You little shit!' Motorbike Man's face was turning purple and he looked about to have a fit. 'I'm going to kill you very slowly. First the money, then the statue, now the notebook. You've got ten seconds to tell me where they are.'

Quentin could feel his eyes bulging and the blood pounding in his ears. For the first time in his life, he couldn't bluff or lie his way out of a situation, couldn't even run away; images of his mother in their family home flashed into his mind.

'Is this what you're looking for?'

The voice wasn't Walberg's. It was low and feminine – the sweetest sound Quentin had heard that day. He gasped when the knife nicked his chin as Motorbike Man jerked his arm away and whirled round.

'And if I were you, I'd drop that knife, now,' Wanda said from the doorway. 'I know how to use this.' She raised one hand slightly, indicating the gun she held.

Motorbike Man stood motionless, poised as though preparing to spring at Wanda but eyeing the gun tentatively.

Wanda raised her other hand, brandishing the greenish-brown coloured notebook it held. 'You're wrong, you know,' she continued, her voice steady. 'We didn't have it. I found it just now, outside in the bushes. You must have dropped it yesterday. I'm quite happy to hand it over if you set my friend free.'

Motorbike Man's eyes darted from Quentin to Wanda and the gun, like a trapped animal desperately seeking escape. Nothing else moved except the rise and fall of Walberg's chest as he struggled to breathe.

'Let him go,' he managed to gasp. 'Get the book.'

'Shut up,' snarled Motorbike Man. 'You want me to set him free to go running to the police? I can take *her*.'

'I wouldn't try it,' Quentin said, feeling braver without the threat of cold steel against his neck. 'She's a good shot.'

'Drop the knife,' Wanda said, raising her arm and levelling the gun at Motorbike Man's chest.

'The book first.'

Without taking her gaze from her target, Wanda dropped the notebook and kicked it sideways, away from her but well out of Motorbike Man's reach.

'Drop the knife, untie my friend, then come and pick the notebook up.'

Motorbike Man looked incredulous. 'And then what?'

'Then you can walk out.'

'Just like that?'

'Just like that.'

'And why should I believe you?'

'Because a gun's quicker than a knife.'

There was a tense pause, then the knife clattered to the floor, skittering away. Quentin gazed at Wanda in admiration. For the umpteenth time he marvelled at her ability to stay calm in a desperate situation. He should have known she wouldn't stay at home while he was on a potentially dangerous job.

'Let me get the book, then I'll push off and you'll never see me again.'

'What about your associate?' Wanda asked, nodding towards Walberg.

Motorbike Man shifted his weight. 'I can't take him. He's ill.'

'So you'll leave him to his fate then, like you did yesterday?' Quentin butted in. 'Lucky for him we came when we did. He'd be a goner if Wanda hadn't kept him alive until the ambulance turned up.'

Walberg lifted his head and stared at Wanda. 'You,' he croaked, 'at the station…'

'Yes,' snapped Motorbike Man, 'at the station, on the motorway, here, every-bleeding-where!'

'That's enough!' Wanda's voice was sharp. 'All right, get the notebook, then leave. One false move and I'll shoot.'

'Wanda, no!' shouted Quentin as Motorbike Man moved forward. The panic in his voice seemed to trigger Motorbike Man into action. His careful, creeping steps turned to a lurch, not for the book but for Wanda. He dived for her legs, flinging one arm up and knocking the hand that held the gun, and throwing the other round her knees and pulling her over.

In his panic Quentin rushed to stand up, forgetting that he was still lashed to the chair. He managed a half standing position, stumbled a few steps then crashed to his knees with the chair on top of him. The wooden chair back hit his neck as it rebounded from the fall, and he moaned. Hearing a clunking noise, he twisted his head and saw the gun sliding across the laminated flooring towards the settee.

'Gotcha,' he heard Motorbike Man grunt, and jerking his body in the direction of his voice, saw Wanda trying to break out of his grasp. For a moment it seemed she would succeed, because one of Motorbike Man's hands disappeared from sight. It returned before Wanda could wrench herself free, and this time it held the knife. Wanda's efforts to escape him ceased.

'Think you're so clever, don't you?' Motorbike Man hissed. 'Caught me by surprise before, but you won't get away from me today. Where's the money, bitch, and where's that statue? Tell me, or I'll kill you.'

'No, you won't. Not her.' Walberg's voice was weak, but his words made Motorbike Man look at him in surprise. Quentin looked at him too. He seemed to have recovered some energy, enough to have retrieved the gun from where it had come to rest by his feet. He held it now, pointed directly at Motorbike Man.

'What d'you mean, not her?' Motorbike Man jeered. 'She's as bad as he is.'

Walberg wheezed noisily. 'Let her go and get out while you can.'

'Going soft in our old age, are we? Well, it won't wash. It's them against us, remember?'

Walberg seemed to waver, and for a moment Quentin thought he might relinquish the gun.

'It's more like him against you,' he said to Walberg. 'To save his neck he tried to palm you off with fake money yesterday, and left you to pick up the pieces.'

'Don't listen to him,' Motorbike Man snapped. 'Or don't you care about getting banged up for years? Oh no, I suppose it doesn't matter to you in your state.'

Walberg sat forward on his seat, the gun in front of him, his gaze flickering to Wanda before returning to Motorbike Man. 'Exactly,' he said, his voice louder and steadier now. 'If I shoot you, I'll never get to trial, so I've got nothing to lose. Let her go.'

Something in his tone seemed to make Motorbike Man understand he was serious. Even though Walberg was ill, it didn't take much effort to pull a trigger, a fact that his partner in crime must have recognized, because he drew the knife away from Wanda's throat and laid it on the floor. Pushing himself into a kneeling position, the chair still weighting him down, Quentin watched. His stomach churned as his panic resurfaced. Motorbike Man had relinquished the knife before, but he'd still managed to disarm Wanda. Quentin didn't believe he'd give up and go quietly now. He was bound to try something.

'What about the job?' Motorbike Man said, still holding onto Wanda's arms.

A faint snigger escaped Walberg. 'I don't care about the job any more, or the money. What good would it do me? I just want to see my daughter before I die. Thanks to this lady, I might be able to. Now let her go.'

Motorbike Man didn't move. He stared at Walberg as if trying to think of a way out of his predicament.

'I mean it,' Walberg said, his voice rising. 'I'll count to ten. One, two, three–'

'All right, all right,' Motorbike Man interrupted. 'I'll let her go. Here.'

Instead of releasing his grip on Wanda, Motorbike Man pushed her forward with a mighty thrust, rolling on top of her and ending up just short of Walberg's feet and a foot away from Quentin. Still kneeling, Quentin shuffled, lurched forward, twisted sideways and brought the back of the chair down on Motorbike Man's shoulder. It gave a satisfying crack, and Motorbike Man squealed in pain. He scrambled up, facing the front window as he did so. Instead of turning and going for Walberg as Quentin expected, he launched himself across the floor to where the notebook lay and scooped it up.

Quentin, his head ringing from its bang on the floor as he'd brought the chair down, watched helplessly as Motorbike Man sped out of the room towards the front door. What's going on? Quentin thought groggily.

Pale and shaken, Wanda came into his vision. She started towards him, then turned as a commotion from outside reached their ears. It quietened, and a voice called, 'Hey, you two, I could use some help here.'

'Bloody hell,' Quentin muttered. He'd never been so glad to hear Colin's voice since the day they'd met.

Chapter Twenty-one

Confusion filled Quentin as he tried to make out what was happening. He felt a rush of air and saw Wanda run outside. Colin was out there, wasn't he? Yes, he'd heard his voice. Why were Colin and Wanda outside when he was in here unable to move? Quentin let his head rest on the floor, closed his eyes and tried to breathe normally. A movement roused him and his eyes flew open. Walberg! He'd totally forgotten about Walberg. With the weight of the chair still on him, he raised his head and shoulders as far as he could. Walberg was slumped back in the settee, the gun clasped loosely in a hand that lay in his lap. His breath came in ragged gasps and there was a blue tinge around his lips.

'Wanda!' he shouted as loudly as he could. It seemed a long time before Wanda appeared, breathless and red-faced. She approached the settee, her face changing when she saw Walberg lying there. Side-stepping Quentin, she stood over the sick man and felt for his pulse. From his position Quentin could see Walberg's eyes flicker, then open. As though recognising Wanda, he looked at her and whispered, 'Helen, my daughter…'

'It's all right, we'll find her. I'll ring for an ambulance.'

'No good. Thanks… for trying.'

His head lolled and a grimace contorted his grey face. He tried to speak again, and Wanda lowered her ear to his mouth. When she raised it again, she met Quentin's gaze and shook her head. The ragged gasps had ceased. Jumping up, she pushed Walberg down so he lay flat on the settee and began to pump his chest as she had done the day before. Quentin could see it was useless. There was no way back for Walberg this time.

'What's going on in here then?'

Quentin's head had twisted so many times he was beginning to think he was at a tennis match. His neck ached and his knees hurt, and when he saw Colin standing with a grin on his face, something in his brain snapped.

'For God's sake, is anyone going to untie me from this bloody chair?' he yelled.

'Phone an ambulance, Colin,' Wanda commanded. 'Heart attack.'

Colin took out his phone and started the call. As if taking pity on Quentin, he rolled his eyes, wedged the phone between his chin and shoulder, strode across and unbuckled the belt. When he'd pulled the belt free, he lifted the chair away, and Quentin grunted in relief.

While Colin finished the emergency call, Quentin sat on the floor rubbing first his wrists and then his knees. 'I won't be able to walk for a week,' he groaned. 'What a farce. After all this, the man we thought might help us can't tell us anything and Motorbike Man's got away again.'

'No, he hasn't,' Colin said, looking smug. 'What do think I was doing out there while you were, em, otherwise engaged?'

'You mean you've got him?'

'Of course.' Colin spoke as though stopping criminals in their tracks was an everyday occurrence. Quentin stared at him.

'So where is he? You haven't left him on his own?'

'Oh, he's not going anywhere.'

Grimacing at the pain that shot through his knee as he stood up, Quentin limped to the front door and looked out. Motorbike Man was sitting propped up against the fence, his arms bound behind him with a multi-coloured length of material, the end of which was secured to the gatepost. A flowerpot sat on his head, obscuring his face and from which bits of compost fell onto his shoulders.

The brightly coloured material Quentin recognized as a scarf, and a slow grin spread over his face. After his threatening behaviour earlier, it was strange to see Motorbike Man helpless like this, his head with its flowerpot crown flopping to one side. He was either unconscious or dazed, Quentin calculated. Laughter bubbled up inside him, and he leaned against the door frame for support.

'Oh my God!' he choked as Colin appeared behind him. 'You certainly made a good job of that!'

'Yeah, well, I always knew scarves were meant for more than keeping you warm. It's Emma's. Pretty, isn't it? I saw Wanda arrive and go in, so I came and looked in through the window. I saw her on the floor struggling with our friend.' Colin nodded towards Motorbike Man, then continued, 'Then he rushed out, so I grabbed a flowerpot, tripped him up and bashed him with it.'

Amazed, Quentin shook his head. 'Well,' he said when he'd got to grips with Colin actually having faced danger and done something useful, 'I suppose we'd better call Philmore.'

'No need,' Colin told him airily. 'I've done it. He's on his way.'

Faces had appeared at the windows of several neighbouring houses. A door across the road opened and two people peered out.

'It's all right,' Quentin called. 'There's been a break-in. The police are on their way.'

Within minutes the street resembled a scene from EastEnders. Sirens wailed and blue lights flashed as an ambulance and a police car arrived simultaneously, causing more doors to open and a knot of curious neighbours to form on the pavement. A second car pulled up, and Detective Chief Inspector Philmore and DS Francis got out.

They came through the gate and stood in front of the man slumped against the fence. Philmore lifted the flowerpot to reveal the dirt-streaked face underneath.

'Bill Adamson,' he said sourly, and let the flowerpot slip down again.

DS Francis's face twisted into an expression of suppressed laughter, but Quentin's spirits plummeted when Philmore sent him a look he couldn't fathom. Anger or gratitude? Why would he be angry when they'd captured a major player in a gang, one who could possibly tell them who the ringleaders were?

Beating back the questions he burned to ask, Quentin led him into the house, where the paramedics were taking over from Wanda's frantic pumping at Walberg's chest. After several minutes of attempted resuscitation, they declared him dead. Wanda looked upset. She sat on the chair that Quentin had been tied to.

'Poor bloke,' she said. 'I knew he was gone, but I had to try.'

'You did well, love,' one of the paramedics said.

'Looks like you did all you could,' said Philmore. 'And not for the first time.'

'No,' said Colin, who'd come into the room. 'She saved his life.'

'And he saved mine today,' Wanda said, her voice stilted. 'Lord knows what would have happened if he hadn't challenged Motorbike Man.'

Philmore's gaze drifted to Walberg. 'Challenged him, in his condition. How?' He went over to the settee. 'Ah. What's this?' Reaching into his pocket, he drew out a pen and bent down. When he stood up, the gun swung by its trigger guard from the pen. He stared at it, then at Wanda.

'This was his challenge? But it's not real. You can tell from the weight. Anyone handling this would know it's a replica.'

'Yes,' agreed Wanda. 'It's mine. Well, my nephew's actually. I borrowed it last year and I've never returned it. It's a useful deterrent.'

'But Walberg must have known–'

'Probably, but our friend outside didn't.'

'Right,' said Philmore, his expression suggesting that he'd been caught in the eye of a hurricane and landed on stage in a pantomime. He looked from Wanda to Quentin, then at Colin. 'It was you who rang me, wasn't it, Mr Ward? I'll need to speak to you. All of you.' His phone rang, and he stepped away. When he came back he said, 'I have to go now. I'll ring to tell you when to come in and we can get to the bottom of why you just happened to be here – and why you're in possession an offensive weapon.'

'I've just told you,' Wanda began, then stopped under Philmore's glare.

'Make sure you're available.' Philmore cast a meaningful look at Quentin and began to walk out as DS Francis came in. He told her to send for the SOCO team and question the paramedics before they took Walberg's body away. 'I'll see Adamson off then I'm going,' he added as he moved away. 'See you back at the office.'

Quentin followed him out and stood next to him while they watched Motorbike Man – or Adamson – being relieved of his flowerpot helmet and the scarf replaced by handcuffs. At a nod from Philmore, the captive, having come to his senses, was bundled into a waiting car by a uniformed officer. Catching sight of Quentin, he glowered at him, a menacing glare that threatened revenge.

Stare all you like mate, Quentin thought, the memory of a knife at his throat and his ungainly position on the chair burned into his brain. You deserve everything you've got coming.

As Philmore made to walk to his car, Quentin said, 'So you know him, then?'

'That really doesn't concern you, Quentin.'

Quentin bridled. 'Now hang on a minute. I've been threatened with a knife, slapped round the face and tied to a chair. I think I'm entitled to know something about someone who does that to me.'

The DCI gave an impatient toss of his head. 'None of that would have happened if you hadn't interfered. All right, yes, we've had dealings with him before. Walberg told us Adamson was involved a few weeks ago. He's on our records but we haven't been able to track him down or get any information on the ringleaders, hence the plan we put in place – the one you've managed to destroy.'

'It's not my fault Walberg collapsed next to us and that Adamson snatched our holdall,' Quentin said hotly. 'We were just innocent bystanders, there for perfectly legitimate reasons.'

'So you were.' Philmore's tone was sarcastic. 'Taking a dead cat to the vet's.'

Without waiting for a reply, Philmore strode to his car. As he drove away, a plethora of thoughts blossomed in Quentin's mind. They had found the money, rescued the statue and delivered one of the criminals into police hands while another was dead. What was left for them to investigate? Was this the end of the case?

He pressed his lips together hard. How could it be the end with the ringleaders still at large? It couldn't be. Too many loose ends.

And Quentin didn't like loose ends.

Chapter Twenty-two

'Lucky you thought to bring that gun – I'd forgotten about it,' Quentin said as they arrived home. He'd opted to travel back with Wanda, leaving Colin to follow alone.

'I hope they give it back,' Wanda said, opening her front door. 'It's not really an offensive weapon – it doesn't even take real bullets and it wasn't loaded. I should have taken it back and hidden it, though I suppose Motorbike Man will mention it in his version of events.'

'Yeah. He'll probably make us out to be the aggressors. Still, they've got his knife. That's aggressive enough.'

When Mozart had stopped his boisterous greeting and Wanda had put the kettle on, Quentin continued, 'Who'd have thought Colin would clobber Motorbike Man like that? I never imagined him getting involved with fisticuffs. Mind you, it was probably because he knew you were in the house. He may not have been so keen to rescue me.'

Wanda rolled her eyes. 'I don't know why you've got such a downer on him. He's a perfectly decent man who's led a perfectly decent life and likes to do the right thing.'

'Huh. The gospel according to Saint Colin, you mean.'

'Oh shut up, Quentin. You're just jealous because he's financially secure, had a good career, had a family, got a nice house and is qualified to work again if he chooses.' She handed Quentin a cup of tea. 'Well, come on, admit it.'

Quentin was incensed. 'Certainly not. I've never wanted a conventional career. I like what I do and I've got a nice house too, and a family.' Even if they are ten thousand miles away, he added silently, but not missing the implication that he hadn't generated a family of his own. Neither had Wanda, so who was she to talk?

'And,' Wanda went on, 'you don't like the fact that he's the one who stopped Motorbike Man from getting away while you were belted to a chair. I hope you'll be giving him credit for it.'

'Course I will. I've already thanked him,' Quentin said grudgingly.

He knew Colin was a decent man and that seeing the danger in things was sensible – especially if you had someone else to consider, as Colin had. Quentin guessed that having a daughter brought out the protective gene in most men. But it was Wanda who was the issue in this emotional conflict. Although she insisted that she had no intention of remarrying or living with someone permanently, Quentin wasn't naïve enough not to realize that, should she change her mind, Colin had a lot more to offer than he did.

'We don't have to call him Motorbike Man anymore,' Wanda said, breaking his train of thought. 'His name's Bill Adamson. He doesn't look like a Bill.'

'Really? And what do Bills look like?'

'Like my uncle. Round-faced, jolly and kind.'

'Hmm. Well, sorry to shatter the illusion. Philmore knows this Adamson, apparently, but hasn't been able to get him or the ringleaders. That's why they hatched this plan with the microchipped statue.'

Wanda nodded. 'They pulled Walberg in and he agreed to turn informant. Why did they pull him in?'

'I wasn't privy to that information. Philmore's not happy with us. We've stopped Adamson leading them to whoever he was meant to pass it on to.'

'He could have got away if we hadn't,' Wanda pointed out. 'If they had moved in on the big boys, Motorbike Man – I mean Adamson – could have done a runner if he was still free. I suppose it would depend on how they set the plan up. Anyhow, with Walberg dead so is the plan. The ringleaders must know by now that they're not going to get their hands on that statue.'

'You're right, Wanda. And what about the person Walberg was supposed to take the money to? What does he think has happened to it? If only we had a name. The only two we know are Walberg and Adamson.'

Wanda put down her teacup and stared at him. 'Names,' she muttered, then louder, 'Names! That's it!'

'What is?'

'When Walberg was dying, he said something.'

Quentin screwed up his face, trying to recall what Walberg had said. 'That's right. He said his daughter's name – Helen, wasn't it?'

'Not that. I mean his last words. I could just about hear him.'

An image of Wanda leaning down and putting her ear to the dying man's mouth came to Quentin. 'So – what did he say?'

'I thought he said, "It's a riddle," but he might have said "It's Riddle." As I said, I could hardly hear him.'

'It's a riddle? Was he having the last laugh, do you think?'

As if she hadn't heard him, Wanda carried on, 'Suppose Riddle's a name?'

Quentin jerked himself upright. 'A name?'

'Yes. Well, why not? It makes more sense than it's a riddle. Oh, there's Colin.'

She got up to answer the doorbell. Quentin watched her, impatience settling on him. Colin would be more insufferable than ever now he'd pulled off Adamson's capture single-handed.

'Hello, Quentin,' Colin said as soon as he saw him. His grin was so wide it almost pushed his cheeks into his eye sockets.

'Hello, Colin,' he said, determined to be civil no matter how superciliously Colin acted.

'Tea, Colin?' Wanda asked, disappearing into the kitchen when he nodded.

Swallowing his reluctance, Quentin told him what they'd been discussing.

'Right,' Colin said when he'd finished. 'So you think Riddle might be a name and could be connected with the gang?'

'It could be,' Wanda said, coming back with his tea. 'I didn't think it was important considering everything else that was going on, and anyway it didn't make sense. But suppose he was telling me something?'

'Like the person he got the statue from, the bloke waiting for the money?' Quentin asked. 'If they're one and the same, that is. They could be different people.'

Wanda shrugged. 'Maybe. Who knows? Could be his daughter's surname. He was concerned about her.'

'Yeah, I suppose,' Quentin said. 'Philmore will have his daughter's name and address, surely, if they struck a deal.'

'Yes, of course he will. I imagine he'll give her the bad news. I wouldn't have minded doing it – I told him I'd find her. I wish he hadn't died there, right in front of us. I know he was a criminal, but all the same…' Wanda chewed at her lip, as if recalling those last few minutes of Walberg's life. 'Riddle,' she murmured. 'It's not much to go on, is it? If only we knew if it is a name.'

Quentin slapped his hand down on his knee. 'The notebook! Bloody hell, I'd forgotten it. What happened to the notebook?'

'I don't know,' Wanda admitted. 'I was busy with Walberg. I didn't see what happened after Adamson ran out.' She caught Quentin's eye, and they both turned towards Colin.

'Notebook?' Colin looked baffled, lifting his eyebrows enquiringly while reaching into his jacket. 'You mean this one?'

Quentin practically fell on him and snatched the book from his hand. 'You listened to us wittering on and you had this all the time?'

Colin leaned back in his chair. 'That's what I like about you, Quentin. You're so grateful when people help you.'

Quelling his desire to study the notebook immediately, Quentin looked at the older man. He should be grateful. Colin may just have handed him an opportunity to carry on with the case.

'You're a genius, Colin, a real genius,' he told him, and for once he meant what he said.

'You didn't hand it over to the police?' Wanda asked.

'He dropped it when I tackled him,' Colin said. 'I didn't know if it was important, but I thought it wouldn't do any harm to read through it first. I can always say I put it in my pocket and forgot about it.'

'You're really sounding like one of us now,' Wanda told him. 'Well done. Come on, Quentin, don't keep it all to yourself.' She stood beside Quentin and peered over his shoulder.

'It's mainly dates and times,' Quentin said, flicking through the pages. 'Have you looked at this, Colin?'

'Only briefly. There's one thing I noticed, which meant nothing to me then, but it might now, after what Wanda said. Look at the last two entries.'

Starting from the back, Quentin thumbed through the pages until he came to one sporting forward-sloping text written in a shaky hand. *'Riddle,'* he read.

'Riddle!' Wanda said triumphantly. 'It *is* a name connected to the gang.'

Turning to the previous page, Quentin looked at the entry. The writing was the same but more defined.

'*Sat, 9th September, 11.30 a.m., Eltham station*,' he read aloud. 'And there's something else.' Screwing up his eyes, he tried to see through the thick inked line that obscured most of the words. 'It looks like, twelve-thirty, something place.'

'September 9th,' said Colin. 'That was Saturday just gone, wasn't it?'

Wanda's eyes gleamed. 'Yes, the day this all kicked off. Don't you see? Walberg was meant to exchange the statue for the money at Eltham station, then hand the money over to someone at twelve-thirty, either all of it or part of it at least, if some of it was his own payment. Except he couldn't, because at twelve-thirty he was still recovering from whatever caused his collapse, and he still had the statue, not the money.'

Quentin took up the narrative. 'That's why the last bit is crossed out, because he didn't make the rendezvous to pass the money on. He'd have gone back to Catford with the statue. When I heard them talking, he told Adamson he called the person he got his instructions from and told them the exchange would have to be rearranged.'

It made perfect sense to Quentin. Walberg had written down what he was meant to do, then deleted the part that hadn't taken place, possibly the next day. That would also explain the shaky handwriting on the last page – his collapse had weakened him, left him unsteady.

'Called the person he got his instructions from?' Colin queried. 'Does he mean Riddle, do you think, or someone else?'

Quentin shrugged and continued leafing through the notebook. 'Perhaps Riddle supplied the statue, but that doesn't mean he was involved with arranging to steal it. He's probably just a middleman. He's mentioned on other pages as well, but I can't see any other names in full. There're some initials, written at least twice – BLS/G. There're other dates too, a few months apart. They might coincide with other artefacts going missing.'

'I expect Philmore would know,' Wanda suggested.

'I daresay he would,' Quentin agreed, 'but he hasn't got the notebook. We have.'

There was a silence, and Quentin knew they were both thinking the same as him. They had the notebook, but what were they going to do with it?

Chapter Twenty-three

It was several minutes before anyone offered a suggestion.

'We'll have to give it to Philmore,' Wanda said, eyeing the notebook thoughtfully. 'We'll be done for withholding evidence or obstructing the course of justice if we don't. If only we could make use of it first.'

Another silence. Thoughts whirred in Quentin's head, jumbled, crazy thoughts, interrupted only when Wanda stood up and cleared her throat.

'Time for some brainstorming,' she said. 'We'll go through the notebook, make sure we haven't missed anything, write down our findings and analyse them.'

'And then what?' Colin asked doubtfully.

'And then we'll formulate a plan. OK with you, Quentin?'

'Hmm? Oh yes, good idea. We'll photocopy it, then we'll have a copy when we give the book to Philmore.'

'I'll do it now.'

Twenty minutes later, Wanda came down from the spare bedroom where her computer and scanner were, the notebook and some sheets of A4 paper in her hand. She sat down at the table and beckoned Quentin and Colin to join her, a satisfied smile on her face.

'There are just notes of dates, places and times, except for this,' she said, pointing to a single line on one of the sheets of paper. 'I kept it separate so we could find it easily.'

Quentin heard Colin's sharp intake of breath and gave one of his own. 'A telephone number!' he said. 'No name?'

Wanda shook her head. 'It's just there on its own. Could be anyone's.'

'On its own?' Quentin persisted. 'You mean on a page on its own, or does it relate to something else on the same page?'

Wanda picked up the notebook and turned to where a folded piece of paper marked the relevant page. 'Here we are. It's on the opposite side of an entry dated 11 August this year. There's the time and place, and the name Riddle again.'

'So,' said Colin thoughtfully. 'It could be a number connected to the transaction shown on that page.'

'Yes,' said Wanda, 'it could be Riddle's, as he's mentioned on this page, or it could be a number that Walberg used several times and just jotted it down so he wouldn't forget it. But if it was a frequently used number surely he'd write it somewhere more prominent, at the back or the front of the book, rather than searching through to find it.'

'Unless he just wrote it down and then memorised it,' Colin suggested.

Wanda nodded. 'I suppose that could be it. What do you think, Quentin? Quentin?' She tapped Quentin's forehead with her fingertips. 'What's going on in there?'

The action brought Quentin out of the trance he'd fallen into. 'I think… I don't know about the number, but whoever was expecting that statue knows there's something wrong, and whoever was expecting the money does too.'

'Are we assuming that the plan was for Walberg to get the statue from this Riddle and then take the money to him?' Colin asked. 'It seems daft to me – why would Riddle give the goods to Walberg then wait about for him to bring the money? He might as well just make the exchange himself.'

Quentin had been wondering about that. 'Not necessarily. Perhaps he thought making the exchange was too risky.'

'It's no more risky than handing over the statue or accepting the money,' Colin countered.

Quentin was stumped. 'Well, we can only guess at their reasoning, but we can make a fair assumption about one thing. Neither the supplier nor the receiver of the goods knows where they are unless Motorbike– I mean Adamson, has told them, and from what I overheard I'm sure he hasn't, so as yet they won't have any idea what's happened to it. I mean the gang'll find out soon enough about Walberg's death, but they can't know about Adamson being arrested yet.'

Wanda gave him a cool look. 'And your point is?'

'I reckon, that is, what I would do if I were Philmore, is bargain with Adamson – get him to take the statue so it leads them to the ringleaders.'

'In return for a lighter sentence, you mean? Good thinking, but what if Adamson doesn't want to play ball?'

'Shouldn't think he'd have much choice, unless he likes the idea of a long spell in prison. It's what Philmore should do if he's got any sense–'

'Hold on a minute,' Colin interrupted. 'What are you saying, Quentin? You're going to suggest a way to do a deal and catch the ringleaders to Philmore? You can't do that. It's not up to us to tell the police how to do their job.'

'But they can't just leave things as they are,' Quentin said, frustration mounting. 'They've gone to all the trouble of microchipping the statue, so they should use it to their advantage.'

'They probably will when they've got the info out of Adamson,' Colin answered.

Quentin clicked his tongue. 'Who knows when that will be? We should do something now.'

Wanda nodded. 'Yes, so why don't we?' she said. 'We've got a telephone number – it might be this Riddle, but even if it's not we could ring the number, say we found their number with the statue and would be willing to meet them and hand it over, you know, for a small reward. There must be loads of people who find things and aren't too fussy who they give them to as long as there's something in it for them.'

Excitement rose in Quentin. 'That's a brilliant idea, Wanda!'

Colin gave a meaningful cough. 'Only one problem – well, two really.'

Wanda caught his meaning. 'Yes. We don't have the statue and we don't have a clue whose number it is. We're only guessing it's Riddle's.'

'They don't know that, do they?' Quentin pointed out.

'Now just a minute.' Colin's voice took on an incredulous tone. 'You're not actually going to ring that number, pretend you've got something you haven't and arrange to meet them?'

'That's the general idea,' Quentin snapped.

Colin shook his head. 'Ridiculous! How are you going to explain yourself if the number's nothing to do with the stolen goods? It could be a friend's number – anyone's.'

'I'm sure we could get round it somehow, say it's a wrong number or something,' Wanda assured him. 'I'm thinking we should let Philmore in on it though.'

'Now you're talking sense,' Colin said. 'It would be stupid to risk handing over imaginary goods to a dangerous criminal.'

'If we tell Philmore, they wouldn't have to be imaginary,' Wanda said. 'He could arrange for us to have the statue and the police could be in at the kill.'

'It could well be the kill if they rumble us,' Colin complained. 'Philmore will never agree.'

'He might,' Quentin said, his enthusiasm growing. 'If we had the statue, it would make it easier for him to follow us to the handover point. They'd just track the microchip.'

'I can't see a Detective Chief Inspector trusting a member of the public to lead them to a gang they've been after for ages,' Colin insisted, taking off his glasses and cleaning them with the bottom of his shirt. 'They'd be more likely to get one of their own to do it.'

'Maybe, but I've done it before.'

Colin tossed his head impatiently, then replaced his glasses. 'But he's got Adamson. He might have talked, told them everything he knows, in which case he can lead them to the gang, can't he?'

Wanda sat back in her chair and crossed her legs. Quentin could see she was mulling things over.

'They've only just got hold of Adamson,' she said eventually. 'It could take hours, days, for him to tell them what they want to know. That's if he tells them anything.

And today's Tuesday. The money's been missing since Saturday.'

'Yeah,' Quentin agreed, 'but Walberg told Adamson he'd phoned the person he got his instructions from to let them know the situation. The exchange was rearranged for Monday at Walberg's house, so as far as the bosses are concerned they've only be waiting for the goods since then – yesterday.'

'Even so,' Wanda insisted, 'if Philmore did get Adamson to contact his boss how would he convince him that he's only now able to hand the goods over?'

Quentin had been wondering about that too. 'It depends what he's told them already. Like I said before, he must have reported Walberg's collapse at the station, and another time was arranged for the exchange, so he couldn't have told them he'd lost the money. He spent Sunday following us to try and get it back and when he didn't he made up bundles of paper to look like banknotes so he could fool Walberg. Then he lost the statue as well – he'd have wanted to try and get that back before the gang found out. Anyway, that's why Wanda's idea's better. I'll ring that number and say I've found the statue. The higher ups will think Adamson's been stalling for time because he's lost the goods, which is true. I think I'll go and see Philmore.'

'And he'll say no,' Colin said, his mouth set in a stubborn line.

'Not if we ring that number first. Chances are it's Riddle's, as his is the only name in the book. If we can find out, ascertain that it belongs to one of the gang, perhaps even make some sort of arrangement with them, and *then* go to Philmore–'

Colin looked about to make a sharp retort, but seemed to change his mind. Instead he got to his feet and said, 'Make an idiot of yourself if you like, Quentin. I've done my bit capturing Adamson and getting the notebook. As far as I'm concerned, we can't do any more.'

'If you think that, why did you keep the notebook?' Quentin asked irritably. 'Why didn't you give it to Philmore at the time?'

'Yes, Colin, why didn't you?

Colin reddened under Wanda's gaze. 'Impulse. Oh all right, if you must know he annoyed me when he arrived at Walberg's house. Went on about amateurs trying to do the job of professionals instead of thanking me for nailing a wanted man. That's how I know he won't agree to your scheme. Even so, I know he's right. Just hand the book over and let them get on with it. Anyway, I'm meeting Emma at five. We're going to see *Les Misérables*. We've waited ages to see it so I can't let her down.' He rose and kissed Wanda on the cheek. 'Bye love. I'll call you in the morning.'

'So much for wanting to help us,' Quentin muttered to himself. Colin heard and rounded on him. 'I have helped, and surprising as it may seem to you, Quentin, there is life outside Greenwich. Unlike you I've got other commitments.'

Seeing Wanda's warning look, Quentin bit back a sarcastic reply. 'Yes, of course you have. Give Emma my love and enjoy the show.' He waited while Colin collected his things, then watched as he strode to the door and let himself out.

'I'm glad you said that,' Wanda said when he'd gone. 'We asked him to help, not become a full partner in the business. He's already been arrested, sat in a parked car half the night and got himself handcuffed into the bargain. I expect he's had enough.'

Quentin grinned at the images her words conjured up. 'I know. I don't mean to keep having a go at him. He's been useful, but he's just so– so correct all the time.'

'Not all the time, or he would have given that notebook to Philmore,' Wanda pointed out.

'That's true. OK, credit where it's due, he did well. Anyway, I think we should go with your idea about ringing the number in the notebook.'

Wanda looked doubtful. 'It's a good idea in theory, but now I've thought about it I'm not sure we should go it alone. The police have ways of tracing numbers. It's a mobile, and if we liaise with Philmore he should be able to track it when they answer the call.'

That was true, but Quentin was desperate for them to solve the case themselves and was sure they could do it.

'What have we got to lose if we ring the number ourselves? Let's assume the number is Riddle's. Even if it isn't, I think it must be someone to do with the gang. It should provoke some sort of reaction.'

'Yes,' said Wanda, her original enthusiasm returning. 'We should be able to judge from their tone and what they say whether we should go on to mention the statue.'

Quentin frowned in concentration. 'We won't mention it unless they are concerned about there being a notebook with their number in it. Then we'll say we found the holdall as well.'

'And then what?'

'Play it by ear, I suppose. Maybe do what you said, act as if we want a reward. Depends what reaction we get. If it *is* Riddle, he–'

Wanda interrupted. 'Or she,' she said.

'Point taken. OK, *they* must live in London, or not far away, to be able to deliver the statue to Walberg at Eltham station by eleven-thirty in the morning, like it says in the notebook.'

Wanda chewed at her lip. 'Mmm. Don't call from the landline, they might find our address from that. But then they'll see the mobile number if you use that.'

'I can change the settings so our number is withheld,' Quentin told her, reaching for his phone. He played with the setting facility for a few minutes, then rang Wanda's mobile to check he'd done it correctly.

'Number withheld,' Wanda read. 'OK, all systems go.'

'Do you want to ring, Wanda? It was your idea.'

'No, it's all right, you do it. What if you get voicemail?'

'Then we'll call back. It's no good leaving a message. Right. Here we go then.'

Taking the copies that Wanda had made, Quentin found the number and keyed it in. He held his breath when the ringing stopped, praying he wouldn't get voicemail.

'Hello?'

Quentin was surprised. Despite Wanda's comment earlier, he hadn't expected a female voice.

'Hello,' said the voice again.

'Er, is that Mrs Riddle?' Quentin saw Wanda's look of surprise at his words too.

The woman at the other end sounded wary. 'Who is this? How did you get this number?'

Quentin felt uncomfortable. Perhaps this woman was nothing more than Walberg's girlfriend. He hesitated. Go for it, he thought.

'Actually,' he said, 'I found a holdall with a couple of things in. There was a notebook with the name Riddle and this number in it.'

The ensuing silence was palpable. Quentin could almost hear the woman's brain ticking, wondering what to make of what he'd said. When she spoke, her tone was cautious. 'A notebook?'

'Yes.'

'Where did you find it?'

By now Quentin was certain that she had something to do with the gang. He decided to dangle the carrot before she took fright and cut him off.

'I found it in a street in Catford.' He waited to see if she would ask him where Catford was. When she didn't, he guessed she was either in London or knew the city well enough to know its boroughs.

'What else was in the holdall?'

She was fishing, Quentin knew. Oh well, he thought, in for a penny in for a pound.

'Only an ornament. Look, if it's not yours I'll hand it in to the police as lost property.'

'No!' the woman cried out.

Quentin raised his eyebrows at the note of panic he detected.

'No, it's all right, it *is* mine and I'll be glad to get it back.'

I bet you will, Quentin thought wryly. 'All right then, Mrs Riddle,' he said, remembering she hadn't actually said her name was Riddle. When she didn't contradict him, he continued, 'Where do you live?'

'As it happens I'm just going out. Could I meet you somewhere?'

'Yes, if you're in London.'

'Where would be convenient for you?'

It was obvious to Quentin that she didn't want to disclose her location, and seemed willing to travel to anywhere he suggested.

'Well, I'm busy this afternoon,' he said, suddenly realizing that if he wanted back up he'd have to give Philmore time to get organised. 'It'll have to be tomorrow.'

'Can you make it tonight? Any time will do.'

Quentin glanced at his watch. Nearly three-thirty. Could Philmore have back up arranged by tonight? It would be tight, but if there was a problem he could always ring back and rearrange it for tomorrow – she was hardly in a position to argue.

'I can't make it before seven-thirty,' he said.

'Seven-thirty's fine. Where?'

Quentin thought quickly 'Do you know the café opposite the children's play area in Wanstead Park?' he said, unwilling to give his location away either and remembering the park not far from where Colin lived. As far as he knew Adamson was the only one who knew he lived in Greenwich.

There was a pause, as though the woman was trying to work something out. 'OK,' she agreed. 'I'll meet you outside the café at seven-thirty. What's your name?'

Quentin's mind went blank. 'Freeman,' he blurted, saying the only name he could think of that shouldn't immediately be associated with him or Wanda. 'John Freeman. How will I know you?'

'I'll know you, won't I, because you'll have the holdall. OK, Mr Freeman, I'll see you outside the café at seven-thirty. I'll be so pleased to get my things back.'

The line went dead.

'Well?' demanded Wanda.

'Seven-thirty outside the café in Wanstead Park.'

'Outside? What's wrong with inside?'

Quentin shrugged. 'Probably wants to take the bag and disappear. And it might not be open at that time of night.'

'You don't think she suspects anything? I mean did she believe what you said about finding the holdall?'

'She seemed to. If Adamson's been stalling them then she probably worked out that he'd lost it somehow. Or maybe she's more concerned with her name being in a notebook. Either way she freaked out when I said I'd take the stuff to the police, so she can't know Adamson's in custody or that the police have got the statue. And she was pretty keen to get hold of it.'

Wanda's brow wrinkled. 'So we were right. Do you think she'll turn up on her own?'

'Shouldn't think so. If I thought she would…' Quentin tailed off, trying to think of any way he could meet with the woman alone.

It would be great if he could go to Philmore with some vital information, something that would lead to the arrest of all the gang members. But how could he? Visions of keeping Riddle talking, trying to elicit information, even surreptitiously photographing her from a hidden camera, flashed into his head. Then what? So they'd know what she looked like, but she'd know what he looked like too.

'Don't even think about it, Quentin,' Wanda warned. 'Call Philmore, tell him what you've arranged and what we thought about using the statue for them to follow.'

She was right, he knew. It would be stupid to get there without the statue. Sighing he reached for his mobile.

Chapter Twenty-four

After he'd endured the expected earbashing from Philmore, Quentin looked at Wanda and grinned.

'You sounded like you were in the secret service, the way you practically spoke in code,' she said. 'What did he say?'

'He's fuming,' he told her. 'He's sending a car for me.'

'Is he now? And a pretty sight he'll have to behold. You've got a bruise on your cheek.'

'So would you have, if you'd been hit round the face and bashed your head on the floor.'

'You haven't had anything to eat either. At least let me make you a sandwich.'

Quentin glanced at his watch. 'Might not be time. Got any crisps?'

'I'll have a look. I don't suppose he wants to see me as well?'

'No, 'fraid not.'

Feigning offence, Wanda flounced into the kitchen. 'It's all right for some, isn't it, Mozart?' Quentin heard her say. 'Never mind, I'll take you for a nice walk, and then we'll have dinner together, just you and me.'

By the time she returned with two packets of crisps and an apple her sarcasm had been replaced with concern.

'Watch what you say to Philmore,' she advised, 'and be careful what you agree to. I don't want to be running this detective agency on my own.'

Quentin grinned. 'Don't worry, it'll take more than a gang of criminals to keep me away from you.'

* * *

'So we're all set then?' Quentin said to Philmore in his office two hours later. 'I meet this woman, hand over the statue and you let her go off with it so you can follow the microchip. Or you could nab her. You'd have two members of the gang then, and this woman might tell you everything you want to know.'

Philmore looked at Quentin steadily, brown eyes unblinking. 'She might or she might not. She might not know much.'

He had listened to Quentin's account of how he'd come by the notebook (Quentin said he'd found it and kept it, not Colin), how he'd rung the number shown in it and spoken to a woman called Riddle. The DCI had looked as though he would explode. After gazing at Quentin as if he didn't know what to do to stop his interference, he'd agreed to Quentin meeting her.

'So you're in for the long haul,' Quentin said. 'You don't want to rely on Adamson or this woman telling you who the ringleaders are. But now you've got Adamson, how do you know the transaction will take place?'

The door opened and DS Francis entered the office. Philmore gestured her to sit down, then replied, 'Adamson's arrest has been kept quiet. We only pulled him in this morning, so with any luck this Riddle and the people Adamson reports to will think he's either trying to recover the goods or is lying low somewhere. They may even think he's absconded with the money. Like you, I don't believe he's told them he's lost the money, or they'd have been after him. That's why we need to move quickly, before they find out we've arrested him.'

‘I see.’ Quentin sat back in his seat and frowned. ‘So you want me to keep up the pretence of knowing nothing about all this? I’m just someone who came across an abandoned holdall containing an ornament and a notebook – a good citizen with a social conscience.’

‘That’s about it, yes.’

‘Right. But you’ll be there, behind the scenes, in case…’ In case of what, he asked himself. He was just an ordinary member of the public returning someone’s property. Riddle had accepted that on the phone, so why should she think differently when they met? The only person who could identify him was in police custody.

‘We’ll be there,’ Philmore assured him. ‘What you have to do is act normally, show a little curiosity but not too much, keep it short, give her the holdall and leave.’

‘What if she’s not on her own?’

Philmore shrugged. ‘Hopefully it won’t make any difference. If anyone else is there they’ve got no reason to doubt you’re anything but what you say you are. You’re sure you didn’t give anything away when you spoke to her?’

When Quentin shook his head, Philmore carried on, ‘Should be nothing to worry about, then.’

The earlier scenes Quentin had imagined of gaining glory and bringing the criminals to justice single-handed were replaced by pictures of burly men materialising from nowhere and setting about him. Suppose they decided to eliminate him for no other reason than he had seen the statue and the notebook?

As though reading his thoughts, Philmore said, ‘Don’t worry, Quentin. I wouldn’t let you do it if I thought anything untoward would happen, but if it does, we’ll deal with it.’

‘Fine. Well then, better get going.’ He reached for the holdall and stood up. ‘Where was this statue stolen from anyway?’

'All in good time, Quentin. Now don't forget, don't try to pump her for information. Just deliver the statue and walk away.'

'She'll know I read the notebook, though. That's how I got her number.'

'Nothing in the book makes sense, Quentin. It just looks like a list of appointments.'

Reassured at his words, Quentin said, 'It does. So I'll just continue to play dumb.'

A snigger escaped DS Francis. Quentin stared at her, and after a warning look from Philmore she composed herself. 'Sorry,' she murmured.

Quentin smiled in spite of himself. After the fiasco that had played out the last time he'd been here and the one in the alley behind Mrs Freeman's house, he could hardly blame her for thinking he was dumb. Somehow, that made him more determined to prove her wrong.

'OK,' he said jauntily. 'What are we waiting for?'

* * *

His bravado was short-lived. When he was a few yards from the rendezvous, the police back-up officers were concealed at a safe distance and he was alone. Despite the semi-darkness, he felt exposed and vulnerable as he approached the café, the holdall swinging from his left hand. He had a vague notion that he should keep his right hand free in case he needed to punch his way out of a surprise attack.

A woman in flat shoes and a denim jacket came out of the dusk, walking slowly from the opposite direction. As she drew nearer and spotted him, her pace quickened. She stopped in front of the café and waited for him.

'Mr Freeman?' she called when he neared her. Resisting the urge to look beyond her to check no one was preparing to pounce on him, he nodded. The café was closed, but in the light from its veranda he judged her to be between thirty and forty, short reddish hair, though it could have been dyed, with thick dark eyebrows and thin lips.

'Mrs Riddle?' he asked.

'Yes. It's so good of you to go out of your way to return my things. I'm sorry if I was rude on the phone. I've been getting a lot of nuisance calls lately.'

'That's all right. I get a lot of those myself.'

'Well I'm very grateful. I hope you didn't have to come too far.'

'Not that far,' Quentin answered, anxious not to give her any information that could lead her back to him. 'Did you?'

'No. Well, thanks again.' She held out her hand for the holdall.

'That's all right. I know what it's like when you lose something. Lucky your number was in that notebook.' Slowly, Quentin raised the bag and, almost reluctantly, handed it to her. He wished there was something he could say to get more information from her.

Should he show more curiosity? He'd referred to the statue as an ornament. Should he mention it?

Before he had time to make a decision, she stepped away from him. 'I must go now,' she said starting back the way she had come. 'Thanks again for all your trouble. Bye.'

Quentin stared after her, watching until the encroaching dusk had swallowed her up. As he turned and made his way to the park entrance, lamp posts snapped into life, their yellow light casting shadows all around. A figure emerged from one, and Quentin tensed before recognising Philmore.

'That was quick,' Philmore said. 'What did she say?'

Quentin repeated the gist of the conversation. 'I don't think she suspected anything,' he finished. 'She seemed pretty anxious to get away.'

Philmore nodded. 'Good. Now it's just a case of waiting.'

'Do you think she'll deliver it tonight?' Quentin asked.

'Depends where she has to take it. Probably not, if it's out of town.'

'Yes,' said Quentin, a variety of possibilities opening up in his mind. 'Yes, when Motorbike Man–'

'Motorbike Man?'

'Adamson, when Adamson came to make the exchange he came by train, so if we find out where that train started–' he stopped when he saw Philmore's expression. 'OK, he could have got on anywhere along the line, but still…'

'How do you know he came by train? Did you actually see him come through from the platform?'

A flush rose to Quentin's face. 'No, the first I saw of him was when he grabbed my bag, but because he ran onto the platform and got on a train, I thought… You think he just jumped on the train as the quickest means of escape? That he might have got there another way?'

'You're the one who called him Motorbike Man,' Philmore said quietly.

Quentin cast his mind back to the events at the station. 'I assumed he had a ticket to get on that train, but given the crowds, he could have got on without a ticket. People do. And he wasn't in motorbike gear, but I guess he could have left that off so he would look the same as everyone else.'

'Anyway,' Philmore continued, 'we're checking the train route. You know, Quentin, if you could learn to play by the rules, you wouldn't make a bad copper.'

Quentin couldn't think of anything worse than having to write reports or justify his every move, but he appreciated the comment. 'Thanks,' he said, his ego swelling.

'That doesn't mean I won't have you arrested for obstructing a police enquiry if you keep doing things off your own bat when you've been told not to,' Philmore added.

'Thanks again,' Quentin quipped. 'What now? You'll be tracking the statue so you or one of your team will be up all night just in case it stays on the move?'

'Something like that. If she takes the statue home for the night we won't be doing anything until the morning, but we'll be ready whatever time it is.'

'Right.'

DS Francis appeared and looked at Philmore questioningly.

'Tell the others to get back to their cars, Debbie, and keep in radio contact. You can go now, Quentin.'

Feeling he was being dismissed, Quentin said, 'Just a minute, isn't there anything else I can do?'

'You've been very helpful, Quentin, but we can take it from here.'

'I'm sure you can, but–' he stopped, then blurted, 'couldn't I come with you?'

'Absolutely not. My team will follow the signal, but if Riddle takes the statue home, they could be sat in the car all night waiting for the signal to start up again. Don't worry, Quentin, I'll keep you informed. Please don't do anything – anything – without checking with me first. OK? You must have other cases to be getting on with.'

'Nothing important,' Quentin mumbled, dismissing the mundane cases they'd handled this year. 'I'd much rather be seeing this through.'

Philmore edged away. 'As I said, I'll keep you informed. Go home and leave it to us.'

Leave it to us. The phrase echoed in Quentin's head. Despite their recent bad press he had a great deal of respect for the British police force, and an even greater respect for Philmore. But he couldn't help thinking that if they listened to members of the public more, especially reliable ones like himself, they might achieve more success.

Chapter Twenty-five

'Well?' Wanda demanded when he got back.

Quentin slumped onto her chaise longue. 'Well nothing.'

'But you rang me and said Philmore had agreed for you to meet Riddle.'

'Yes, and I did. I handed the statue and notebook over and off she went. Philmore and co will be monitoring the signal and following it. He said we had to leave it to them now.'

Wanda hovered in front of him for a moment, then went to kitchen and returned with a tumbler quarter-full with whisky. 'Here,' she said, handing it to him. 'And I've saved you some dinner. I'll heat it up.'

'Thanks. I thought something smelt nice.'

Quentin knocked back the whisky and waited until Wanda brought his dinner on a tray. Although he shared Magpie's fondness for tinned sardines, he never cooked fish himself. When Wanda presented him with trout in white wine sauce, it looked and tasted like a cordon bleu recipe.

'That was delicious,' he told her when he'd eaten and they sat side by side drinking coffee. 'You know, I really thought Philmore would let me go with them. They wouldn't even have the statue or know anything about Riddle if it weren't for us.'

'I expect he's got his reasons,' Wanda countered. 'It's been a long day. It seems ages since we left here this morning. You need to rest.'

'Rest?' Quentin snorted. 'Rest while they're using our information to track down the criminals? Anyway I won't sleep yet. It's not even ten o'clock.'

Putting her hand on his knee, Wanda looked at him from under her lashes. 'Who said anything about sleep? I'm sure we can find something else to relax us.'

'Now that's the best offer I've had all day,' Quentin said, suddenly feeling better, 'but I ought to go and check on Magpie first.'

'Magpie's fine,' Wanda murmured, walking her fingers up his thigh. 'I didn't know how long you'd be so I went in and fed him earlier.'

Quentin settled against the back of the chaise longue and closed his eyes. 'Did I ever tell you that you're the most wonderful woman in the world?'

His pulse quickened when he felt her breath on his face and the swell of her breasts against him.

'No,' she whispered, 'and don't tell me now. Show me.'

* * *

A male figure dressed in black chased Quentin through an alleyway. Quentin ran and ran without gaining ground, like an athlete on a running machine. Ahead of him was another figure, a black spectre with outstretched arms pointing towards him. He could hear himself panting, feel himself sweating as he ran on, desperately seeking escape.

A strong smell of fish assailed him, and as both figures closed in on him he yelled, 'No!'

'Hey!' Wanda's voice broke his dream and he sat bolt upright. His pursuers had disappeared but the fishy smell hadn't. He stared at Wanda, who stood by the bed in a blue satin dressing gown with several sheets of paper in her hand.

'What is it?' she asked. 'Were you dreaming?'

Plopping back on the pillows, Quentin said, 'Yeah. What's that smell?'

'Fish, of course, or did you forget you had trout for dinner? I've just put the leftovers in a bag for Magpie.'

'What time is it?'

'A quarter to twelve.'

'Right. What's that you've got there?'

Wanda sat on the edge of the bed. 'It's the copy I made of the notebook. I was just checking to see if we'd missed anything.'

'And?'

Frowning, Wanda glanced through the notes. 'There's nothing really. Apart from Riddle and Eltham station, there are no other names or places – only those initials we couldn't make sense of.'

Quentin sat up and ran his fingers through his tousled hair. 'Initials?' he repeated, trying to fight his way through the fog in his head. 'What were they again?'

'BLS/G.'

Grunting, Quentin made his way down to the bathroom and splashed his face with cold water. 'BLS/G,' he said to his reflection in the mirror above the sink. 'Could be anyone. Or anywhere.'

As he emerged from the bathroom Mozart trotted up to him and barked. 'Sorry, Mozart, did I wake you up?' He watched while the Highland terrier retreated to the kitchen and barked again. 'Shush,' he warned, but followed the dog to where he sat looking up at the worktop expectantly. Quentin saw the leftovers of tonight's dinner in a polythene food bag on the counter. 'Ah, it's the trout you're after. I'm sure your mistress has fed you already, and anyway that's for Magpie. Sorry, Mote, the answer's no.'

Mozart whined and didn't move. He looked at Quentin so pathetically that Quentin laughed. 'All right,' he said, untying the bag. 'You can have half.' He cut off a piece of the fish and placed it in Mozart's food dish.

'You're as bad as Magpie,' he muttered as he rinsed his fingers. 'Dogs, cats, fish, initials–' He broke off, a thought coming to him. Fish and initials. Initials and fish. Could it be?

'Wanda!' he called as he rushed back upstairs. 'Did you say BLS/G?'

Wanda looked up from where she still sat on the bed. 'What? Oh, BLS/G. Yes. Why?'

'Well it's just a thought, but…'

'Come on, out with it.'

'Do you remember when we had the bag with the money in? The one we brought from the station?'

'I'm hardly likely to forget that, am I?'

'Do you remember what we said about it? About the smell?'

Wanda eyed him sceptically. 'I'm pretty good at sniffing out money, Quentin, but I don't recall that hundred and fifty grand having a particular odour.'

Quentin clicked his tongue. 'Not the money, the bag. It smelled of fish.'

'Did it? Yes, it did, faintly. So?'

'BLS/G,' Quentin said deliberately. 'Billingsgate.'

'Billingsgate?'

Quentin's excitement at discovering a possible link between the money bag and a location gave way to impatience. 'Come on, Wanda. Billingsgate fish market.'

'You mean the money came from Billingsgate or stolen goods have been delivered there at some point?'

'Not necessarily, but something like that. So let's think. The money was brought by Adamson to Eltham, we assumed by train. But he may have come by bike and just ran into the crowd towards the platform. When he spotted me after him he could have kept going, hid in the toilets and got on the first train that came in. He might have got off at the next station and gone back for his bike for all we know.'

Wanda nodded. 'He could have. That doesn't mean he got the money from someone at Billingsgate, only that the bag had been near fish at some point. I think I said that before.'

'You did, but the more I think about it the more I'm convinced there's a connection between the smell and the gang, and with those initials…'

'BLS/G. That's more likely to be someone's initials, isn't it, like, I don't know, Bill Leonard Simon Gates, for example.'

'Or Big Lazy Stupid Giant, or any old thing,' Quentin countered. 'And if it's a person's initials why the slash?'

Wanda's mouth tightened. 'Sarcasm doesn't suit you. All right. The fact that the initials are in the notebook must mean something so it could be Billingsgate. If it were me, I'd write B/gate. After all, Walberg wrote Riddle and Eltham in full, so why not Billingsgate?'

Quentin shrugged. 'Who knows? There were loads of dates and times on the early pages, but nothing else. If he intended to hand the notebook over to the police, wouldn't he have recorded more details?'

Wanda looked perplexed. 'He should have, but perhaps he was afraid to in case any of the gang found out about the book. If they suspected him of being an informant they'd have killed him, wouldn't they?'

'Probably. So… The times and dates – they might be when he was sent to collect or deliver goods or money, like we thought in the first place. He could have told his police contact when and where any exchange was to take place. He needn't have given any names – he might have drawn the line there.'

'But if the police knew the times and places of these transactions why didn't they act sooner? They could have pounced at the time of the exchange.'

'Yes,' Quentin agreed, his mind slowly clearing. 'Yes, but they didn't want to catch tiddlers, they wanted to catch the big fish red-handed. Philmore knew about Adamson, I'm sure, but when I questioned him after Colin was arrested he wouldn't say anything. After Walberg turned informer, they decided to wait until they could set a trap somehow.'

Wanda picked up on his trail of thought. 'And that's exactly what they've done with the statue. Somehow they found out they were going to steal the statue and bugged it so they could track it. How did they know the statue was going to be stolen, I wonder?'

'I haven't a clue,' Quentin answered. 'It doesn't matter. What matters is the statue's back with the gang and likely to lead the police to the top brass while we're here talking about it. Well, we can't follow the tracking device, but we can follow our lead.'

'What lead? You don't mean Billingsgate?'

Quentin reached for his clothes. 'That's exactly what I mean, and that's where we're going if I find out the Riddle woman's still got the statue.'

'Why?'

'Because if she's still got it there's a good chance she'll be handing it over in the morning. And if I remember rightly, Billingsgate Market opens to the public at five am.'

'She may have handed it over already. The criminals could all be in police hands for all we know.'

'They might, but Philmore said he'd contact me if they had any luck.'

Wanda unfastened her dressing gown and let it slip to the floor. 'That doesn't mean he will, especially at this time of night. How do you intend to find out?'

Sighing, Quentin forced his gaze away from her nakedness. 'Simple. I'm going to ring him.'

'You can't ring him now. He could be in bed asleep.'

'Not if I know Philmore.' Quentin located the DCI's mobile number and pressed the call button. The ring tone went on for some time before a groggy voice answered.

'Hello.'

Quentin knew immediately that the statue hadn't moved further than wherever the woman he'd given it to had taken it. If it was being tracked, or had been tracked to someone higher up the chain, Philmore would want to be there.

'Is that you, Quentin?' Philmore said, as if he'd just read the number on his display. 'What are you playing at?'

'Sorry, I just wondered… you said you'd let me know if anything happened.'

'I did and I will, when it does.'

'So she– Riddle's still got the statue, then?'

'Yes. Now for goodness' sake get some sleep and let me get mine.'

The line went dead, and Quentin looked at Wanda triumphantly. 'No action tonight, so it'll be the morning. She'll want to get that statue to where it's supposed to be. My guess is they'll be pretty anxious to lay their hands on it as soon as they can. They're already behind schedule.'

'Hmm.' Wanda sucked in her cheeks. 'So we're going to Billingsgate on the off chance that the handover will take place there?' When Quentin nodded she continued, 'Billingsgate is just across the river. Why do we need to go now?'

'We don't, but I'm going home for a shower and some clean clothes.'

Wanda lay on the bed. 'You don't have to go yet,' she pouted. 'I'll set the alarm, and you can have a shower here.'

Quentin felt the familiar magnetic force drawing him towards her. Oh, what the hell, he thought, and pulled his T-shirt off again.

Chapter Twenty-six

The alarm shrilled at three-thirty. Quentin kissed Wanda's bare shoulder, donned his T-shirt and jeans and went next door to his own house. He looked for Magpie and found him curled up on his bed. The cat sat up, mewed, then curled up again.

'Is that all the greeting I get?' Quentin said, his voice still thick from sleep. 'What about – how are you Quentin, I've been worried about you. No chance, eh?'

Magpie lifted his head and eyed him disdainfully.

'Don't look at me like that. It's all right for you, lazing around all day. Some of us have to work for a living.'

After showering, he dressed, fed Magpie, made tea and toast, then googled Billingsgate.

The place covered thirteen acres and had over ninety stands, some thirty shops as well as cafés, fridges, cold rooms and an enormous freezer store. Thirteen acres! His hopes of finding any of the gang there faded, especially when he read that the market had its own police. He guessed they were like the railway police, empowered to handle situations on site. Surely they'd be on the lookout for thieves and troublemakers, not members of organised gangs that had nothing to do with fish. Logging out of his computer, he collected his wallet, keys and Swiss Army knife and went out. As he reached his gate, Wanda's door opened.

'I hope you weren't thinking of going without me,' she said, pulling her door shut and joining him on the pavement. She smelled fresh and despite the darkness Quentin could see her hair lay close to her scalp where she'd washed it. She wore trousers, a short coat and a scarf, nothing that would make them noticeable.

'I thought you might have gone back to sleep,' he told her. 'I should have known better. I'll go and get the car if you like, and come back for you.'

'Or we could take my car,' Wanda suggested. 'It'll save time and it's easier to park.'

Quentin pulled a face. Wanda's Toyota was nippy, but he'd had enough of his long legs being cramped into a space that felt small after the BMW. 'All right,' he said reluctantly, 'that makes sense.'

They walked to the parking bay along the road, Wanda breaking into a run to keep up with Quentin. 'Slow down,' she puffed. 'You're not on one of your runs. Aren't you supposed to be a retailer or something to get into this place?'

'No, it's open to the public as well, though I don't suppose they get many takers. The gates shut at nine-thirty. We'll mingle with the crowds, keep our eyes peeled for the Riddle woman.'

They reached the car and ten minutes later they were heading towards the Blackwall tunnel. The early hour meant that traffic was light, and it wasn't long before they were behind a line of traffic queuing to gain entrance to Billingsgate's parking area. When they'd parked, they threaded their way through the lines of vehicles and joined the growing bustle of people entering the market. The low-level building with its canopied entrances, looked incongruous against a backdrop of the towering edifices of Canary Wharf.

Quentin was immediately struck by the number of people already crowding the market hall. The smell and the noise filled his senses, and the sight of such a variety of fish, many of which he'd never seen before, conjured up pictures of the exotic dishes produced by Michelin-star chefs he'd seen on TV cookery programmes. As well as the fish laid out on the counters, live crabs and lobsters waved their claws in containers, and eels wriggled about in tanks of water. Traders stood behind their stalls and porters with barrows stood by to transport fresh supplies from cold stores or fridges to the counters.

'I didn't know it was so big,' Wanda said as they walked up and down the rows of stalls. She wrinkled her nose at the sight of some sort of shellfish that writhed from side to side as though they were performing a mating dance. 'Well, you can't get much fresher than this, can you? It's so cold in here. I suppose it has to be. I wish I'd put an extra layer on.'

‘So do I,’ Quentin said, pulling up the collar on his anorak.

‘I thought I got a whiff of bacon along there, at the end of the row,’ Wanda said.

‘There are some cafés, just outside the hall,’ Quentin told her. ‘I looked it up. I suppose people get what they want, then go for breakfast. Are you on the lookout?’

‘I would be if I knew what to look out for. You’ve seen this woman, I haven’t.’

‘I only saw her briefly, and it was more or less dark. She’s average height, short hair, red I think, dark eyebrows. That’s all I can remember. There aren’t many women here, so that should make it easier. Just look for someone with a holdall that looks like ours, or anyone you think looks suspicious.’

Wanda raised her eyes heavenwards but said nothing. Quentin guessed she thought they were chasing wild geese. She’s probably right, he mused as they trudged on. This place is huge. Even if Riddle is here, we’d never see her in these crowds. Half the fishmongers and restaurant owners in the country must be here. For all we know we could walk right past another member of the gang and not realize.

‘Perhaps we should split up,’ he said, feeling agitated. He must have been mad to suggest getting up before dawn and dragging Wanda around one the busiest markets in England. ‘You go over the other side, call me if you find anything.’

Nodding, Wanda disappeared among the throng of traders and buyers. Fighting the urge to call her back and go home, Quentin stood still and looked about him. He needed to be higher. Glancing up, he saw the upper floor, like a balcony with a glass frontage. Remembering they’d passed a flight of stairs, he went back to where he’d seen them. Minutes later he stood looking down into the market hall, its green floor hardly visible beneath the mass of people. A huge clock, which reminded Quentin of the face of Big Ben, was suspended from the ceiling, hanging like a guardian over its precious charge.

He gazed into the mass of people but saw nothing of note, certainly no sign of the woman he'd met last night. He thought he spotted Wanda's blonde head, but from where he stood he couldn't be sure. A man in a tabard with a radio attached stood against a wall. The market police, Quentin assumed. What a job, standing around in this cold for hours. He watched for a few more moments, then made his way back the way he had come.

Joining the crowds again, he moved slowly along stalls, listening to the glib talk of the traders and watching as they deftly handled their wares. Someone elbowed their way past him and seconds later a voice said, 'You in the queue, mate?'

'What?' He turned to see a man with a florid complexion eyeing him impatiently.

'Oh no, sorry.' He moved aside to let the man nearer to the stall he was standing by. Despite his mounting frustration, this place fascinated him. He'd never seen so much fish, and it was disappearing fast. He understood now why trading stopped at eight – if stocks kept going at this rate there wouldn't be a lot left after seven.

He carried on until he was at the end of a row of stalls. The crowd in this part had thinned, and he took a long breath and tried to collect his thoughts. He was just wondering whether to call it a day and go for some breakfast when he saw a porter come from an opening behind the stalls, pushing a barrow loaded with polystyrene boxes. Moments later another porter, in identical white cap, overalls and rubber boots but without a barrow, went into the same opening. Practically all the traders and porters he'd seen were men, but the shape and step of this one told him it was a woman. He felt a stirring of excitement. Could it be?

Edging his way over to where he'd seen her disappear, he entered a sort of corridor with a row of floor to ceiling refrigerators lining the wall on one side. The corridor was empty, but the steel door of a fridge at the far end stood open. Whipping out his mobile, Quentin called Wanda.

'I might have found her,' he whispered when she answered. 'I'm in a corridor full of fridges. I'll call you again when I'm sure it's her.'

Thinking he may be able to peer into the fridge without its occupant spotting him, he moved closer. He could hear movement coming from inside, and icy cold air wafted through the gap. He was almost level with the fridge when the woman came out, her arms clasped around several boxes stacked on top of each other. She tried to kick the door shut with her foot but missed and stumbled, dropping the boxes. Lids flew off and fish and pieces of ice were jolted out of the boxes, reaching Quentin and splattering his jeans and shoes. Hoping he could exit the corridor at the other end, and thinking it would be quicker than going back, Quentin darted forward in an effort to get past the woman before she had a chance to see him properly. Skidding on a piece of ice he almost collided with her, and as he regained his balance and stepped back he looked into the face of the woman he knew as Riddle.

Recognition flared in her eyes and she gasped. Caught off guard, Quentin teetered as the woman launched herself at him, knocking him sideways. He fell awkwardly, his upper body sprawling into the opening of the fridge. Dazed, he tried to get to get up, but before he could he felt his legs being pushed by something heavy. A metallic sound echoed through the air as the refrigerator door clanged shut.

Quentin struggled to his feet and banged on it. 'Hey! Let me out!' He kept shouting for a minute or so, then gave up. Unless someone was passing close by, he wouldn't be heard.

Turning, he gave a cursory glance around him. The fridge was about the size of a large van, the ones used to make home food deliveries. The wall on one side was lined with white oblong boxes, filled with fish, Quentin assumed. On the other side there were gaps, presumably where some had been removed. He could see no way out except the door. Shivering, he felt for his mobile and he rang Wanda's number.

'No signal,' he groaned, panic rising. Calm down, Quentin, he thought. Someone will be here sooner or later to collect more fish.

Would they though, he wondered. Did more than one porter come in here?

Wrapping his arms around himself, he tried to make sense of things. Riddle must work here. Why else would she be dressed as a porter and have access to the fridge? His impetuous decision to come to Billingsgate had been based on nothing more substantial than a faint fishy smell on the money bag and some initials in the notebook. The possibility of a member of the gang actually working here hadn't occurred to him, but if the market was being used for illicit dealings what better cover was there for the transactions? She would be here legitimately and could meet her contact at any time during working hours. He hadn't noticed any sort of smell on Riddle last night. If anything he'd been struck by a whiff of something clean and fresh, like scented soap or shower gel. But then she would wash thoroughly after a morning at the market. Today she'd recognized him immediately, and obviously realized that he wasn't there to buy fish. It would have been too much of a coincidence. Had she already handed over the statue, or was she waiting for her contact to appear?

He looked around him again. There must be a way out, or an intercom, something to raise the alarm if someone got left inside. He could see nothing, except the door. He would just have to wait. It shouldn't be long. After all, the market was heaving and someone would want to replenish their stall sooner or later. He hoped it wouldn't be later. His teeth were already chattering, and his hands were starting to feel numb. Should he do exercises to keep warm? But then he would use up more air, and he didn't know how much there was in here. Perhaps it was sealed, airtight to keep the temperature constant. He shivered uncontrollably now. Suppose nobody came? Suppose he was trapped here until tomorrow? No one knew he was here except Wanda, and she didn't know exactly where he was.

Visions of being found dead from hypothermia rose in front of him. Random, unaccountable thoughts chased themselves round his head. Who would take care of Magpie if he died? Would Wanda be running the agency on her own after all? Or would she invite Colin to join her? What would his mother say? And his father? He thought of the blustering ex-army officer ordering his mother around as well as Quentin when he had the chance. Only his sister Shelagh got away without a lashing from his sharp tongue. What would Shelagh think, nicely tucked away in an affluent corner of Australia as she was? Would she miss him? Would any of them? Yes, he told himself, Mum would be devastated. Shelagh would be sad, but can you really miss someone you haven't seen for nearly four years?

Winding his arms tighter around himself, he leaned against some empty pallets piled high in a corner. I must do something, he thought desperately. I must attract attention. Stepping sideways he placed numb hands on the middle section of the pallets, then pushed with all his might. They tumbled to the floor with a tremendous crash, taking with them several of the polystyrene boxes of fish that were stacked next to them.

When the sound had stopped echoing round the fridge, Quentin's ears picked up another noise. He whirled round to see the door swinging open. 'Thank God,' he whispered. Then, running forward, he shouted it. 'Thank God!'

He had to wait until the door was fully open before he could greet his rescuer. 'Bloody hell,' he said when a man with greying brown hair and dark eyes came into sight. 'Philmore! What are you doing here?'

Chapter Twenty-seven

It was several seconds before his numb brain was able to work out the answer. The police had been alerted that the statue was on the move and had followed it here.

Pleased though he was to see the Detective Chief Inspector, something about his demeanour told him Philmore wasn't happy.

'She was here,' he blurted. 'Riddle. She locked me in here. You should be going after her.'

'Don't tell us what we should be doing. We're on it. Don't stand there gawking, man. You'll have to be quick if you want to be in on the action.'

Philmore turned and strode away. Quentin stepped gratefully out of the refrigerator and there was Wanda, an anxious look on her face.

'Oh my God, Quentin,' she gasped. 'Are you all right?'

One of the market police who had been with the DCI came forward. 'There's always a door release button inside,' he said, stepping into the fridge. 'Ah. It's behind these boxes. They shouldn't be stacked there, really.'

Quentin groaned. 'So I could have got out then. Where's Philmore rushing off to?'

Wanda grabbed his arm and marched him out of the corridor into the crush of people in the market hall. 'Come on,' she said. 'We'll lose them.'

'What's happening?' Quentin shouted, his mind in turmoil.

'Later,' she shouted back, and kept pushing forward.

As they moved towards the exit the crowd seemed to disperse. Quentin spotted Philmore ahead and ran to catch up with him, Wanda at his side. Philmore slowed when they reached him.

'Got your mobile?' he barked. When Quentin nodded he went on, 'Good. Keep it on. Riddle's got a black Mini Cooper, registration' – he lifted his hand and looked at the number inked on the back – 'GL04 RLZ.'

Opening her handbag, Wanda produced a pen and an envelope and jotted the number down.

'For God's sake don't let her see you,' Philmore continued. 'We don't want to spook her. Wait here until you get a call to say it's OK for you to leave. We'll be tailing her, you stay behind us. We'll ring and let you know where we're going. Don't do anything except follow without checking with me first. You don't need to keep us in sight, just go where we tell you.' Pausing, he looked directly at Quentin. 'And don't forget what I said yesterday. You get anywhere near where you're not supposed to be and I'll have you arrested. Got that?'

Without waiting for an answer, he strode through the gates and disappeared.

Quentin looked at Wanda in confusion. 'What the hell's going on? Why did he tell me to get a move on and then wait here?'

'He won't want us going out until Riddle's gone in case she sees you. It's better she thinks you're locked up where you can't follow her or call the police.'

'OK. So how did he know I was in that fridge?'

'I spotted DS Francis,' Wanda explained. 'I knew if she was here Philmore would probably be here too, and I didn't want to blot our copybook any further. If they were looking for Riddle they wouldn't want us muscling in on their operation, so I thought I'd better come clean and let her know you thought you'd seen her. Lucky you said where you were or we would never would have found you.'

'You took long enough,' Quentin said, blowing on his hands.

'Well, she had to call Philmore first, and alert the market police. Then we had to work out exactly where you were. I suppose it was quite a while by the time we got to the corridor and the fridges. Luckily we heard a crash and guessed it was you.'

Warmth gradually returning to his body, Quentin grunted and said, 'Right. So if Philmore thought Riddle was here, why would he waste time coming to let me out?'

'He didn't waste any time. He wasn't far away and he had back up in place. The market police have had Riddle under surveillance since she arrived this morning.'

'Shame they didn't follow her to those fridges, then I wouldn't have been left there to freeze.'

'You weren't there long enough for that.'

Quentin's fingers were starting to tingle as the blood began to circulate. 'So what made Philmore say we could go with them?'

Wanda pursed her lips. 'I begged him to let us follow them. I pointed out how useful we'd been in the past, and reminded him that we'd taken all sorts of risks to try to get to the bottom of the case–'

'In other words you charmed him into it.' Quentin couldn't keep the admiration out of his voice. It didn't surprise him – he was quite sure Wanda could charm the entire Metropolitan Police Force if she put her mind to it. And really, what did it matter to Philmore if they followed Riddle when he had his own people in place? After all, they appealed for help from the public all the time – they even had a TV show dedicated to reporting crimes and asking for anyone with information to come forward. As long as no one got in their way or put themselves in danger it shouldn't make a difference to their operation.

They looked towards the car park in front of the building. Quentin could see why Philmore hadn't been in more of a hurry. There was a tailback of vehicles trying to get to the exit. Riddle was probably still in the car park.

'Very convenient,' Quentin said, eyeing the queue.

'Convenience didn't come into it,' Wanda told him. 'Philmore contacted the Billingsgate police and asked them to arrange a hold up at the barrier to stop cars leaving.'

'Genius,' Quentin said. 'So by the time our friend collected the statue from wherever she'd stashed it and got to the car park, the exit was blocked? She did have the statue here, I take it?'

Wanda shrugged. 'As far as I know, yes. I mean, if she'd given it to someone else, Philmore would be following them, wouldn't he?'

'Yeah, I suppose, but what if she didn't have it here? Did Philmore actually say they followed the signal, or did they just follow Riddle?'

'Your guess is as good as mine. He didn't give me a running commentary. I must admit, I'd want to go home to have a shower and get changed after working with fish for four hours.'

'I think they've got showers here, but she wouldn't have wasted time with that today. After seeing me she'd have wanted to get away as quickly as possible.'

The line of vehicles started moving slowly. Not long afterwards Quentin's mobile vibrated in his pocket.

'OK.' DS Francis spoke curtly. 'You can go now.'

They made their way through the car park, slipping between the rows of remaining cars and vans. When they'd located the Toyota Quentin eased it out to join the queue of vehicles still trying to get to the exit. Some drivers were becoming impatient and sounded their horns, as though hoping the mass of traffic before them would part like the Red Sea.

'Is Philmore stuck in this lot as well?' Quentin wondered.

'Shouldn't think so,' Wanda replied. 'I'm sure he turned the other way when he left us. Probably parked up the road somewhere outside waiting for Riddle to pass them. Police can park on yellow lines, you know.'

'All right, all right, no need to go on. Ah, here we go. Take my mobile, Wanda, and keep hold of it.'

Finally getting to the exit, they eased out onto the road. Quentin frowned. Which way were they supposed to go? As if answering his question, his mobile rang.

'Inspector? … Yes, OK, thanks.' Wanda lowered the phone. 'Back through the Blackwall tunnel then south onto the A102.'

Quentin filtered into the correct lane and made the turn. They drove on, Wanda taking directions from Philmore's instructions.

The sun made an appearance between the clouds, lightening the sky and making the autumn day seem brighter. Crazy thoughts and unanswered questions chased around in Quentin's head, until Wanda's mobile sang out its tune. She rummaged in her bag and pulled it out. Quentin huffed when she said, 'Hello, Colin.'

'Not now, Wanda,' he said. 'Say you can't talk.'

Ignoring him, Wanda went on, 'No sorry, we went out early … Billingsgate … No, not for fish, because we thought our lady with the goods might be there … I can't explain now … In the car, and I don't know yet where we're headed … Sorry, Colin, got to go.'

She ended the call as Quentin's mobile rang. 'The A20? OK, Inspector.'

'The A20,' Quentin repeated, checking the mirror and indicating. 'So it's the south-east then.'

'Not necessarily. She could go anywhere – she might join the M25 further down.'

'I bloody hope not. I had enough of that the last time.'

The last time. It seemed weeks since they'd given Motorbike Man the slip on the motorway, not the few days it had actually been. It also seemed a long time since they'd had what Quentin called a normal day, a day when he'd worked at the agency, had a leisurely meal and a good night's sleep. Last night's lack of sleep was catching up with him, and he stifled a yawn.

He cast a sideways glance at Wanda. Lack of sleep didn't seem to be affecting her – she looked as cool as ever in her well-groomed and sophisticated way. As far as he could remember he'd only seen her ruffled and upset on a few occasions, and that was during their case in the previous year.

'Quentin!'

Wanda's voice jolted him back to the moment. He braked hard as he saw the traffic ahead had slowed.

'Concentrate, Quentin,' Wanda said.

'Sorry. I bet it's the south-east though. Dover or Folkstone would be my guess.'

'The ferry port or the channel tunnel, you mean? It makes sense if she's planning on leaving the country – it's a straight run down to Dover from here. On the other hand, it's a bit obvious, now she's seen you. She must know someone's on to her.'

'Me, yes,' Quentin agreed. 'But as far as she knows I'm the only one who is. She doesn't know we went to the police.

'She might have worked it out though. She knows something's wrong, that's why she's running.'

There was silence until the phone rang again. Wanda lifted it to her ear. 'Inspector? … The M25 south. OK. Not Dover or Folkstone then,' she added when the call ended, casting a meaningful look at Quentin.

Quentin tutted. 'Oh no. We could get stuck there for hours if the traffic's bad.'

'So will she,' Wanda pointed out.

'Some consolation that is.' Quentin followed the signs to the motorway and soon they were merging into the moving traffic. 'I'm glad we're not going the other way. There's a tailback as far as I can see.'

He wondered how far behind Riddle Philmore was. Having the bug to track made things so much easier.

As he drove, a plethora of unanswered questions came into his mind. Why hadn't Riddle handed over the statue at Billingsgate? Surely that's what she was meant to do or why would she take it there? Or had she planned to deliver it somewhere else immediately after she finished work? What did she think had happened when Adamson hadn't appeared with the goods? He'd obviously stalled her on Saturday, when the original exchange was planned, blaming Walberg's collapse. But later, when Quentin had rung and said he'd found the statue in a holdall?

'Whatever you're thinking, Quentin, don't. Concentrate on driving, or pull onto the hard shoulder and let me drive.'

'I am concentrating, Wanda,' he said, knowing she was right to caution him. What had brought them this far didn't matter. What mattered was staying on Riddle's trail and seeing her caught, hopefully with any accomplice she may be meeting.

With no instructions to the contrary, they kept driving. Quentin looked at the blue signs as they passed them. 'I'm getting this feeling of déjà vu,' he said when they passed the Clacket Lane services.

'Me too, except this time we're not being followed by a motorbike. And you never know, maybe Riddle always comes this way to deliver the goods.'

'Mmm… Maybe, but that doesn't feel right to me.'

'Doesn't it? What does feel right to you, mastermind?'

'Dunno really, except I'm pretty sure she was meant to hand over the statue at Billingsgate, perhaps not inside, maybe in the car park or somewhere just outside. It's a busy place, teeming with people like the railway station was, easy enough to make a swap or a delivery without being noticed, especially if the transaction takes place early. Once out of the car park and surrounding area the recipient could get on the road before the rush hour traffic built up.'

'True,' Wanda agreed. 'But other places are busy too. The handover could just as easily take place outside London.'

'Today, yes, but I'm talking about what was meant to happen. Still, as we said, even though she was shocked to see me and obviously smelt a rat, she doesn't know anyone's following her. I mean, she probably thought that by the time I got out of the fridge she'd be long gone, and–' Quentin stopped as another sign came into view. 'That's it. I bet that's it.'

Wanda looked mystified. 'What is?'

'The M23. Gatwick.'

'Gatwick? You think she's heading for the airport?'

'Why not?'

'Because if she'd filtered into the M23 lane we would have heard by now. They must be past it already.'

Wanda was right, Quentin realized. The turn off for Gatwick wasn't far ahead.

'Perhaps they've forgotten to call us,' he muttered. 'Ring Philmore.'

'No, I don't think we should. He won't thank us for pestering him. I'm sure he wouldn't let us miss the turning if they were heading to the airport.'

'Too late now,' Quentin said as they left the turn-off behind. 'I hope you're right.'

They travelled on westwards, past the signs for Reigate, then Leatherhead. The traffic was better than he'd feared, sluggish but moving steadily. The tailback on the eastbound side they'd seen when they joined the motorway had petered out a while back, and he wondered what had caused it. Feeling uneasy about Philmore's lack of contact for what seemed an age, he switched on the radio. Pop music played for a few minutes, then was interrupted by the hourly news bulletin. He turned the volume up as he heard the word Dover. An incident at Dover ferry port overnight, the newsreader announced, meant that ferries departing from Dover were delayed, causing a queue of traffic, mainly lorries and commercial vehicles, back to the junction of the M20 with the M25.

'What sort of incident?' Wanda said. 'A bomb scare, do you think?'

'Don't know, but it explains why Riddle wouldn't go there. If she listened to traffic reports, she'd know about the problem and avoid it. Maybe that's what that tailback was– there's the phone.'

Quentin turned off the radio and listened while Wanda answered the call.

'OK, Inspector. Thanks.'

'Well?'

'She's turning onto the A3.'

The A3. Where did that go? he wondered. He wasn't sure, though he knew it led to the south coast. He'd been to the Isle of Wight once, and remembered going on a hovercraft from Southsea.

The overhead sign showed they were nearing the A3. Guildford and Portsmouth, he read. Glad to be leaving the monotony of the motorway, he pulled into the inside lane and turned off accordingly. They hadn't gone far when the mobile rang again.

'Yes, Inspector? … So what do you want us to do? … OK.'

'What is it?' Quentin asked.

'The signal's static. They think she's pulled into the next service station.'

'So can we do that? I hope so. I could use the loo.'

'You'll have to hold on. He wants you to stay in the car in case she sees you.'

'Oh great. I wonder how much further she's going.'

'She might not be going any further,' Wanda pointed out. 'She might be meeting someone here.'

'Do you think so? You think she arranged a meeting for here after seeing me at Billingsgate?'

There was a beat before Wanda answered. 'Maybe, but I think she was scared off before that. She was expecting the statue from Adamson, not some stranger who claimed to have found it in the street. She would have tried to find out where Adamson was, or she may have tried to contact Walberg. She wouldn't have been able to contact either of them, so she's got no idea what's going on, except she must know something's wrong.'

'Here's the service station,' Quentin said, flicking the indicator switch. He drove in, swinging round past the petrol pumps and noticing a black car by the air pump with its bonnet propped up and smoke coming from it.

'Someone's in trouble,' he said. As they drew closer recognition swamped him. He couldn't see her face, but – it was a woman, with reddish hair…

'It's her,' he gasped. 'It's Riddle.'

Chapter Twenty-eight

'Are you sure?' Wanda said, craning her neck to look round as they carried on towards the parking area.

'Pretty sure. It was a black Mini Cooper.'

'We'll soon find out,' Wanda said, lifting her handbag from the floor and searching inside. 'Now where's that number – ah, here it is.'

Quentin found a parking space and drove the car into it. 'What?' he asked.

Wanda unfolded an envelope and read, 'GL04 RLZ I'll go and see.'

'I'll come,' Quentin said, pulling the keys from the ignition.

'No, Quentin, she might see you. She doesn't know me. You stay here with the phone in case Philmore calls. I'll just have a quick look.'

She got out, and Quentin sat tapping his fingers on the steering wheel, annoyed that he couldn't go with her. He was tempted to ignore Philmore's order and go to the gents but decided against it. If it wasn't Riddle he'd seen and the signal started again, he should be ready to go. He leaned against the headrest and relaxed a little as the sun came through the window onto his face. Tiredness crept over him. He shook himself, and asked himself the same questions as before but found no answers. A tune rang out, interrupting his thoughts, and it was several seconds before he recognized it as Wanda's mobile. He picked up her handbag and found the phone, but the ringtone had stopped.

'Colin,' he muttered, reading the display. 'Well, he can jolly well wait.' With a pang of guilt, he changed his mind and rang back, but now the line was busy.

What on earth is she doing? he wondered when Wanda hadn't reappeared after ten minutes.

At that moment he saw her. 'At last,' he murmured, then his eyes widened as he saw DS Francis with her. He got out as they approached, grateful to be able to stretch his legs.

'What's going on?' He looked from one to the other, fearful for a moment that Riddle had been arrested and he'd missed a showdown.

'It was her you saw,' Wanda told him. 'She's got engine trouble, that's why she pulled in here.'

'Your partner here had an idea and we're going to try something, if you agree,' DS Francis said.

'Try what?'

'We're pretty sure she's heading for the ferry port in Portsmouth, to go abroad or meet someone. She's got her passport with her.'

Quentin was amazed. How did they know she had her passport?

'She's probably arranged a time if she's meeting someone, or she'll have a time slot if she's going to France or Spain. She could go to either one from Portsmouth–'

'She won't want to be held up for too long,' Wanda interrupted. 'She doesn't know me so if I offer her a lift, say I'm going to wherever she's going, she might accept.'

'Ooh, I'm not sure about that, Wanda.'

'I'll be all right.'

'We'll be right behind her,' Francis assured him.

'What about me?' Quentin demanded.

'The chief says you can come with us,' Francis said, looking as though she didn't approve of her boss's suggestion. Or perhaps it had been Wanda's suggestion. He didn't care whose it was, or whether the detective sergeant approved – he wasn't going to be left out.

'You remember what to do, Mrs Merrydrew?' Francis continued, turning to Wanda.

'Wanda, please,' Wanda said. 'Yes. I go and get petrol, go over to ask if she's all right or get talking somehow, find out where she's going, then say I'm going there and ask if she wants a lift.'

Francis nodded. 'Yes. Have you got a phone? The chief says you should have one.'

'Take mine, Wanda,' Quentin offered. 'Philmore's number's in my contacts. I'll keep yours.'

'Good idea,' Francis said. Stepping backwards, she scribbled down Wanda's registration number. 'OK,' she said. 'Let's go before Riddle decides on a different course of action.'

She gestured to Quentin to follow her. 'Be careful, Wanda,' he called over his shoulder, then hurried to catch Francis up. If anyone could pull this off, Wanda could, but he still felt uneasy about her getting into a car with a criminal.

'Hello, Quentin,' Philmore said when Quentin and Francis reached his Audi.

'Hello, Inspector,' Quentin grinned.

'It's Detective Chief Inspector,' Francis said pointedly.

'Don't split hairs, Debbie,' Philmore growled. 'We haven't got time. Go and check on Riddle.'

Francis disappeared round the corner of the service building and Philmore turned to Quentin. 'Debbie's a bit overzealous at times,' he said. 'She's a good cop for all that.'

'I'm sure she is,' Quentin answered, making a mental note not to call her Debbie. 'So you think Riddle's headed to the ferry port? How do you know she's got her passport with her?'

'We have our methods, Quentin.'

'Why can't you tell me?' Quentin said, irritated. 'I'm not about to broadcast it on national TV. I'm a detective, not a journalist.'

Philmore raised his eyebrows. 'In that case you should be able to work it out for yourself.'

Quentin thought for a moment. 'OK. Riddle works at Billingsgate. She must have had her passport in her handbag or something. While she was working, she left it somewhere she thought was safe, a locker probably, or somewhere workers can leave their things. You opened her bag and searched it. The holdall with the statue was probably there too, unless she left it in her car. How am I doing?'

'Quite well so far.'

'Right, so–' Quentin stopped as Philmore's mobile sounded.

'Yes, Debbie?' he heard him say. 'OK. Stay there until they drive off, then leg it back here.'

'What's happening?' Quentin asked.

'She seems to have taken the bait. Riddle had some bloke looking at the engine but Mrs Merrydrew – Wanda – went up and spoke to her. Lord knows what she said but our suspect's taking a handbag, a holdall and a suitcase from her car and is going with her. Quite a woman, your partner. Must be a good asset to have in your line of work.'

'She is,' Quentin agreed. 'But then she'd be an asset in anyone's line of work, even yours.'

Ignoring this comment Philmore said, 'I need to get on to control, get them to alert the authorities at the ferry port.'

He spent the next few minutes barking instructions into the radio. When Francis hadn't appeared after he'd finished, he said, 'What's keeping them? I'd have thought Riddle would have been keen to get going.'

'Probably gone to the loo,' Quentin said. 'Do you think I've got time to go?'

'Not if you want to come with us. I'm not waiting around if the signal starts again.'

Quentin had almost forgotten about the signal. He'd got used to receiving instructions over the phone. He ran his tongue over his lips. 'I'm thirsty,' he murmured. 'And I really need the loo.'

Philmore shot him an exasperated look. 'I'm sure you can last a bit longer. Here, have some water.'

'That won't help, will it?' Quentin grumbled, but he took a few mouthfuls then gave the bottle back.

A bleeping sounded. Francis returned and scrambled back into the driver's seat. 'They're off,' she panted, switching on the engine.

'About time,' Philmore grunted. 'What kept them?'

Francis was silent while she concentrated on reversing out of the space. Then she said, 'Riddle was talking to someone in the garage, about leaving her car there, I presume.'

After she'd driven forward a few yards the signal was static again. Francis brought the car to a halt.

'Now what?' Philmore asked.

'Perhaps they've gone into the main parking area for some reason,' Quentin said.

'No, she's moving again,' Philmore said as the bleeping filled the air. The tracking device, Quentin realized, feeling a thrill of excitement. The thrill deepened when he spotted a round object with a transparent top, which Quentin took to be a blue flashlight. He imagined flying along the motorway with the blue light pulsing, the siren screaming and all other vehicles moving aside to let them pass as they chased after a carful of dangerous criminals.

A people carrier pulled out in front of them and barred their way. It stopped between the two lines of parked cars while the female driver turned and remonstrated with a child in the back.

'For goodness' sake!' Philmore said. 'Get out of the way, woman!'

Francis sounded the horn and the woman looked round. She mouthed a 'sorry' and continued her exit.

When they got to the slip road leading onto the main road, DS Francis slowed, waiting for a chance to merge into the traffic.

'Go, go, go!' snapped Philmore. 'We can't afford to be too far behind.'

With a peremptory glance in the mirror, Francis pushed her foot to the floor and roared out from the joining lane, wedging the Audi in between two fast moving vehicles and earning an angry beep from the one behind.

'Oops,' Quentin murmured, and immediately wished he hadn't.

'It may have escaped your notice, but we're in a hurry,' Francis said, indicating out into the fast lane.

Quentin had the distinct impression that Debbie Francis thought of him as a nuisance. Or perhaps she was sarcastic with everyone.

'We don't want the local plods messing things up or taking the credit,' Philmore muttered, more to himself than anyone else.

Quentin felt his anxiety. He understood how it would feel to set something up, come close to apprehending the suspects only to be beaten to it by someone else, even if they were on the same side. He kept quiet though. He didn't think Philmore would appreciate any more comments on police methods.

The sky darkened, the bright day overshadowed by grey clouds and the first spots of rain. It wasn't long before the rain was heavy and visibility was poor. Headlights took the place of the sun's rays and wipers beat a tattoo on the windscreen. Quentin noticed another car behind them, one that had followed them out of the service station and kept pace with them.

'It's an unmarked traffic car, in case we have to stop Riddle on the road,' Francis said when he mentioned it. 'CID aren't allowed to stop cars in transit.'

They travelled on, changing lanes and dropping their speed as the signal grew louder. Wanda wasn't a fast driver as a rule, Quentin knew, and if they continued driving the way they were they would overtake her.

'That's them, I think, up ahead,' he said, seeing a glimpse of a blue Toyota.

'We're on track now, Debbie,' Philmore said. 'Stay in this position if you can.'

They cruised at moderate speed, passing Guildford, Hindhead and Petersfield. The traffic built up as the road merged into the A3M towards Portsmouth.

'Looks like we were right,' Philmore said. 'I'll let control know.'

He lifted the radio handset, fiddled with the knobs and spoke into it. He gave the registration number and a description of Riddle as a suspect in her late thirties with short reddish hair, dressed in navy-blue trousers and a turquoise jumper.

Quentin was impressed. Someone on surveillance that morning had been very observant. When he'd seen Riddle earlier, she'd been wearing a white overall and her hair had been scraped back under a white cap. He felt a beat of surprise when Philmore went on to explain that Riddle was travelling with an attractive female companion with blonde hair, who wasn't a suspect. It earned him a sidelong glance from Francis too, though she said nothing.

'Understood,' came the crackly reply. The radio went quiet and Philmore replaced it. He stared straight ahead, and from where Quentin sat, he could see his face had set in a determined mask. They were close to the port now, and he obviously had his mind on what lay ahead.

'How do we know she's definitely going to Portsmouth?' Quentin queried. 'She could carry on to Southampton from here, couldn't she?'

'She could,' Francis answered. 'But she'd have been more likely to have used the M3. It's more direct.'

'But even if she goes to Portsmouth she needn't be going abroad,' Quentin persisted. 'She could be meeting someone, or going to the Isle of Wight.'

'You don't need a passport for the Isle of Wight,' Philmore snapped. 'We have to work with what we've got. We need to alert the authorities just in case. It's no good leaving it to the last minute.'

Feeling like a schoolboy who'd been told off, Quentin muttered, 'No, I suppose it isn't.'

Annoyed that he'd mentioned this when he'd already convinced himself that Riddle was likely to go abroad, he decided not to speak to Philmore unless he had something important to say. He was here at the DCI's discretion, and he had no right to question his judgement.

As they neared the end of the A3M the city of Portsmouth came into view, and Quentin saw a tall white spire piercing the skyline. 'That wasn't there the last time I came,' he said.

'It's the Spinnaker Tower,' Francis told him. 'And that building next to it is called The Lipstick. My cousin lives not far from here.'

'Forget the tour, Debbie,' Philmore growled as the radio crackled into life. 'Bloody typical,' he said, after a terse conversation. 'The special branch police who look after the port are held up at Southampton airport. They cover both sites, so we may have to get back up from the local force. Otherwise, apart from the port's security, we're on our own.'

At the bottom of the A3M they turned west onto the M27, then slipped into the lane for the M275, proving Philmore's reasoning right. The road ran south along the western side of the city towards the cross-channel ferry port. As they crossed the narrow stretch of water between the mainland and Portsea Island, Quentin's excitement mounted. He felt like a huntsman closing in on his prey. Something had to happen, and soon.

They may have been close, but it took an agonising amount of time to get into the port, with all sorts of vehicles trying to get to the same place. Quentin had never seen so many lorries, a great number with foreign registration plates. There were just as many cars and caravans.

'Busy,' Francis commented. 'Maybe people have diverted here from Dover. Oh, the signal's static again.'

Philmore was clearly agitated now. Quentin guessed at his frustration. They couldn't use the blues and twos, as the police lights and sirens were called, in case Riddle took fright. She could easily run and lose herself in the ferry terminal, or even dump the statue somewhere rather than be caught with it.

He imagined himself cornering Riddle, discovering who was behind the operation and recovering the statue single-handed. Philmore would congratulate him then, maybe even consult him on difficult cases–

His daydream was interrupted when Philmore slapped his hand on the dashboard. 'Come on, come on,' he said. As if responding to his demand the traffic in front surged forward. As the same time the radio crackled and Philmore snatched it up.

'Go ahead.'

'Ferry port officials report blue Toyota registration LL03 UDR entering the port,' announced a muffled male voice.

'Find out when the next sailing is,' Philmore said.

From the amount of traffic entering the port Quentin guessed that any vehicle coming in now would have no chance of getting the next sailing, even though more than one company operated ferries both to France and Northern Spain. It would be different for a foot passenger though. Unless Riddle was meeting someone with their own transport, being a foot passenger was her only option. His excitement mounted and his pulse raced with anticipation.

'Toyota proceeding to drop-off point,' the radio voice announced. There was a pause, during which the signal flattened. The voice resumed. 'Suspect getting out the car, also the driver. The driver opening the boot and taking out a suitcase.'

'What about the holdall?' Quentin blurted before he could stop himself.

'Shut up,' Francis hissed.

'Repeat please,' Philmore said.

'Suspect lifted out a holdall. Now talking to driver.' A pause, and then, 'Suspect entering terminal.'

'The signal's still static,' Francis said.

It took a second to understand the significance of her words. If Riddle was walking into the terminal, surely the signal would still be moving. They had entered the port themselves now and were driving towards the drop-off point.

'Pull up by the terminal entrance,' Philmore ordered.

As they approached the entrance, they saw Wanda standing by the Toyota talking to a port worker. They pulled up behind her.

'Wanda's got the holdall,' Quentin said. 'What on earth…'

Philmore and Francis got out, and Quentin scrambled after them.

'Thank goodness you're here,' Wanda said, raindrops dripping from her hair. 'She's taken the wrong bag. I was just trying to explain to this gentleman' – she indicated to the port worker – 'that I'm not parking here, I'm just trying to give our friend the right bag.'

Philmore produced his identity card and flashed it at the port worker. 'Police business,' he snapped. 'We've been in touch with the port authorities.' The man nodded and signalled the OK to a fellow worker nearby.

'What's going on?' Philmore asked Wanda.

Thinking the same thing, Quentin looked at her and saw something he'd rarely seen – Wanda blushing and looking embarrassed. 'It wasn't my fault,' she said. 'I gave her the suitcase, but she took the holdall out herself. It wasn't until she'd gone inside and I went to shut the boot that I realized.'

'What?' Francis said, sounding incredulous. 'You had another bag in the car?'

'Yes. Riddle put hers in and I put her suitcase in front of it. My holdall was pushed to the back but it must have slipped forward while we were travelling. I wasn't really looking when I took the suitcase out – I was too busy looking at her and wondering when you were going to show up.'

'So if you've got the statue,' Quentin said, his brain whirring, 'what the hell has Riddle got?'

Chapter Twenty-nine

Everyone turned to Wanda. 'My wedding dress,' she said, her blush deepening.

For a moment nobody spoke. Then Philmore snapped into action.

'Go in after her, explain about the mix up and give her the holdall. Go now, before she notices her mistake and comes looking for you.'

Wanda turned to go, then turned back again. 'She's meeting someone,' she said. 'When I picked her up, she made a call and said there was a change of plan because her car had broken down. She said she'd meet them inside the terminal.'

'Them? Did she give them a name?' Philmore asked.

Shaking her head, Wanda said, 'She just said "it's me" and afterwards she told me she was meeting a friend. That's all. She didn't talk much.'

'All right. Take the bag in now.'

Wanda whirled round and headed for the door, reaching it just as several people were coming out. She stood aside to let them pass, was about to start forward again when Riddle approached the glass doors from the inside. The door opened but she stopped, one foot over the threshold.

'Bloody hell,' Quentin murmured, panic rising as, instead of going to Wanda, Riddle looked directly at him. It was as though the moment was frozen in time. Quentin, Philmore and Francis stood by the cars, Wanda a few feet in front of the door, while the person they were all focusing on shifted her gaze between each of them. Then Riddle turned and fled back into the terminal.

'Come on!' shouted Philmore. He sprinted into the building pursued by Francis. Quentin followed, knowing that keeping out of sight was no longer a priority.

Bursting through the entrance Quentin moved forward, his eyes searching for Riddle. Wanda came up beside him, the holdall still over her arm. 'Can you see her?' she asked.

'No. There's Philmore, over there. We'll split up.'

Quentin walked through the crowded hall towards the information desk then on past the ticket desk. He wondered whether Riddle had a ticket, whether she'd booked in advance and whether she even intended boarding a ferry. But she'd brought a suitcase and her passport so surely she must be taking a ferry. Or perhaps, because of the unexpected way she'd received the statue, she'd arranged to hand it over here and come prepared in case she had to make a hasty escape.

Quentin spotted the toilets, desperate to go in but not wanting to miss anything. He turned towards the waiting area, where people sat on rows of fixed plastic chairs. His gaze went up and down the rows, though he didn't expect Riddle to be there. Hiding in plain sight was fine if you didn't need to make a quick getaway, and anyway, she may be looking for whoever she'd arranged to meet.

A robotic voice from the tannoy announced that the Pride of Cherbourg, due to sail at 12.30 p.m., was now ready for boarding. Drivers should return to their vehicles and foot passengers should proceed to the embarkation area. A swathe of people stood up, gathering their belongings and shuffling their way to the ends of the rows of chairs. Soon the entrance to the embarkation area was filled with people and Quentin cursed. If Riddle was in that lot he'd never see her. He needed to be on the other side, near passport control. If she was boarding the Pride of Cherbourg, she would have to go through there.

But then she needn't have gone that way at all, he mused, sweeping his gaze around the hall once more. He needed a clearer view, so he gripped the back of one of the recently vacated chairs and stood on the seat. So many people, most toting rucksacks, suitcases on wheels and bags of some kind. And holdalls. Holdalls of all colours and sizes. The words 'needle' and 'haystack' came to him. Suddenly he saw her, carrying her suitcase as well as Wanda's holdall, pushing her way around the edge of the rows of chairs against the surge of people.

Before he had time to react, he spotted Francis weaving in between the passengers after her. He jumped down from the chair, colliding with a man carrying a child as he landed. 'Sorry,' he called, not stopping but chasing after Riddle and Francis. When he saw them again Riddle was nearly at the exit. Francis was almost on her, but before she got there, Riddle turned and threw the suitcase at her knees. Francis, poised to lunge forward, tripped over it and fell sprawling onto the floor. By the time Quentin reached Francis, Wanda had appeared from the other side of the entrance and was rushing out through the door.

He followed and yelled as he saw Wanda take a flying leap at Riddle just as she made it to the Toyota. Riddle fell backwards against the car and kicked out, catching Wanda in the stomach. Wanda recoiled, teetered sideways and clutched at herself, dropping the holdall in the process. Quentin ran forward in time to catch hold of Riddle's shoulder as she opened the Toyota's door. He tugged hard, forcing her back against him. Just then someone came at him from behind.

He felt hands yanking him away from Riddle and pushing him sideways. He reeled several feet, then slipped in a puddle. Breaking his fall with his arms, he looked up to see Riddle drop into the Toyota's driver's seat while a man scooped up the holdall Wanda had dropped, ran round the car and flung himself into the passenger seat. Seconds later, the engine spluttered into life and the Toyota sped away. The whole thing happened so quickly that Quentin couldn't take it in.

While he recovered his balance, Wanda straightened up. 'Did that really happen?' she gasped. 'Has Riddle just stolen my car?'

'And who the hell was that guy?' Quentin said, wondering if he was dreaming. 'Did you leave the keys in the ignition?'

For the second time that day Wanda sounded embarrassed. 'I didn't expect to go chasing round the terminal. I thought I'd just be getting Riddle's things from the boot.'

DS Francis appeared, limping up to them with Riddle's abandoned suitcase in tow. Just then a blue light flashed and the traffic car that had been with them on the journey from London, and had been parked further along, screamed its way through a three-point turn and raced off after the Toyota.

'Where's Philmore?' Quentin asked.

'At passport control,' Francis said despondently. 'We should be going after them, but he's not here and my ankle–' She winced and tried to move her ankle, which was already beginning to swell. 'I don't think I can drive.'

'I can,' Quentin said. 'Give me the keys.'

'You can't–' Francis began.

'Argue later, unless you want to miss a chance of arresting them,' he said, holding out his hand. He took the keys as she handed them to him and made for the Audi. Wanda, having regained her breath and recovered enough to walk, opened the passenger door, took the suitcase and waited while Francis got in beside Quentin. Then, the engine already running, she tumbled into the back.

'Wait!' Francis shouted as the car jolted forward. 'There's the chief.'

Quentin turned to see Philmore running towards them. Winding down the window, Francis blurted, 'Riddle and her accomplice have taken Wanda's car. Traffic are after them.'

The look on the DCI's face was something Quentin would remember for a long time. He expected to be ordered out of the driver's seat, but evidently speed was more important. Wrenching open the back door, Philmore leapt in beside Wanda.

'Go!' he yelled.

Quentin drove off at a screech while Francis took the police light, turned it on and placed it on the roof via the window. Over the shriek of the siren a fast bleeping sounded. The signal. It was leading them out of the ferry port.

Once outside, Quentin pushed his foot to the floor, disregarding the speed limit and most of the highway code. It felt good knowing that however he drove would be justified in the name of the law, and the adrenaline that coursed through his body had more effect than several glasses of whisky. He could have gone on for hours, undertaking vehicles, weaving in and out of traffic and causing other vehicles to make way for him. Francis was barking into the car radio, ordering an alert to all cars in the area. Quentin felt like he was in the middle of a detective film.

It wasn't long before a blue light flashed ahead of them and the air was filled with the wail of another siren. They'd almost caught up with the traffic car, and Quentin wondered how far in front the criminals were.

'My car will be hammered the rate Riddle's going,' Wanda said. 'Bloody cheek, pinching my car after I gave her a lift, not to mention kicking me in the stomach.'

'Are you all right, Wanda?' Quentin asked, positioning the mirror so that he could see her.

'Just drive will you, we haven't got all day,' Philmore said, then leaned forward to hear the message coming over the radio. 'What was that?'

'Traffic are arranging a roadblock on all roads going out of town,' Francis told him. 'But I think it's too late. We're nearly back where we came in.'

The traffic going out of the city was much lighter than when they'd entered, and the five miles back towards the M27 flew past. It had stopped raining, and Quentin pulled the visor down against the sunlight.

'They're going west,' Francis said.

Seeing the road divide into east and west lanes, Quentin veered to the left and followed the road round, expecting to be back on the M27 westbound. The blue light disappeared, then reappeared as they emerged from a bend.

'This is an A road,' Quentin said, wondering why the fleeing suspects hadn't taken the motorway. It was far more difficult to escape on a road with traffic lights and roundabouts to negotiate, but then if Riddle and her companion didn't know the area it was easy to take a wrong turn.

'Now we'll get them,' Philmore said, sounding happier. 'Good. And are you going to tell me why a civilian is driving a CID car, Sergeant?'

Before Francis could answer Quentin swung the Audi dangerously onto the other side of the road to overtake a van, which, unlike other vehicles, had failed to pull over to let them pass.

'Moron!' he shouted over the siren, then instantly forgot it as the blue light ahead disappeared.

'They've turned off,' Francis said. 'Next left.'

Portchester Castle, Quentin heard Wanda murmur as he took the corner at speed. Francis was thrown against him as they hurtled round, but she straightened up and said nothing. Quentin followed the signal until it stopped and the road curved. Minutes later he saw the grey flint walls of the castle ruins across an open green area. The traffic car was there, its flashlight still pulsating. Quentin brought the car to a halt behind it just in time to see the two officers chasing two figures running around the outside of the castle wall.

Philmore flung open the back door, leapt from the car and started after them. Quentin followed him, breaking into a run and gaining on him. He could see Riddle, her progress impeded by the holdall, while her male companion raced ahead of her. Despite her load, Riddle was surprisingly agile, jumping over stones and tussocks of grass that obstructed the dirt path. She managed to get right round to the far side, where the creek water lapped at the edge of the land, before Philmore and the two officers were nearly on her. She turned, and seeing she couldn't escape, she heaved the holdall up and threw it into the water. Quentin slowed as he came up to them.

'He's getting away,' Philmore panted, pointing to the back of the unknown fleeing man.

Pushing past him, Quentin ran on, grateful for his running experience. He quickened his pace, determined not to let this criminal escape. He could see now that he had a holdall too, though he was coping with it better than Riddle had. It didn't make sense to Quentin – why they'd brought both holdalls and not just the one with the statue seemed stupid, unless they hadn't had time to check which was which. Whatever the reason, this man wasn't getting away if Quentin could help it. He might be the brains behind the whole business.

Spurred on by this thought, Quentin ran faster while the fleeing man was obviously tiring. The man half turned, saw Quentin and turned to carry on, tripping over a protruding tree root. He sprawled forwards, giving Quentin precious time to catch up with him. He sprang up again, leaving the holdall on the ground and covering the way ahead with increasingly slow steps. Vaulting over the tree root, Quentin scooped up the bag and went after him. A few yards further on the path split in two. The man ahead of Quentin broke his stride and hesitated – just for a few seconds, but long enough for Quentin to launch himself at him. He misjudged the distance and fell heavily onto his front, his elbows taking the brunt of the fall and the holdall cushioning his torso.

Cursing, he got up and resumed his pursuit as the man took the path that led round the castle wall towards the green area. A mistake on the man's part, Quentin realized, because ahead of them several police officers appeared and barred the way. Either Philmore or Francis must have called for more back-up. The man stopped and turned, seeing he was trapped. As if deciding Quentin was a safer bet than the police he ran back towards him, attempting to push him aside and take the other path. This time Quentin grabbed him, dropping the bag and sustaining a vicious punch to his shoulder before managing to push the man to the ground. He kept him there, struggling, until a couple of police officers reached them and hauled the man to his feet.

Gasping for breath, Quentin sat up and looked at his adversary. He was the same height as Quentin but older and heavier, with a definite paunch showing over his belt. His brown hair was thinning and his unremarkable features were set in a scowl. Pretty ordinary, Quentin thought, just like any other man in the street.

Wanda appeared, supporting DS Francis on one arm. Leaving Francis behind, Wanda rushed up to Quentin just as Philmore and the two traffic cops came from the other direction with a defeated-looking woman between them. Riddle looked at her partner in crime for a few seconds, then turned her gaze away as if she was afraid to meet his eyes. One of the traffic cops was wet up to his waist, and he held a holdall that dripped murky-looking water onto the ground.

Philmore sprinted the last few feet towards Quentin and the man he had felled. 'Well done,' he said to the uniformed officers either side of the suspect.

'Thank you, sir,' one of them said. 'Actually it was this man who stopped him.' He indicated towards Quentin.

Quentin stood and Philmore nodded but said nothing. Instead he looked at the uniformed officers. 'Has he given his name?'

When the officers shook their heads he looked directly at the man they held. 'Name?'

The man glared at him defiantly.

'You might as well tell me. Your friend will, if you don't.'

The look the man sent to Riddle told Quentin exactly what he was thinking; that whatever else she was, Riddle was no friend of his at this moment.

'All right,' Philmore said. 'I'll tell you. George Barrow. Right?' When there was no answer Philmore asked again, 'Are you George Barrow?'

'Yes,' came the sullen reply.

'George Barrow, I have reason to believe you are in possession of stolen goods.'

Philmore picked up the bag Quentin had dropped and thrust it at Barrow. 'Open it.'

'Open it yourself.'

Philmore didn't move. 'Open it.'

Barrow stared at him, then at the cordon of police in front and behind him. As if realizing there was no way out, he began to tug at the zip, his face full of hatred. His expression changed when he looked inside. He hesitated, seeming unsure what to do. Then, eyes bulging, he put his hand in and pulled out a handful of white chiffon. For a moment he lost his composure and looked across at Riddle with visible incredulity. Recovering, he pulled out the rest of the wedding dress and held it up. There was a titter among the watching officers.

'So you're going to arrest me for being the receiver of a woman's dress?' Barrow scorned. He tipped the bag upside down. Two satin shoes, a tiara and some magazines fell out.

Quentin resisted the urge to laugh. Why on earth hadn't Riddle ditched the bag when she'd seen what was in it? Barrow apparently thought that too, because he looked at Riddle as though he would have liked to hit her.

'Stupid bitch,' he snarled.

'George–' Riddle's voice was pleading, but Barrow continued to glare at her.

DS Francis limped up to them, took the holdall and stuffed the things back inside. Philmore thrust the wet second bag at Barrow. 'Open it.'

'Why?' Barrow jeered. 'Is it the bridegroom's outfit?' Another titter from the observers, but Barrow's eyes were constantly moving, darting glances all around as though looking for a last-minute chance of escape.

Philmore seemed unruffled. 'Open it,' he repeated, his voice quiet.

Barrow's fingers curled and uncurled into fists several times before he eventually took the wet holdall and unzipped it. 'I don't know what this is,' he said, peering inside.

'I'm pretty sure I do,' Philmore said grimly. 'And it's not a wedding present.'

Barrow looked from Philmore to Riddle. 'I've never seen this before. It's nothing to do with me. She's the one you should be talking to.'

This brought a gasp from Riddle. 'She said she had something for me,' Barrow went on. 'I didn't know what it was, I swear–'

Suddenly ceasing his claim to innocence, he pushed his hand into the bag and yanked out the statue. Side-stepping Philmore, he lunged at Francis, dropping the bag and wielding the statue like a weapon. She reeled sideways, and the blow that Barrow delivered found Quentin's hand as he caught her and pushed her aside. Philmore made a grab for Barrow from behind, but their attacker swung round and brought his weapon up under Philmore's chin. While Philmore yelled and was thrown back, Barrow dodged a police officer and made for the water's edge. He began to wade through the reeds in an attempt to reach the open water. Alarmed that Barrow may get away after all his efforts to catch him, Quentin went after him. So did several of the uniformed officers, two of them reaching the man before Quentin got to the water's edge. Seeing they had the criminal well in hand, Quentin retrieved the statue, which Barrow had dropped in his haste to escape.

'Are you all right, Quentin?' Wanda asked anxiously when he went back to the others.

Quentin gave a rueful grin. 'Just about,' he said. 'I've probably broken my elbow, put my shoulder out and had my hand smashed, but who's counting?'

After they'd watched Barrow and Riddle being handcuffed and taken away, Quentin turned to the cop who'd fished the holdall with the statue out of the water. 'I see you drew the short straw then.'

'It got stuck in the reeds,' the cop said, water still dripping from him.

'Won't the water contaminate the evidence?' Quentin asked Philmore. 'I mean, the fingerprints will be wiped, won't they?' Not giving Philmore a chance to reply, he went on, 'Still, maybe that was the idea. Fancy chucking a valuable object like that in the water, after all the trouble they've taken to get it.'

Rubbing his bruised chin, Philmore looked at him almost pityingly. Quentin held his gaze, baffled, and suddenly he knew. 'It's not valuable is it? It's a fake.'

'Of course!' Wanda blurted, sounding as though she understood too. 'When you knew the statue was going to be stolen, you planted a copy in its place.'

Still fingering his chin, Philmore nodded. 'It was risky, but we could hardly plant a tracking device in a genuine artefact.'

'But what if they'd examined it before they took it abroad?' Quentin demanded.

'We hoped to catch the criminals before it got that far,' Francis put in. 'We might have done it a lot sooner if–' she stopped. Quentin guessed she'd intended to say *if you hadn't interfered*, but thought the better of it.

'If Walberg hadn't collapsed when he did?' Wanda finished for her.

Francis winced in pain as she shifted her injured ankle. 'Yes. Anyway, chief, about the car–'

Quentin could feel her embarrassment as she explained more fully what had happened at the ferry port and why she'd allowed Quentin to drive the CID car.

'Sorry, sir,' she said finally. 'I thought you'd rather I went after them than risk losing them.'

'Good initiative, if you ask me,' Quentin said, feeling sorry for her despite her apparent antipathy towards him.

This earned him a frosty retort from Philmore. 'I think I know how to handle my own sergeant, thank you. When I want your opinion, I'll ask for it.' He whirled round and started walking towards his car.

There's gratitude for you, Quentin thought, weariness overcoming him. The idea of a hot bath and a large whisky suddenly seemed very inviting.

Francis started to walk away, then turned, stepped forward and placed her hand on Quentin's arm. She swallowed, as if it was hard for her to think of what to say.

'It's lucky you were here,' she said, 'otherwise I might have had my head bashed in.' She lowered her gaze to his hand. 'You should get that looked at.' Moving back, she smiled at Wanda and continued, 'Don't mind the chief. He's just upset because he missed the action at the ferry port.'

With that she turned and limped after her boss.

Quentin looked at Wanda and grimaced. 'At least one of them's grateful. Philmore didn't even offer us a lift back to London.'

'Why would he when he knows my car is here?' Wanda said. 'Anyway, I don't feel up to going back yet. Let's find a pub, have a meal and a drink.'

'Good idea,' Quentin agreed. 'But I can't wait that long.' Going back behind the castle wall, he cast a cursory glance around, then sighed deeply as he relieved his aching bladder.

Wanda raised an eyebrow at him when he rejoined her. 'Sorry,' he said, 'but I've been holding on for ages. OK, a pub and a meal, and after that let's get a room for tonight and go back tomorrow. I think we passed a hotel up the road. We've been on the go since four o'clock this morning.'

Quentin's phone rang, and realizing that she still had it, Wanda dived into her bag, fished it out and handed it to him.

Quentin groaned when he read the display. 'Oh, bloody hell! It's Colin.' He put the phone in his pocket. 'Pub,' he said. 'Lead on, Macduff.'

Chapter Thirty

'I can't believe they wanted me to pay for those crates of fish I tipped on the floor,' Quentin complained to Wanda two days later.

They were safely back at his house after a tedious journey from Portsmouth to Greenwich the previous day. Having spent most of today giving their statements and learning as much as Philmore thought they should know, they were relaxing and trying to piece things together.

'Honestly,' Quentin went on, 'there was nothing wrong with them. The fish were practically frozen anyway. All they had to do was scrape them up and put them back in the crates.'

Wanda shook her head. 'That's hardly the point. How would you like eating fish that's been all over the floor?'

Quentin made a face. 'I expect I have. Who knows where it's been before it gets to our table?'

'Don't even think about it. I still can't understand how that woman managed to get you in there in the first place.'

'I told you, I was so shocked, seeing her there right in front of me, I was confused for a minute. She dropped a crate – well, they're boxes really – knocked into me and sent me off balance. The door was open and I fell in, that's all.'

Raising her eyebrows Wanda said, 'That's all? Surely it would have been better to run away than get locked in a fridge.'

A huff of protest escaped Quentin. 'Now wait a minute! I'm the one who nearly froze to death.'

'Exactly. And how do you think I would have felt if I'd been happily wandering around Billingsgate while you were dying? I've had one man die on me this week. I don't want another. I'll be getting a complex.'

Noticing the edge to her voice, Quentin softened. She really had been concerned when she'd seen where he'd been trapped.

'Someone would have had to come in to get supplies at some point,' he said, 'and I would have found the door release if some bright spark hadn't stacked boxes in front of it. I couldn't believe my eyes when I saw Philmore. And by the way, you haven't told me why your wedding dress was in the boot of your car – I know Philmore gave it back to you that day in his office, but he kept the holdall it was in.'

Wanda pursed her lips. 'That bag was Colin's. I borrowed it when we went back to his after he was arrested.'

Quentin rolled his eyes. 'How many holdalls do you think we've handled in the last week? Never mind, I can't be bothered to work it out. All I know is I don't want to see another one for a very long time.'

Wanda gave him a mischievous smile. 'Oh, I don't know, I think it made things rather fun. At least it wasn't boring, and you never know what you might find in a holdall, especially if it's not your own.'

There was a rap at the door. 'That'll be Colin,' Wanda said, standing up. 'I said he could come round to hear the whole story. Don't look like that. We wouldn't have caught Adamson or got the notebook if it hadn't been for him, *and* he came over to feed Mozart and Magpie yesterday.'

She was right, Quentin knew.

'Hello, Colin,' he said when she'd let him in. 'Thanks for feeding Magpie yesterday.'

Colin gave him a look that said he should be thanked for more than feeding Magpie.

'And for your help on the case,' Quentin added after a meaningful glance from Wanda. 'Especially when you clobbered Adamson.'

'I'm glad you appreciate it,' Colin muttered. His gaze fell on Quentin's bandaged hand. 'Been in the wars, then?'

'You could say that.'

'He should have gone to A&E,' Wanda said.

'No, I shouldn't. Nothing broken, and you're a good nurse.'

'Huh!' was all Colin said.

'Coffee or tea, Colin, or something stronger?' Quentin asked, determined not to antagonize him.

'Tea, I suppose, as I'll have to drive again later.'

Another meaningful look from Wanda.

'Well…' Quentin cleared his throat. He watched as the older man turned hopeful grey eyes on him. 'You can eat here and stay over with me if you like?'

'Brilliant idea,' Wanda enthused. 'Why don't we get a takeaway for a change and just chill out? I've got some beers at my house if you want some.'

'And I've got whisky,' Quentin said.

'All right, that'll be great if you're sure you don't mind, Quentin.'

Quentin did mind, but he didn't say so. Instead he poured Colin a whisky.

'So,' Colin said, 'I've told the police everything I know about what happened at Walberg's house, now I want to know what happened from then on. Why on earth did you go to Billingsgate?'

Quentin explained about putting the initials in the notebook together with Billingsgate, and what happened there and afterwards. When he got to where Wanda gave Riddle a lift to the ferry port Colin looked shocked. 'You let Wanda get in the same car as a criminal? Alone?'

'It's all right, Colin, I was perfectly safe. Quentin was right behind with DCI Philmore and DS Francis.'

'Quentin rode in the police car?'

Quentin grinned. 'Yep. More than that – I drove it. You should have seen it, Colin. It was so exciting–'

'I don't believe it,' Colin spluttered, bringing his whisky glass down on the arm of the chair. 'You're making it up.'

'He isn't, Colin,' Wanda said, and went on to relate the rest of the story.

'I missed the action again, then? What is it with you two? You could have rung me, told me what was going on. I could have driven down to Portsmouth, caught you up.'

'You wouldn't have caught us up, and once we got to the port it all happened so quickly,' Wanda told him. 'Honestly, Colin, you couldn't have done anything, and you'd done so much already. We wouldn't have got that far if it hadn't been for you.'

Colin seemed to melt under her beguiling look. That look, those eyes and that sultry voice. Wanda could charm the leaves from the trees.

'So that's it then?' Colin said, holding out his glass for a refill. 'The bloke on the motorbike and the one in Catford, they were just middlemen?'

'Yep,' Quentin said. 'From what Philmore said earlier, a worker at the museum where the statue was on display arranged to switch off the alarm after closing, steal the statue and pass it on to Walberg. What the thief didn't know was that the police found out, probably through Walberg, that the statue was earmarked to be stolen and they planted a duplicate in its place. Walberg should have exchanged it for his share of the money, maybe the museum worker's share as well, which he would have passed on to him.'

Colin sat forward, a frown creasing his forehead. 'So the theft was an inside job. But why did they need Motorbike Man, Adamson or whatever his name is? Why couldn't Walberg go straight to Riddle?'

Quentin spread the fingers on his unbandaged hand. 'Because it was Walberg's job to keep the goods until it was safe to pass them on.'

'How do you know?' Colin demanded.

'Because,' Quentin said patiently, 'that's what Walberg said when he turned informer. In due course, Riddle contacted him and told him where and when to make the exchange. He knew her name and had her number, but Philmore thinks it's possible they never met.

'Adamson was the go-between, and the strong arm of the gang. He wouldn't think twice about roughing someone up, whereas from what I saw of Walberg he was far more refined. I don't think our friend on the motorbike would know the Venus de Milo from a chalk model of Mickey Mouse.'

'Right,' Colin said slowly. 'So then the woman made the final handover to the bloke she met at the ferry port? I'm guessing that under normal circumstances he would take it abroad and sell it on?'

'That's what the police think,' Quentin said. 'They've had their eye on Barrow for a while but they couldn't get any evidence. That's why they set this trap – they had to catch him receiving the goods.'

Colin closed his eyes and leaned back in his chair as though trying to take this all in. 'OK,' he said eventually, 'but who financed the gang? I mean, they had the money you found in the holdall before they were given the goods. Who supplied that?'

'We wondered about that ourselves,' Wanda said. 'We won't know for sure until the police have made Barrow talk, if he ever does. It doesn't matter anyway. They all got their cut. Whoever supplied the money would have recouped it and made a huge profit when the statue was sold on.'

Colin gave a low whistle. 'A nice tidy little racket then.'

'Yes,' Quentin said. 'Philmore reckons Barrow, Riddle and Adamson will get quite a few years inside between them.'

Colin threw him a sceptical look. 'And of course, he told you all this. How come you're so privileged? And don't say it's because of that case last year.'

'All right, I won't.'

'It isn't just that,' Wanda said. 'Quentin stopped Barrow from escaping.'

'Hmm. Oh well, I suppose I should say congratulations, seeing as you acknowledged my help for a change,' Colin said grudgingly. 'But I want to be in at the kill next time.'

'I don't suppose cases like this come up very often,' Wanda sighed. 'It'll be back to divorce and missing dogs next week.'

Quentin pushed that thought away. He was still bathed in euphoria. He didn't want the reality of everyday work at the agency spoiling it.

'At least you'll get paid for that,' Colin pointed out.

Quentin's euphoria faded a little. It faded even more when Colin continued, 'Is the spare bed made up, Quentin? I assume that's where I'll be sleeping.'

'Of course it is,' Wanda said. 'It'll be fine. We could all do with good night's sleep, couldn't we Quentin?'

'Yes,' Quentin said, interpreting the coded message. He poured himself another drink. If he couldn't spend the night with Wanda he might as well drink enough to make him sleep. A least he wouldn't hear Colin snoring.

Chapter Thirty-one

The following morning, after Colin had gone home, Quentin sat on the sofa with Magpie curled up on his lap. After all the excitement he felt the need for a quiet day, time to regain his energy and reflect on the success of the case.

He couldn't believe it was only a week since it had all started. Tomorrow he would go to the office, pick up the work he'd left in limbo even though it was Sunday, but now he was going to relax, perhaps call his mother, even speak to his father and tell him that he'd helped crack a big case.

Until his resentful recognition of Quentin's part in last year's case, which had made UK headlines, his father had made it clear that in his opinion Quentin had achieved nothing in his life. To him, Quentin was someone who'd let the family down, dropping out of university and drifting from job to job. Yes, he would enjoy telling his father that he'd helped the police, perhaps embellish the story a little, and his mother would be proud.

His mobile rang and he sighed. He was just starting to enjoy being alone in the comfort of his own home. He glanced at the display, but the number was withheld. Resisting the temptation to cut the call off, he pressed the green connection button.

His breath stopped when a well-modulated voice said, 'Mr Cadbury.'

There was a beat before he found the courage to answer. 'Y-yes,' he faltered, wondering if he had made a mistake.

'I said you hadn't heard the last of me, Mr Cadbury,' the cultured voice went on, 'and you haven't. Quite the opposite, in fact.'

No mistake. Quentin's blood whooshed in his ears. It almost drowned out the sound of the caller's breathing. Almost. Memories of his previous encounter with this man, Whitelaw, flooded him, and a cold prickle ran down his spine. The head of a ring of criminals, he had escaped justice last year when Quentin had been involved in tracking down some of the gang and putting a stop to their activities.

'What do you mean?' he asked, hoping he didn't sound as shaken as he felt.

'Well now, Mr Cadbury. I believe that once again you've been poking your nose into things that don't concern you.'

Confusion filled Quentin's mind. How could this man, Cultured Voice as Quentin thought of him, possibly know anything about the case he'd just been caught up in?

His own voice cracked when he said, 'It did concern me. My bag was stolen, and my friend was mugged.'

A snigger sounded in Quentin's ear. 'Ah yes, the delectable Mrs Merrydrew. How is she?'

Determined not to be drawn into a conversation about Wanda, Quentin said, 'What do you want?'

Whitelaw's sardonic tone hardened. 'What I want, Mr Cadbury, is to be able to conduct my business in peace, without an incompetent idiot like you getting in my way.'

Quentin's shock at hearing from a devious criminal mastermind gave way to anger. How dare this man call him incompetent? I'm the one who's broken up two criminal gangs and put some of their members in prison, he wanted to shout. Instead he said, '*Your* business? Don't tell me you're behind this whole thing. That operation's been shut down now.'

'So it has, thanks to you and your interfering, and it's none of your business what I'm behind and what I'm not.'

'Given up your previous occupation then, have you? Isn't it good enough for you now?'

'As needs must, Mr Cadbury. Let's just say I have interests in many things. Fortunately I'm still at liberty to be able to indulge my interests, unlike some of my acquaintances.'

Quentin's temper began to boil with the injustice of it. However indirectly, the man had obviously been involved in this latest case. Since his near capture last year, he had apparently decided it was safer to keep away from direct action.

'So you've left your so-called acquaintances to take the rap,' he said sourly. 'Honour amongst thieves and all that.'

'That's rather an old-fashioned adage, I must say. One can't afford such high-minded principles these days. And thanks to you, I can't afford as much as I'd like.'

'Nor can I, but I don't steal things just because I can't afford them.'

There was a pause. Quentin knew he had pushed the boundaries, but he didn't care. Time to call a spade a spade, and a thief a thief, no matter how clever or cultured.

The rage Whitelaw had been suppressing exploded in Quentin's ear. 'Enough of the shilly-shallying, you jumped-up little nobody. This is the second time you've deprived me of a lot of money. Well, you'll be sorry. I was prepared to overlook your first interference, to a degree anyway, but now I'm going to have to put a stop to it.'

Quentin's mouth ran dry. 'Is that a threat?'

'Watch your back, Mr Cadbury. Watch it very carefully. Because I'll certainly be watching it. I'll be watching it until it's carried away in a coffin with the rest of you.'

The line went dead. As dead as Quentin knew he would be if Whitelaw carried out his threat. And this man, whatever name he was using now, wasn't in the habit of making idle threats.

His stomach churning, Quentin had a sudden urge to go to the toilet. When he returned, feeling weak at the knees, he collapsed onto the sofa. He sat for a moment, staring straight ahead, wild imaginings swamping his brain. Then, hand trembling, he picked up his phone and called Philmore.

* * *

'Don't worry, Quentin,' Wanda soothed when he told her about the phone call. 'You can go away for a while, lie low. He can't be everywhere at once. I'm sure he's got better ways to spend his time than tracking you down. What would he gain from killing you except adding murder to his list of offences?'

'I shouldn't think it will make much difference to him. He won't do it himself anyway – he's too clever for that. But he's powerful. He can post his spies and hire a hit man.'

Wanda shuddered. 'Now you're scaring me. Perhaps we should move, both of us. He knows where we live from the last case, and even if he didn't, he'd soon find out. We'll be sitting ducks if we stay here.'

'Yeah, I guess so, but the idea of my keeping the same mobile number was to give him the chance to contact me with a view to finding out where he is. I agreed to act as bait, so I should stay and see what happens.'

'That was when you'd upset his plans the first time. You've crossed him twice now, so it's a different kettle of fish. He's threatened to kill you.'

'That's what Philmore said,' Quentin admitted. 'He's run it past his superiors and been told it's too risky. He's offered us police protection.'

'What, plant someone to watch us all day, every day? How long would they keep it up for? I don't fancy that.'

'Well, the alternative is to change our identities, to disappear altogether.'

'Absolutely not,' Wanda said. 'That would be awful. I don't want to be somebody else, and we've got the business to think about.'

'We could operate the business from anywhere,' Quentin pointed out. 'But I agree with you. I don't want to be anyone else either. Or live anywhere else, really.' He gazed around his lounge, his eyes lingering on the china cabinet and winged upright armchair, legacies from his late Aunt Josie. He'd grown fond of the place in the two years he'd been here, and he loved the location. Why should he be driven out of his home?

'I think it's time for an extended holiday,' he said after a further moment's thought. 'We'll disappear for a while and decide what to do when we come back. With any luck our friend will have been caught by then. He can't be infallible.'

'Holiday? Where do you think we'd be safe? The moon?'

Quentin didn't even have to think about it. 'Australia,' he said, realizing that he actually wanted to go, and not just because he needed a safe haven.

'Australia,' Wanda muttered, looking bemused. 'Ten thousand miles, and all because of a dead cat.'

'The good thing is we still have each other,' Quentin whispered, catching her hand and pulling her to him.

For once Wanda didn't contradict him or try to dilute his assertion that they were a couple. They stood together for a moment, united in mutual apprehension.

A knock at the door broke the spell. Releasing Wanda's hand, Quentin went to answer it. A small woman with wispy hair stood there, her face showing signs of a recently acquired suntan. Quentin's heart plummeted.

'Hello, Quentin. I've come to collect my Lucky. I hope he hasn't been any trouble.'

Swallowing his trepidation, Quentin shook his head. 'Trouble? Of course not, Mrs Freeman. No trouble at all.'

THE END

AUTHOR'S NOTE

Billingsgate now opens at 4 a.m. It is scheduled to be relocated to Dagenham Dock in East London.
In 2006 it was 5 a.m. before fish could be moved.
The police station in Wanstead closed in 2013.
Portsmouth ferry port terminal has been rebuilt since 2006.

If you enjoyed this book, please let others know by leaving a quick review on Amazon. Also, if you spot anything untoward in the paperback, get in touch. We strive for the best quality and appreciate reader feedback.

editor@thebookfolks.com

www.thebookfolks.com

More fiction by the author

THE MYSTERY OF THE HIDDEN FORTUNE (Book 1)

Quentin Cadbury, a useless twenty-something, is left to look after his late aunt's London house when his parents head to Australia. But burglars seem determined to break in, and not even the stray cat he befriends can help him. As the thieves are after something pretty valuable, and illegal, he must grow up pretty fast to get out of a sticky situation.

THE MYSTERY DOWN UNDER (Book 3)

Evading a London gangster, private investigator Quentin Cadbury and his sidekick Wanda Merrydrew visit Australia to catch up with Quentin's family. Yet when they discover a burglar is causing upset in their quiet Sydney suburb, they can't help but get involved. Can Quentin catch a thief and prove his mettle to his ever-disappointed father?

FREE with Kindle Unlimited and available in paperback!

Other titles of interest

MURDER IN HAMPSTEAD
by Sabina Manea

After ex-lawyer, now interior designer, Lucia Steer accepts a job renovating a large London house, she has no idea she'll discover the owner dead. Lucia is determined to unlock the secret of this closed room mystery, no matter the trouble she'll inevitably land in.

FREE with Kindle Unlimited and available in paperback!

MURDER ON A YORKSHIRE MOOR
by Ric Brady

Ex-detective Henry Ward is settling awkwardly into retirement in a quiet corner of Yorkshire when during a walk on the moor he stumbles upon the body of a young man. Suspecting foul play and somewhat relishing the return to a bit of detective work, he resolves to find out who killed him. But will the local force appreciate him sticking his nose in?

FREE with Kindle Unlimited and available in paperback!

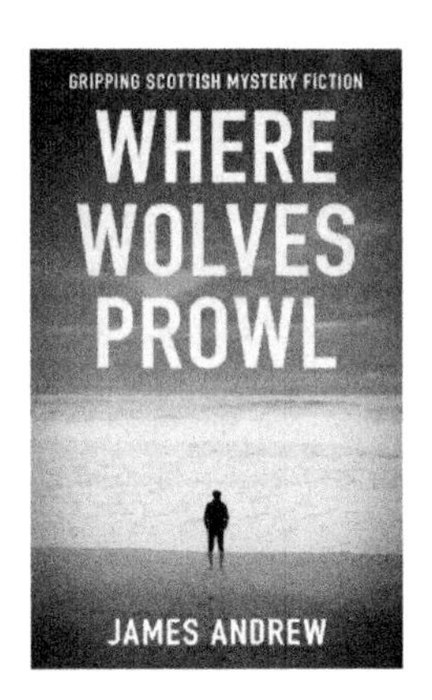
GRIPPING SCOTTISH MYSTERY FICTION
WHERE
WOLVES
PROWL
JAMES ANDREW

THE
BOOK
FOLKS

Printed in Great Britain
by Amazon